A NOVEL BASED ON THE LIFE OF
LAURA BASSI

BREAKING BARRIERS

Jule Selbo

THE
MENTORIS
PROJECT

Breaking Barriers is a work of fiction. Some incidents, dialogue, and characters are products of the author's imagination and are not to be construed as real. Where real-life historical figures appear, the situations, incidents, and dialogue concerning those persons are based on or inspired by actual events. In all other respects, any resemblance to actual persons, living or dead, events, or locales is entirely coincidental.

Barbera Foundation, Inc.
P.O. Box 1019
Temple City, CA 91780

More information at www.mentorisproject.org

ISBN: 978-1-947431-29-4

Library of Congress Control Number: 2020934628

All net proceeds from the sale of this book will be donated to Barbera Foundation, Inc. whose mission is to support educational initiatives that foster an appreciation of history and culture to encourage and inspire young people to create a stronger future.

The Mentoris Project is a series of novels and biographies about the lives of great Italians and Italian-Americans: men and women who have changed history through their contributions as scientists, inventors, explorers, thinkers, and creators. The Barbera Foundation sponsors this series in the hope that, like a mentor, each book will inspire the reader to discover how she or he can make a positive contribution to society.

Contents

Foreword

First and foremost, Mentor was a person. We tend to think of the word *mentor* as a noun (a mentor) or a verb (to mentor), but there is a very human dimension embedded in the term. Mentor appears in Homer's *Odyssey* as the old friend entrusted to care for Odysseus's household and his son Telemachus during the Trojan War. When years pass and Telemachus sets out to search for his missing father, the goddess Athena assumes the form of Mentor to accompany him. The human being welcomes a human form for counsel. From its very origins, becoming a mentor is a transcendent act; it carries with it something of the holy.

The Barbera Foundation's Mentoris Project sets out on an Athena-like mission: We hope the books that form this series will be an inspiration to all those who are seekers, to those of the twenty-first century who are on their own odysseys, trying to find enduring principles that will guide them to a spiritual home. The stories that comprise the series are all deeply human. These books dramatize the lives of great Italians and Italian-Americans whose stories bridge the ancient and the modern, taking many forms, just as Athena did, but always holding up a light for those living today.

Whether in novel form or traditional biography, these

books plumb the individual characters of our heroes' journeys. The power of storytelling has always been to envelop the reader in a vivid and continuous dream, and to forge a link with the subject. Our goal is for that link to guide the reader home with a new inspiration.

What is a mentor? A guide, a moral compass, an inspiration. A friend who points you toward true north. We hope that the Mentoris Project will become that friend, and it will help us all transcend our daily lives with something that can only be called holy.

—Robert J. Barbera, President, Barbera Foundation
—Ken LaZebnik, Editor, The Mentoris Project

Part One: Genoa

BOLOGNA
CITY IN THE PAPAL STATES
ITALIAN PENINSULA
1716–1728

Chapter One

Laura Maria Caterina Bassi tried to step lightly. She didn't want her mother or any of the other women in the parlor to look up from their needlework to ask her where she was going. She was glad her new soft, leather-soled shoes—given to her yesterday on her fifth birthday—made no sound. And that her blue silk dress, with its stiff petticoats, could be pressed to her sides to muffle the rustling crinoline. Luckily, her mother and the hostess—one of Bologna's most renowned, the imperious and beautiful Signora Mucchi—were gossiping and nibbling on *panforte*, the chewy fruit and nut confection that her mother could not resist. Laura slipped past the parlor door and raced down the long, wide hallway.

She reached the library and peeked in. She could glimpse Count Luigi Marsili's tall form, his wide chin, and his bulbous, piercing eyes. He wore a shoulder-length periwig of cascading black curls and a waistcoat adorned with military medals. His commanding voice filled the room.

"Gentlemen, *il mio uomo*. The University of Bologna, and especially its work in scientific study, is stagnating. Set in the old ways. Science cannot stand still!"

A number of the men nodded, some raising their hands. "*Ben detto! Ben detto!* Well said! *La scienza vive!*"

Laura leaned in. She liked that word: *science*. Her father told her it was the study of how everything in the whole world worked. She wanted to know more about this science.

Marsili spoke loudly, like he was rallying his troops for battle. "As you know, as of this year, 1716, I've retired from the Pope's army and am now concentrating on work in geology and ocean science. But the university's facilities are lacking and Bologna is suffering!"

Laura saw scowls. It was apparent not everyone agreed, that some resented his words.

A thin man with a humped back, his matted gray wig slipping to one side of his bony face, stood. "Do not speak ill of the oldest university on the Italian Peninsula! It ranks as one of the finest in Europe. Our city is called *La Dotta*, the city of 'the learned.'"

Marsili's voice rose. "And now resting on its reputation, Dottore Salti." He forged ahead. "England and France are gaining. Will Bologna fade into the background?"

The supporters of Marsili shouted, "No! *Non per noi!*"

Marsili raised his hands high into the air. "I propose a new Institute of Science! And I offer my palazzo as its home."

Marsili's supporters, elated, stood on their feet. "*Bravo!*"

"We must study science the way it should be studied," Marsili nearly shouted. "With resources! With an open mind!"

Laura felt the excitement in the room. Her eyes searched for her father—his well-tailored coat, linen shirt, and flowing red wig. Finally, she located him . . . and cringed. For his gaze was not on Count Marsili; it was on her. Giuseppe Bassi's eyes sent a silent but strong message. *Daughter, do not think about entering. Go to where you are supposed to be.*

Laura, disappointed, slipped backwards. She disliked being told where she was "supposed to be"—she wanted to be where her curiosity led her. On the family's walk to the Mucchi palazzo, her father had told her he was most pleased to be invited to this evening's salon where important discoveries and ideas would be discussed. He'd been raised in a poor farming family, but had dared to move to the city, managed to get an education, and risen to become a well-respected, well-paid *avvocato*—a lawyer in Bologna. And even though these salons were exclusive and, for the most part, only for forward-thinking professors and nobles of fine families, his offer of financial support had been accepted and gained him this invitation. He had told Laura he hoped she would be on her best behavior.

Laura frowned. She wanted to behave, but she also wanted to be inside the library. To listen to every word.

Count Marsili held up his hands again for attention. "New ideas and new discoveries lead to a deeper understanding of the world. To this new and great period of Enlightenment."

"Enlightenment? What is that?" one of the nobles asked.

Laura peeked in again, trying very hard not to be noticed. What was that new word?

"A time of reason. Of sensibility," Marsili informed the men. "We all know that science was feared and squashed in the Dark Ages, then ignored and vilified in the more recent Reformation. But it's a new day, a new age. The French have given it the title 'Age of Enlightenment.' Where scientists will lead, they will experiment, they will show that God encourages us—wants us, demands of us—to strive to understand the makeup of the world He has so generously provided. The Enlightenment—with Bologna leading—can be the era of great thinkers."

Laura muttered the word under her breath. *Enlightenment.* It made her feel light and happy.

Marsili's voice rang out. "Our fine city, Bologna, with a new Institute of Science, can and must become a center—in natural history, physics, chemistry, optics, astronomy, military art, anatomy, and more. Open your purses," he urged. "Our new institute will need books. Laboratories. Instruments. Resources. Researchers. Bologna must be the most 'enlightened' city on the Italian Peninsula! In Europe!"

"Hear, hear! *Ben detto!*"

Laura felt a tug on the ribbons of her linen cap. She heard a worried whisper.

"Laura! We're supposed to be in the sunroom."

Laura turned to see her best friend, Eugenia Mucchi. Her dainty, pretty face, framed with the lace of her cap, was pink with worry. "My mother mustn't see us. We'll get in trouble."

Laura put her small hands together, as if beseeching her friend. "One more minute."

Dottore Salti, the grouchy-looking man with the worn gray wig, was growling. "These are very big dreams, Count Marsili."

"*Sì*, Dottore Salti. But without dreams, how does humankind move forward?"

Laura took a deep breath. She had many dreams—going to school, learning languages, history, literature, science. Learning everything.

Eugenia pulled at the sleeve of Laura's dress. "Please, Laura. My mother will be angry."

Laura frowned. She knew that to be true. Eugenia's mother,

Signora Mucchi, expected perfection in manners and fashion. Laura dipped her head and saw specks of dirt on her knitted white stockings. They had been clean when she and her parents had left their home in the early afternoon to walk to the Mucchis' grand palazzo. She should have walked around the rain puddles that had formed in the lower areas of the Piazza Maggiore, but she liked to tap her foot against the water and count the ripples in the small pools.

Laura glanced at Eugenia's stockings; they were pink, clean, and perfectly tight. "I never want you to get in trouble, Eugenia," she assured her friend. "I'll race you."

The girls flitted past the tapestries, fine art, and statues that lined the hallway of the Mucchi palazzo. They crouched, then held their breath, scampered past the women's enclave, and slipped into a sunroom filled with toys.

A group of girls sat in a circle with embroidery hoops, pulling oversized needles and thick threads in and out of thin linen fabric, intent on fashioning flower designs. Eugenia went to join them, but Laura's attention was drawn to the other side of the room. A half-dozen boys flanked a long table; they eyed a line of miniature cast-iron carriages. The boys argued about how many carved wooden horses to place in front of each carriage.

Laura gazed at the configuration and mused aloud, "What if the carriages were all linked together and the front vehicle was an engine propelled by steam. The engine might be strong enough to pull all the carriages so the horses wouldn't have to do such hard work—they could eat hay all day."

"Steam can't do anything. That's just hot air," declared Vincenzo Cruce, an eight-year-old boy with a mass of freckles across his cheeks. He glowered at Laura.

Laura pursed her lips and pointed out in her small, calm

voice. "Steam can be used for power. My father told me there was a Greek named Hero, thousands of years ago, who put water in an almost-closed vessel, then put a flame under the vessel to heat the water. This created steam. This steam made the arms attached to the vessel turn—like a windmill."

Vincenzo snorted. He did not like to be shown up.

Laura, oblivious to his irritation, continued. "And just yesterday, my father read to me about a man in England named Thomas Savery, who invented a water pump that's propelled by steam. He heated water just like Hero did in Greece. And now the Englishman's working on something he calls a steam engine. It's meant to be strong enough to pull things."

The boys stared at Laura; they were confused by this serious girl sharing odds bits of what seemed to be ludicrous information.

Eugenia approached. "Laura? I want to show you my new dolls."

Laura turned to her friend. "We're discussing steam, Eugenia."

"No, we're not," Vincenzo snarled.

The boys quickly moved off to the other end of the table to set up war games with small wooden soldiers. Laura noticed they stood tightly together, leaving no room for her to join them.

Eugenia led the way to a row of shelves. "Laura, sometimes you think of strange things. Everyone knows a carriage will always need a horse to pull it." She waved her hand at the shelves lined with beautiful porcelain dolls. "You pick your favorite and I'll pick mine."

Laura puffed out a long breath. Dolls. She would rather use her time to think of a way to invent a steam engine. Or something just as wonderful.

~

It was the end of the afternoon and Laura and her parents, wrapped in heavy velvet cloaks, walked the short distance to their home. The evening clouds were gathering and the promise of another chilly October rain was in the air. They crossed through Bologna's grand Piazza Maggiore and passed the city's most massive church, the Basilica di San Petronio, and the Fountain of Neptune, its flowing, spurting waters overseen by a giant statue of the Greek god of the sea.

Laura was full of questions. "Papà, what do you think about this thing called the Enlightenment? Will Bologna be part of it?"

"We shall have to see. Our new pope, Clement XI, appears to be open to new ideas. More so than our previous pope, who believed that man should accept God's gifts and not endeavor to understand them."

"Papà, do scientists have to obey the pope?"

Signora Bassi nearly gasped. Her right hand touched her forehead, heart, and both shoulders, making the Catholic sign of the cross. "God speaks through the pope, my daughter. And we must obey God."

Signor Bassi gently took his wife's arm and replied to Laura, "The pope is elected by men to be the spiritual leader, the head of our Church. He's charged with acting in the way he feels God would approve. But in Bologna, because we are part of the Papal States, the pope is also our political and temporal leader. He's in charge of decisions such as war, our trades, our economy. The university needs money to support study and to build laboratories. Many will be grateful if Pope Clement will promise funds to support scientists' work."

"God must see science as worthy," Laura said. "It's so obvious."

Signor Bassi and his wife shared a look, again taken aback by their daughter's precociousness. She had asked to learn to read when she was three years old, and had challenged herself in the family library. She wanted to know how things worked, what they were made of, where and how people in the world lived.

"Papà," Laura continued, "Count Marsili said the Enlightenment is the time for great thinkers. How does a person become a great thinker?"

"The first requisite is to be a great questioner," Signor Bassi said. "Asking questions opens a person to new ideas."

"I like questions," stated Laura. "And I like answers, too."

The Bassis approached their large, stone villa. Suddenly, a great wind blustered and rain began to fall in large drops.

Signor Bassi, always prepared, opened an umbrella made from an oiled muslin. "Gather close for safety, my family."

Laura saw Nucca, their round and solicitous housekeeper, standing in the open doorway. "There's Nucca. Can I run, Mamma?"

"*Mia cara*, you'll get wet," Signora Bassi worried.

But Laura was already running. She bounded up the steps to the stone veranda and into their stately home.

Nucca clucked her tongue, "You're not acting like a young lady, Signorina Laura."

"Rain makes me wonder about clouds, Nucca. And the sky. It's all part of science." Laura skipped up the marble stairs to her bedroom.

"I'll be up to help you out of those wet clothes, Signorina Laura," Nucca called after her.

"*Grazie*, Nucca."

Laura raced to the small desk in her room and quickly took out a thin piece of vellum. She unscrewed the lid on her inkpot and dipped a quill into the dark ink. She printed her letters carefully, trying to get the shape of each just right.

Salutations Pope Clement XI,

My name is Laura Maria Caterina Bassi. I am writing to tell you that I think science is wonderful and it seems to me that God must think so too. I hope He tells you that.

She folded the letter and put it into a drawer. She'd take it to the church; surely it could be sent it along to the pope.

A short time later, Nucca had helped Laura out of her cap, crinolines, stockings, chemise, and hair ribbons and into her linen nightdress and sleep bonnet. Laura climbed into bed and slipped her bare feet under the quilted cotton coverlet. She breathed in deeply.

"I can smell the lavender scent in my pillow, Nucca."

"It is for sweet dreams, *signorina.*" Nucca moved the tallow candle to the bedside table.

Signor Bassi entered. He'd taken off his wig and Laura liked to see his thick, wavy reddish-brown hair.

"Papà, why do men wear wigs?"

"Fashion. Vanity. I think it became the style in Europe when the young king, Louis XIV of France, started losing his hair. He thought a wig made him look more handsome and powerful."

Laura giggled. "Do you like them, Papà?"

"They're hot and expensive. But it's important to fit in, I suppose. To do—and wear—what is expected." He patted Laura's hand. "Did you brush your teeth?"

"*Sì*, Papà. I crushed baked eggshells with sage and salt in Cook's kitchen. Nucca rubbed the mixture on a cloth and I rubbed the cloth on my teeth myself. See?" Laura showed her teeth. "They feel clean."

Signor Bassi nodded to Nucca. "*Grazie*, Nucca." Nucca dipped in a short curtsy. "Signora Bassi could use your help now," he added.

"*Buona notte*, Signorina Laura." Nucca padded out of the room, her ample figure moving quickly.

Signor Bassi reached for the Bible. "What will it be tonight?"

"Genesis, Papà. When God created the Earth. It's like He created science at the same time."

Signor Bassi laughed, "You could be very right to think about it in this way."

Just then, a bolt of lightning formed a ragged line in the sky. The room lit up for a moment, and Laura chortled with excitement.

"Papà!"

"Count for it, Laura."

Before Laura could even begin to count, the thunder clap sounded. She could almost feel its power through her body.

"Papà, where does the lightning come from? And why does the bolt of light come first? Before the sound? And why does the sound come quickly sometimes and much later at other times?"

"Perhaps someday, scientists will be able to explain it."

Laura yawned, her eyes closing. "Perhaps the scholars in the Enlightenment will come to understand the sky and the stars. And even go to the moon one day."

Signor Bassi chuckled. "One day, *mia cara*. Perhaps one day."

Sleepily, Laura mumbled, "Papà, when can I go to school?"

"Girls don't go to school. They learn what they need to know right in their own homes."

Laura was half asleep. "But I want to ask so many questions—so I can become 'enlightened.'"

Chapter Two

On the last Sunday in June, Bologna celebrated with a mass in honor of one of its most beloved saints: Saint Caterina. Laura felt it was an extra-special day for her, too, because one of her middle names was Caterina. She sat between her mother and father; one of her cousins, Carlo, who was a few years older than her and loved to play pranks, sat behind them with his parents.

Carlo leaned forward and teased, "I've got a big spider in my hand . . . shall I let it crawl on your shoulder?"

Laura giggled as Carlo's father pulled him back and reprimanded him.

She saw her friend Eugenia in a straw hat topped with flowers, in the nobles' pews of the Basilica di San Petronio. Eugenia was twisting to wave happily to her. Signora Mucchi, her face stern, leaned into Eugenia and whispered. Laura could see Eugenia's face fall as she turned around and sat up as straight and perfectly still as possible.

"*Benedictus Deus in donis suis, et sanctus in omnibus operibus suis* . . . ."

Laura's cousin, the recently ordained Father Lorenzo Stegani, his white and gold vestments catching the light that streamed through the stained-glass windows, moved to the pulpit to give the opening prayer. Laura loved the Latin language, its stately sounds, how when spoken in church it resonated in the large space and seemed to merge into one long word.

Unaware that her young voice was clear and strong, Laura recited the prayer along with her cousin. "*Qui vivit et regnat in saecula saeculorum* . . . ."

Nearby parishioners cleared their throats, signaling disapproval. Carlo, behind her, snickered.

Signora Bassi put a hand on Laura's arm to caution her. She leaned to whisper into her daughter's ear. "Pray softly, Laura."

Laura dipped her head. "Sorry, Mamma. I forgot to stay quiet."

But Laura was soon transfixed as Father Stegani told the story of Saint Caterina. Three hundred years ago, she had been the daughter of a lawyer, just like Laura. Caterina had loved learning, just like Laura. Caterina had founded a Franciscan convent in Bologna, a religious order of nuns she named the Poor Clares. The convent was a school and hospital, one of the first that was available to the poor. Laura felt pride in Caterina's accomplishments for she, too, hoped to accomplish something just as fine one day. Maybe she, too, could be a teacher.

Father Stegani continued, telling the parishioners he was about to disclose miraculous events. Laura leaned forward.

He raised his bearded jaw and lifted his eyes toward heaven.

"In the days after Abbess Caterina's death, in 1463, many people of Bologna prayed over her body. And, wondrously, sick people were cured of their ailments."

The parishioners touched their foreheads, hearts, and both shoulders in the sign of the cross.

Father Stegani raised his voice. "The cured, awestruck, fell to their knees. When the leaders of the Church witnessed this, they wondered—could these events be connected to Caterina? It was decided to exhume her body."

Laura could hear Carlo behind her, groaning in disgust.

"How long does it take to dig up a body, Papà?" Laura asked.

Her father put his finger to his lips. Laura frowned; she realized her voice, again, had been too loud.

Father Stegani continued, "The body of the Abbess had been buried for eighteen days. When it was taken from the ground, doctors were astounded to see that Caterina's blood still flowed and sweet smells emanated from her body. And then, when the sick approached and touched the exhumed body—all were miraculously cured."

Laura held her breath. The best was yet to come.

Father Stegani's voice echoed in the massive stone church. "And then, a young novitiate of the Poor Clares' order could not contain her grief. She called for Caterina's expired body to join the living again, to sit up!" He paused theatrically before continuing. "The novitiate begged, 'Sit up! Sit up!' And the Abbess's upper body rose and she sat up!"

Laura forgot her parents' admonition to be quiet. She stood. "But how, cousin? How did that happen?"

Signora Bassi quickly pulled Laura back to her place in the pew. Her father pressed his lips together, not pleased.

Laura sighed and settled back in the pew. The hardest thing about being in church was not being able to ask questions when she wanted answers.

After church, Laura stood by herself in the Piazza Maggiore, deep in thought. *How did Saint Caterina sit up after she was dead? Did her eyes open? Did she speak?* She had so many questions.

Other children played in groups—the girls skipped in circles and Carlo was with the boys who raced after each other, playing a game of tag. Laura's parents socialized, catching up on the city's news and gossip. The warm sun was high in the sky. Laura could feel the hard stones of the piazza through her soft leather shoes. She wondered why stones retained more heat than the dirt paths of the city. She wondered why Bologna favored the terracotta color for its buildings. Why did the red-orange hue make her feel soothed? She wondered why the sun, in the days of June, stayed high in the sky for a longer time than during the Christmas season.

Eugenia, out of breath from the skipping with the other girls, joined her and showed off her new dress. "Laura, look at the pearl buttons on my dress. Mamma says they come all the way from China. That's a place far, far away."

Laura remembered a story she'd read about China, a large country in the Far East that the Venetian explorer, Marco Polo, visited four hundred years ago. "Eugenia, did you know that China is the place where fireworks were invented? Fireworks shoot light and color into the sky."

"Maybe we'll sail on a magnificent and fancy ship and see China one day," Eugenia dreamed. She touched her pearls. "To see pearls and fireworks."

Signora Mucchi's clipped, haughty voice rang through the air; it was time for Eugenia to get into the Mucchis' grand carriage. Eugenia kissed Laura quickly on the cheek and skipped toward a waiting groomsman. He offered Eugenia his hand and she daintily slipped into the carriage. Laura liked to walk, but Eugenia had told her that gilded carriages were signs of noble families and her mother thought it was important to make their status clear.

Laura saw Father Stegani join her parents. She hurried over and smiled up at him. "*Buongiorno*, Cousin. Has Pope Clement answered my letter yet?"

Father Stegani leaned down to Laura. "Not yet. I'll let you know when there is a post for you. It was good to hear you join me in prayer in the church."

Laura ducked her head, chastised. "I'm sorry for speaking aloud."

"That I do not mind," said Father Stegani. "But your Latin needs a bit of improvement. Pronunciation is very important in Latin."

Laura frowned. She always wanted to get things right. "What did I mispronounce?"

"Just a few words," Father Stegani said kindly. "How old are you now, Laura?"

"Almost six."

"What if I teach you Latin? That way, when you do speak up, your meaning will be easily understood."

"Really, Cousin?" exclaimed Laura. She rose to her toes in anticipation. Latin was the language used for great learning and only boys of noble families were tutored in Latin.

She looked up to her parents for their agreement. "*Papà e Mamma. Di di sì.* Say 'yes.'"

Over the next year, Laura worked hard on her Latin lessons and soon her cousin decided to add French to her assignments. She practiced every day, following Nucca around the house and garden, stating the foreign names of objects. She learned songs and poems and wrote questions in her notebook for Father Stegani. She also anxiously awaited her father's return from the monthly salons of learning, for he would often bring back pamphlets written in French by Enlightenment scholars. She pored over the articles, but even though she could sound out the French words, she was frustrated because she could not understand their meanings.

One day, when winter had finally departed and the leaves on the trees were beginning to bud, Father Stegani arrived for a lesson. Laura met him at the gate to the villa.

"Cousin, the French Enlightenment mathematicians write of something called 'calculus' and I don't know what it is. Will you teach me?"

Father Stegani stepped back and chuckled. "Laura, I'm a theologian. I know only mathematical basics. Adding and subtracting. Simple multiplication."

Laura look stymied. "Multiplication? I don't know about that. Shall we start there?"

Father Stegani hesitated. He knew that young girls of Laura's station were expected to learn about concerns of home and family. Not mathematical problems. But Laura's face was so open and expectant, he did not want to disappoint.

He leaned into her. "I have an idea: Let's surprise your parents with multiplication skills when we think it's the right time. This will be our secret."

Laura's eyes lit up. She liked surprises.

～

The days turned toward summer and the warm sun encouraged Bologna's gardens; pink bougainvillea and red and creamy-white hibiscus bloomed. Bees darted from blossom to blossom and sparrows and warblers chirped in the trees. The stone streets and piazzas were filled with people enjoying the sun. The marketplaces abounded with vendors of fruits, vegetables, and meats; storefront doors were open to let in fresh air and allow the shoppers to see the fabrics, leathers, and fine wares on display. Laura, in a new felt hat decorated with red ribbon and bows, strolled through the city's main piazza with her father. They were out to shop for Signora Bassi's birthday present.

"Mamma will like a new hat, Papà. I think it should be very big and grand. But not too heavy. Because sometimes she gets tired."

Signor Bassi nodded; it was true, his wife, at times, felt a weakness. But he did not want to share his worries with his young daughter.

"We'll go to the best hat shop—it's over there."

Laura noticed a cluster of boys with school sashes over their cloaks; they followed a corpulent, jowly tutor who held a colored stick high in the air so that the boys could mark his place in the crowds. She felt envy; she wanted to follow them to their classrooms. She wondered what the boys might be learning—could it be calculus, a language like German, or astronomy?

"Signor Bassi." A deep voice thundered through the crowd.

Laura turned to see Count Luigi Marsili stride toward them. She was surprised by how much larger he seemed when he was close up, how his wig was shinier and heavier, and how his voice rumbled from his chest.

"I'll take this opportunity to thank you for your generous donation to the Institute of Science."

Signor Bassi gave a slight bow. "Not as generous as yours, Count Marsili. After all, you gave over your palazzo." He nodded toward Laura. "My daughter."

Laura bubbled with excitement. "I heard you speak at the salon at my friend Eugenia Mucchi's home. You said that without dreams, humankind cannot move forward to the Enlightenment. I thought about that. And I have a question: Will the French thinkers ever come to Bologna? So people can think together?"

Marsili peered down at the diminutive Laura and then let his eyes sweep back to Signor Bassi—clearly ignoring Laura's query.

"I have an appointment. *Scusami.*" The count, his heavy chin leading, strode off.

Laura frowned. "Why didn't he answer my question, Papà?"

Signor Bassi found an excuse. "He's an important, busy man." He wanted to distract Laura. "Look. *Scacchi.*"

Laura looked to where her father was pointing. It was a jeweler's storefront where two men sat at a small table in front of their open shop, concentrating on a board game.

"What is it?"

"Some call it 'chess.'" Signor Bassi moved closer, and Laura followed. "I believe it originated a thousand years ago in the Far East—India or Persia."

They watched the older gentleman, wearing a jeweler's eyeglass around his neck, move a chess piece one square forward. His opponent, a young man wearing an embroidered yarmulke on his head, responded by moving a piece of his own.

Laura studied the game. "The board has sixty-four squares. And the colors of the squares alternate light and dark." She did the math in her head. "Papà, that's thirty-two light squares and thirty-two dark squares."

"That's true." He looked at her curiously. "How did you calculate so quickly?"

Laura, feigning innocence, shrugged. She was not going to give away the secret she and Father Stegani shared.

Their eyes moved back to the rapid play of the opponents. Signor Bassi did his best to explain.

"As you see, each player starts with sixteen pieces. One king, one queen, two towers, two bishops, two knights, and eight pawns. A player must use his pieces to protect his king at all costs."

The older man moved a knight quickly on the board. Signor Bassi was impressed.

"Ah! See, Laura, he has trapped his son's king—there is nowhere to move it for safety . . . ."

The jeweler knocked over the chess piece; the king lay on its side on the board.

"Ah, he has won the game," said Signor Bassi.

"I would like to learn to play scacchi, Papà."

The jeweler waved his hand as if Laura's request was absurd. "Not for girls, not for girls."

A creased formed in Laura's forehead as her father led her away. "Girls live in this world, too, Papà. Why shouldn't I want to learn?"

Signor Bassi kissed her cheek. "Of course you should. But now, let us go buy a big—but not too heavy—blue hat for your mother's birthday."

~

Laura placed the large present, tied with a pink ribbon, in the middle of the dining table. Father Stegani would be joining them, and Laura was helping Nucca set the table for dinner. Nucca kept an eye on where Laura placed the forks and spoons.

"Your mother will inspect the table, Laura. It's the wife's duty. Just as she writes the supper menu for me each morning. I tell the cook—for Cook cannot read—and Cook shops and then prepares the meal. Your mother checks in midday to make sure all is on schedule. You'll do this when you are mistress of a home. It's what a lady does."

Laura nodded, but she wasn't thinking of table settings. She was anticipating the surprise she and Father Stegani had planned before tonight's birthday supper. She spied Father Stegani stride through the gates to their villa.

"There he is!"

"A young lady does not shout, *signorina*," Nucca sighed.

But Laura was already calling to her parents to gather in the parlor. Signora Bassi, wrapped in a warm shawl, took a place on a chaise. The panforte delicacies, put there to tempt her weak appetite, remained untouched beside her.

Signor Bassi poured himself a glass of fine wine and sat next to his wife. "What is this surprise you two have for us?"

Father Stegani lifted Laura so that she stood on a hard chair.

"Be careful, *mia cara*," Signora Bassi warned.

Father Stegani gave a deep bow and announced that Signorina Laura Maria Caterina Bassi would like to share her latest studies. "Since she will be seven years old in just a few weeks, we have decided to concentrate on the number seven. My cousin will answer my questions first in Dante's Italian, then in French, and then in Latin."

Laura's parents shared a look. *What questions?*

Father Stegani started with simple addition. "Seven plus twenty-five is—"

"Thirty-two." Laura said. And then she added "*trente-deux*" and "*triginta duo.*" She grinned at her mother and explained, "That will be your age in seven years."

Signora Bassi gave a light laugh. "Oh dear, don't remind me."

Father Stegani prompted, "Seven plus fifty-seven is—"

"Sixty-four," Laura answered, again using the three languages. "That is a number two times larger than your age now, Papà."

"And now," Father Stegani announced, "the multiplication of seven."

Using her three languages, Laura ran through the multiplication table up to the number twenty-five. She finished with a flourish.

"Seven times twenty-five is one-hundred and seventy-five. That is a large number, but it is not even close to a number that is called 'infinity.'"

"Infinity?" Signora Bassi repeated. She pressed her hands together, anxious. "I've never heard that word. Is that a proper word for a young lady?"

Laura nodded. "It is, Mamma." She turned to Father Stegani, who lifted a lesson board. Laura had drawn an image in chalk. It was an elongated numeral eight that rested on its side. "An Englishman named John Wallis designed this symbol for it."

Laura clapped her hands in glee. "It's a number that never ever ends. It's part of mathematics. In French, it is called *infini*. In Latin, the word is *infinitum*."

Laura's parents were silent. They did not know of another girl in Bologna who was learning multiplication tables. They glanced at Father Stegani.

"Don't ask me anything more about infinity, I don't understand it," Father Stegani laughed. "Laura read about it in one of the pamphlets Giuseppe brought home from the salons."

Signor Bassi, guilty, avoided his wife's questioning gaze.

Father Stegani turned to Laura and applauded. "Well done, Cousin."

Laura hopped off the chair and curtsied. "Now we can eat." Laura took her mother's hand and led her into the dining room. "There's another surprise for you there, Mamma."

Father Stegani hung back to talk to Signor Bassi. "Giuseppe, you can see Laura is special. It would be a shame to not challenge her."

Signor Bassi sighed, worried. His daughter, indeed, was special.

The season's first snow swirled past the windows of the Bassi home. Laura, her lips pursed, sat on the window seat of her room. She was using her abacus to solve her latest mathematical problems. She moved the leaden balls on the wires stretched across the instrument's wooden frame and jotted her answers in her notebook.

"Laura?"

She looked up. Signor Bassi was standing in the doorway.

"Oh, Papà. I'm trying to prove this equation." She lifted

a pamphlet. "If I can figure out how it's been solved, then I'll understand more. But I might need a bigger abacus."

"Already?" Signor Bassi laughed.

It was just last week that she and her father had visited Bologna's newest shop, Divertimenti. He'd told her that the first of these shops had recently opened in London, where an Enlightenment scholar, John Locke, was advocating for educational toys for children. Signor Bassi told Laura, "Locke calls them 'rational amusements' because they're meant to teach as well as entertain. He believes that the mind is a tabula rasa, a blank slate, to be written on by experience and learning."

Laura had marveled at the toys in the shop, the puzzles that formed maps and geographical formations, blocks with letters of the alphabet on them, foldable papers to study shapes, and shelves of other toys. Her father had let her pick one and she had chosen the small, colorful abacus. "Mathematics are important to science, Papà," she explained.

While her father had set up an account with the shopkeeper, Laura had spied the freckled Vincenzo Cruce entering the shop. He was with his friend, Alesso, a boy with a square face and large ears, who followed Vincenzo everywhere. They wore their school robes and sashes. She remembered trying to discuss steam engines with Vincenzo at Eugenia's palazzo, and that he had questioned their veracity. In the store, he had turned to look at her and scowled, crossed his eyes, and stuck out his tongue. Laura, confused, had felt a stab of hurt. Why was he unkind? She had tried to put it out of her mind, but the moment still stung.

But now, it was Christmas Eve and her father was holding a sparkling crystal ornament. "Shall we put this in your mother's basket while she is sleeping?"

Laura's face brightened. "*Sì, Papà.*"

They padded down the marble staircase and entered the library. Laura placed her mother's ornament in a basket near the fireplace. She noticed that in the center of the table, there was an odd shape covered with one of her mother's shawls.

"What is it, Papà?"

Signor Bassi pulled out a chair on which he had stacked two pillows. "This will be your chair."

Laura, curious, lodged herself on the pillows. Signor Bassi, building anticipation, pinched the crest of the shawl between two fingers. With a quick flourish, he lifted it to reveal a magnificent chess set.

Laura gasped, "*Bellisima!*"

The board's squares were made of rosewood veneer; half of the squares were stained a golden amber, the other half glinted in a deeper rosy hue. The frame of the board was fashioned of walnut, rubbed with an inky dye to darken its tone. The chess pieces were carved of alabaster; one set had been dipped in a red tint, the other shone a creamy white. The royal couples of the game—the kings and queens—were represented with stately and stern faces, the knights carved as horse heads, with strong-jawed, implacable glares. The bishops had solemn looks and the towers were topped with impressive parapets. The pawns were carved as foot soldiers, carrying small lances.

"Oh, Papà. You remembered I wanted to learn scacchi! Can we play?"

There was a twinkle in his eyes. "It is my Christmas Eve present to you."

Laura squirmed with anticipation.

"You had observed, Laura, that the game can be approached mathematically," said Signor Bassi. "So, let's examine the board.

Notice there are eight vertical columns—these columns are called 'files.' The rows can be referred to in rising numbers from one to eight."

Laura traced a finger up the side of the board. "Files. Rows one to eight."

Her father continued, "There are also eight squares that are horizontal to the player. These are called 'ranks.' They're identified with the first eight letters of the alphabet." Signor Bassi motioned to her grouping of chess pieces. "You'll play with the lighter colored pieces."

Laura counted the squares. "My queen now sits on the square that is file number one, rank D." She assessed the other pieces, getting their placements set in her mind. "My king is on the file number one, rank E. He has a bishop, knight, and tower to protect his right flank. I have eight soldiers lined across the board, starting in file number two . . . ."

Signor Bassi explained, "They're meant to protect the king and queen and the court. The pawns are considered to be of least value on a chessboard."

"But if the king needs this line of protection, how can they be considered of less value?"

Signor Bassi rubbed his hands together, looking forward to the game. "Perhaps Count Marsili will tell us more about military strategy."

Laura paused, considering her father's words. "Playing chess is like a battle?"

"*Sì*. It's about knowing when to attack and when to hold back."

Laura sighed. "I wonder if Count Marsili will answer me if I get a chance to ask him another question."

Signor Bassi was still rankled at Marsili's pointed dismissal of Laura. But there was nothing he could do about it. The count was an important person in Bologna.

"When you're ready to start, my daughter, you will say, 'White—to play.'"

Laura's eyes narrowed, her voice full of worry. "Papà, what if I win the game?"

Confused, Signor Bassi tipped his head to the side and told Laura there was a winner and loser in every game.

"But Eugenia told me that a girl should always let the boy win."

Signor Bassi chose his words carefully. "Would the game be fun for me if I knew I would always win?"

Laura thought about that. "I don't think so. I think you would grow tired of playing chess with me."

"I think so, too," Signor Bassi said. "Every person should rise to their best possible self. In life. In chess."

Laura's grin was wide. "*Bene, Papà.*" She reached her small hand to move a pawn. "White—to play."

Chapter Three

Laura sat next to her mother's bed, her brow wrinkled with worry. "Mamma, do you want to eat today? Nucca will bring you broth, maybe some bread."

Signora Bassi gave a weak smile. "No, *mia cara*. I'll consider later."

Her parents' bedroom had been Laura's chosen place for over a week now. Signora Bassi's weakness, stomach pains, and sore limbs had kept her from venturing downstairs. Many doctors had visited, but they had offered no relief.

"Do you want me to read aloud again?" Laura asked, reaching for her book. "When Dante spies Beatrice in Paradise, Mamma. Is it still your favorite?"

Signora Bassi nodded her head, closed her eyes, and mouthed the words along with Laura.

"On high looked Beatrice, and I on her; and in the time, perhaps,
an arrow takes to light, and fly, and from the notch be freed,

I had come to a marvel and she was lovely and said,
'Direct thy grateful mind to God . . .'"

"Why do you love this passage so much, Mamma?"

Signora Bassi took Laura's hand. "Your father first read it to me. It is about love. Great love, which I want for you one day."

"The poet Dante loved Beatrice?"

"*Sì*. He first set eyes on her in Florence; she was a young girl and he was not much older. But it was love at first sight." Her mother's voice was barely above a whisper. Laura could feel the coldness of her fingertips.

"Shall I read more?"

"*Sì*. Read to me how Beatrice shows Dante heaven—how she lives inside a rose, on a lovely petal with angels flying around like bees, bringing love and peace to all who reside in Paradise."

Laura heard footsteps on the stairs. Signor Bassi and a tall, fair-haired, bespectacled young doctor, wearing a gray velvet waistcoat and dark breeches, a ruffled shirt, and polished, buckled shoes, entered the room. Nucca was close behind, carrying fresh linens.

Signor Bassi made the introductions. "Dearest wife, Dottore Gaetano Tacconi has recently received his degree from the Collegio di Medicina and has knowledge of the latest skills—in diagnosis and procedures." He motioned to Laura. "Dottore, please meet our daughter."

Laura curtsied and moved to Nucca; she leaned against the housekeeper's solid frame. She hoped that this doctor might find a way to make her mother feel better.

Over the next few days, Dottore Tacconi spent many hours at

the Bassi home. Laura continued to read to her mother for it soothed her as the doctor administered the purgatives—mixtures of aloe and ash to flush unwanted fluids—as he applied lead plasters to her mother's abdomen to reduce swelling and started a course of disambiguation—bloodletting. Laura documented the procedures in her notebook and wrote down his directions for care—in Latin and in French. She wanted to make sure nothing was forgotten.

At the end of the week, Tacconi's curiosity got the better of him. He straightened his finely curled wig and ventured, "Signorina, may I see what you've been writing?"

Laura nodded. Her small hands offered him her notebook.

His pointed chin was tucked to his chest as he turned the pages. "How old are you?"

"I am eight years old."

"And where did you learn languages?"

"My cousin, Father Stegani. And he also teaches me mathematics—as much as he knows. I try to learn more on my own. I read the pamphlets my father brings home from the university salons. Written by those of the Enlightenment. I like the ones on science the best. But some are very complicated for me."

Tacconi, under his breath, murmured, "They're complicated for many."

Laura had been wanting to ask many questions over the past week, and now there seemed to be an opening. "Did you study at Count Marsili's new institute? What are the ingredients in a plaster? And why do you take away blood? Papà says blood replenishes itself, but how does it do that? How many sciences are involved in medicine?"

"Those are quite a number of questions."

"Father worries I ask too many," Laura admitted.

Tacconi noticed the chess set in the corner of the room. "Does your father play scacchi?"

"*Sì*, Dottore. My father and I play sometimes while Mamma sleeps. We don't want her to wake and feel alone."

"Did you say that you yourself play the game of chess?"

Laura nodded. "My father fears I might checkmate him soon." She smiled. "He says that I should try as hard as I can to do so, and so I am."

Tacconi fastened the clasps on his medical bag. "Perhaps I should talk to your father. I believe he said he'd be in his library." He gave a slight bow. "Good day, Signorina."

Laura watched Dottore Tacconi move down the wide staircase and knock on her father's library door. She bit her lip, worried. She hoped she hadn't been too inquiring—or said anything wrong.

Inside the library, Tacconi accepted a goblet of fortified wine from Signor Bassi. "I believe your wife is gaining in health. And your daughter has been a great asset. Her reading, her attention to the timing of bathing her mother's forehead and to the attending nurse's administrations—they are commendable."

Signor Bassi nodded. "Laura is conscientious and she loves her mother very much."

"And young Signorina Bassi seems to have a talent for languages. And interest in many things. Perhaps you'd consider hiring me as a tutor to extend her studies into areas of philosophy. We would stay to the topics that are acceptable for young girls, of course. My fee is negotiable." Tacconi did not tell Signor Bassi that he had unpaid bills at the shops of the tailors and the wigmakers.

Signor Bassi was surprised. "It's unusual for a young girl to have a tutor. I'll think on it. Thank you for your offer, Dottore Tacconi."

Later that night, Laura sat at her window seat, deeply involved in her reading. The thick tallow candle was low; the flame was growing fainter. Her father entered her room.

"Daughter, it's time for bed."

Laura looked up at him. There were tears in her eyes.

Signor Bassi hurried to her. "Are you ill?"

"Oh, Papà, this is a very sad story." She showed him her book. "You know about Hypatia?"

"The Roman scholar? She lived more than a thousand years ago."

Laura nodded. "In Alexandria, Egypt. She was a doctor and a scientist and taught in her own school. And then she was put to death because she wanted to understand God's design of the world. She wrote this." Laura read, *"Life is an unfoldment, and the further we travel the more truth we comprehend. To understand the things at our door is the best preparation for understanding those that live beyond."*

She wiped the salty wetness from her cheeks. "Why was she punished for wanting to learn?"

Signor Bassi hesitated. How should he answer this? "Misunderstanding," he spoke gently. "Misuse of power, perhaps. But the desire to gain knowledge should never be punished. It should be celebrated."

Laura looked out her window and mused aloud. "Sometimes I feel as if I'll never know everything. That feeling makes me so sad."

The candlelight flickered and extinguished. They were in darkness; only a sliver of moonlight illuminated the corners of the room.

Laura moved to her bed and settled her head on her pillow. "*Buono notte, Papà.*" She sighed, closed her eyes, and was quickly asleep.

At that moment, Signor Bassi determined to do the unexpected for his exceptional daughter. He would not listen to those in Bologna who believed in society's strict protocol. He would send word to Tacconi tomorrow and hire him as Laura's tutor.

It was two weeks later and Laura was up at dawn.

"Nucca, I couldn't sleep, not a bit!" Laura's voice was filled with excitement. She pulled on long woolen stockings and Nucca helped her tie silk ribbons below her knees so that the stockings would not slide down and gather at her ankles. "I've made a list of questions to ask."

Nucca helped Laura into a washed-linen petticoat and a rose-colored mantua that buttoned up the back. She pulled Laura's hair gently off her forehead and tied it back with strips of lace.

Laura was impatient. "I'm ready, Nucca."

"Your lesson doesn't start for another hour, Signorina," Nucca said, but Laura was already bounding down the wide staircase into the breakfast room.

"Mamma, you look so pretty. There is pink back in your face." Laura kissed her mother's cheek.

Signora Bassi patted a place at the table near her. "Laura, you must have some cheese and bread so your stomach will not growl during your lesson."

"Nothing will keep me from learning," Laura assured her. She took a bite of cheese. "I like goat cheese, Mamma. But I was wondering about it. Both cows and goats eat grass, but their milk tastes different and so do the cheeses made from their milk. Papà said the milk will reflect the grass the goat or cow eats—but if they eat the same grass, why does the cheese still taste different?"

Signora Bassi smiled. She did not know where these questions came from. "I don't know the answer to that."

"Do you think Dottore Tacconi will know?" Laura took out her notebook. "I'll add the question to my list."

An hour later, Laura sat with her hands folded and watched Dottore Tacconi. He carefully placed his three-sided cocked hat on a chair and smoothed his chestnut-colored, horsehair wig. He lifted books from his leather satchel and nodded to Laura.

"We'll concentrate on your languages and the topics of ethics and logic. A fine young woman, versed in these things, will make an excellent impression. Therefore, we'll begin with Socrates, Plato, and Aristotle, then venture through the centuries."

Laura nodded, wanting to please. "*Grazie*, Dottore. And I've prepared also." She showed him the pamphlets stacked on the parlor table. "These cover subjects I've questions about. Topics that I think about when I am waking and going to sleep. And in between those times, too." She reached for the top pamphlet. "This one is written by the Englishman Edmond Halley about his work. It was first published in English, but I do not know that language, so I read a French and a Latin translation. It's about seeing a particular comet—one with a very long tail—in the sky. This is my question: How can an astronomer like Master Halley predict that the same comet has appeared before and will appear again in the future?"

Tacconi took a moment; this conversation was not part of his lesson plan. He flicked a bit of dust from his waistcoat. "I suppose thinking about the heavens is acceptable for a young girl. I did present a short defense on astronomy when earning my *laurea*."

"What is a *laurea*?"

"My doctorate. My badge of high learning. It's the University of Bologna's belief that scholars should be informed on many subjects." Tacconi raised his eyes to the tall ceilings in the parlor and recalled his information. "It was once thought, actually by Aristotle, that comets were disturbances in the sky. Then it was discovered, by use of theoretical mathematics, that comets were entities that orbited the sun. Astronomer Halley is a theorist. He studied the new ideas of gravity that his friend, another Englishman named Isaac Newton, published—as well as centuries of reports on comets."

Laura checked the pamphlet. "This comet appeared last in 1682. I don't understand how Master Halley can calculate that it will appear again every eight decades or so. How can he know that? He was not alive in 1607 or 1531 or before to see the comet's orbit."

Tacconi leaned back, enjoying the role of instructor. "Theories, young signorina, are reached in various ways. Master Halley read documentation on various comets. He discussed gravity and parallax mathematics with his friend Newton and came to an unprovable but highly possible conclusion."

Laura's curiosity was piqued. "What is parallax mathematics?"

Tacconi waved off the question. "Much too complicated for us to discuss."

Laura decided to concentrate on Halley; she did the calculation in her head. "If Master Halley is correct, the next sighting should be around 1758. That is forty-five years from now."

Tacconi, surprised, realized this girl was quick. "That sounds right."

Laura pressed, "But you said 'unprovable.'"

"That is why it's a theory. Based on research and projections. Theories are expectations of what might be."

"But not really *knowing*." Laura sat back. "I would like to focus on science that can be proven."

"Literature and the more gentler studies will be of more use for you."

Laura was on her own track. "Copernicus theorized that the sun was the center of our world."

"*Sì*, that's true. Copernicus spent three years studying law and astronomy at our University of Bologna. He wrote *De Revolutionibus Orbium Coelestium* here."

"As a theory. And then Galileo proved it."

"*Sì*. Galileo had to invent a telescope to prove Copernicus's theory." Tacconi explained, "Galileo looked through his telescope at a planet we call Venus. He could see that Venus went through phases, like our moon, and realized these phases could only happen if Venus was traveling around the sun. With further observation, Galileo concluded that the Earth also circled the center—the sun."

Laura's brow furrowed. "But then, when Galileo presented his observation, it made the Vatican and the Pope angry. Galileo was put in prison and asked to recant."

"The Inquisition of the time had its purpose," Tacconi said.

"What was that?"

"To combat Protestantism," Tacconi continued, as if repeating a standard, agreed-upon answer. "To keep people from interpreting scripture in their own ways. It was accepted that the

Earth was the center at that time and the Vatican did not want anything to be questioned."

Laura leaned forward. "But now, it's commonly accepted that he was right—but still there are writings of Galileo that the Church bans. Have you read them?"

Tacconi felt a throbbing in his temple—Laura's mind was mercurial and he felt he'd lost control of this lesson. "If the work is banned, it is best to avoid it. There are many other things to study."

Laura leaned forward. "I don't like the idea of scientists—who are only trying to understand God's world—being put in prison for their thinking. Do you, Dottore Tacconi?"

Tacconi sighed. This was a controversial topic. It was known that the sitting pope, Clement XI, was a patron of science, but still, it was never good to criticize past decisions of the Church. Tacconi had aspirations of rising in society and he knew that Bologna's social circles could turn their backs on a scholar who was too argumentative.

He handed Laura a book. "Socrates, Plato, and Aristotle. That is on our agenda. Quill and ink ready? You will want to take notes."

Laura opened her notebook. "*Bene.* The Greeks." She looked up. "That brings me to another question. I would also like to know why certain ideas and inventions of ancient Greeks and Romans disappeared for centuries. Even when they had been recorded. Like using steam for power. And harvesting machines on farms that were more efficient than the ones we use today. And necessary rooms where the unmentionables were swept into a receptacle."

Tacconi's ruffled collar began to feel tight. He was not about to talk to this young girl about toilets. He lifted the pamphlets off the table and put them to the side.

"Signorina Laura, your mind seems to be full of too many things. We must start at a beginning. I've chosen the early Greeks."

"*Bene*. It did help to learn Latin before French," Laura mused. She wrote in her notebook. "I'll write down 'parallax mathematics.' We mustn't forget to discuss that." Her small hand continued to write. "I'm also writing down Sir Isaac Newton. He seems to be an interesting thinker in the Enlightenment."

"Signorina, we must focus."

Laura nodded. "One more thing." She added a sentence to her notebook. "I need to make a list for what one must do to earn a laurea."

Chapter Four

In May 1721, a mass was held at the Basilica di San Petronio to eulogize Pope Clement XI and pray for the new pope, Pope Innocent XIII. Laura sat with her parents as Father Stegani spoke of the recently deceased Clement XI's kindly leadership, his patronage of art, and his passion for archaeology.

"Because of the support of Clement XI, the catacombs of Rome have been opened to us. We can explore the burial places of Christians as far back as the second century. These deep caverns are filled with frescoes, sculpture, and medals of gold . . . ."

Laura, along with many of the parishioners, had her eyes on the front pew—a pew reserved for one of the richest and most eminent families of Bologna. One of its most popular elder sons sat in attendance, his back straight, his hands pressed against his chest in prayer. The impressive Monsignor Prospero Lambertini was famous in the city; at age thirteen, he'd gone to Rome to attend the Collegio Clementianum to study philosophy and civil law. At age nineteen, he'd received laureas in theology and law. Laura wished she could ask him about all he learned, what it was like to dedicate years to study. And what it felt like to excel—almost beyond Bologna's dreams. A dozen years ago, Pope Clement XI, recognizing Lambertini as one of the greatest scholars of Christendom, had appointed him a monsignor and Promoter of the Faith, and then raised him to membership in the Vatican's Sacred Council.

But what was most compelling about him, Laura thought, was what her father told her this morning. Monsignor Lambertini had committed large personal funds to the Institute of Science and loved science as much as theology, just like Laura. Her father had told her that the men at the salons hoped that the monsignor would use his influence in the Vatican, for many were worried that the new frugal and conservative pope, Innocent XIII, would cut funding for scientific work. Laura bent her head and delivered a silent prayer, hoping that Monsignor Lambertini could change the pope's mind.

After Mass, the Bassi family strolled under Bologna's colonnades—the wide, covered walkways with brilliantly painted ceilings that protected the pedestrians of the city from the sun and rains. The colonnades fronted the Palazzo del Podestà, where the city's government had their offices, and the grand Palazzo d'Accursio, one of the city's largest buildings, once the seat to kings and jurists and the symbol of Bologna's political power.

In one of the piazza's small cafés, Laura noticed a group of tables filled with chess players. She pulled at her father's arm.

"Look, Papà. Scacchi." She smiled up at him. "Do you forget we're in the middle of a game? I wonder if you've been too busy to play because you're afraid I might checkmate you."

Signor Bassi tucked his wife's thin hand into the crook of

his arm and laughed. "You're a fine opponent, my daughter. And I'm sorry I've spent too much time lately on business. However, it's now official. I've been appointed the city's governor and chancellor for estates. My clients will include Bologna's senators and vice-legates." He pointed to a high window of the Palazzo d'Accursio. "There's my new office."

Signora Bassi leaned into her husband; she was proud. "Admirable news, isn't it, Laura. It means we will get a fine carriage and the family will receive more social invitations. Our dressmaker will be busy."

They were interrupted. "I am pleased to introduce my uncle, Signor Bassi, and his family."

The Bassis turned to see Father Stegani standing with Lambertini; the monsignor was in his ankle-length black cassock with fuchsia trim and sash. Laura was awestruck. She and her mother dipped into curtsies and Signor Bassi bowed.

Father Stegani took Laura's hand and continued. "This is my ten-year-old cousin I told you about—Signorina Laura Bassi."

Lambertini bent so he was at eye level with Laura. "Ah. I hear you speak Latin and French and are starting Greek. And do mathematics. Why do you study so hard?"

Laura liked his kind, intelligent eyes. "I want to be part of the Enlightenment and be part of the University of Bologna."

Father Stegani chuckled as Signora Bassi inhaled in surprise. Signor Bassi was about to temper Laura's assertion, but Monsignor Lambertini kept his focus on Laura. He smiled. "Have you ever been to the university?"

Laura shook her head. "I dream about it. All the ideas that are spoken of in one place. It seems like it must be like heaven."

"Would you and your father like to see the classrooms that Count Marsili has provided at the new Institute of Science?"

Laura looked to her father, her eyes pleading for his acceptance.

It was a few weeks later, in early June, that Laura sat in the family's new carriage next to her father, headed to the Institute of Science. The warm sun shone on the Piazza di Porta Ravennate and Laura smoothed her soft-green silk mantua, with its overskirt of cream-colored organza. She noticed the tips of her bleached cowhide shoes; she had told Nucca she must wear her softest ones, for she wanted to be able to move quickly and see everything at the university. And now she was almost there.

"Is it really the oldest university in Europe, Papà?"

"It is, and considered one of the most demanding."

"I hope we'll be able to see the laboratories where the experiments take place."

The carriage passed two of the tallest towers in Bologna.

Laura smiled. "I like that the towers are leaning—and lean more every year. That they defy falling down."

"They've stood for over six hundred years. I see it as a tribute to competition and hubris."

"Hubris?"

"Excessive pride. The two families, the Asinellis and the Garisendas, each wanted to show they were wealthier and more powerful than the other. Each of their towers started at seventy meters, but they each kept adding height to outdo each other. The foundations were finally stressed and the towers weakened and began to lean." Signor Bassi smiled. "As the Bible's Book of Proverbs suggests, 'Pride goeth before destruction, and a haughty spirit before a fall.'"

Laura turned to keep her eyes on the towers and they continued on. "I wonder when gravity will win out?"

The carriage turned onto Via Zamboni and Laura was transfixed by the immense Palazzo Poggi. Laura gazed at the newly constructed Specola Tower that had been built for studies in astronomy.

"Look, Papà. Wouldn't it be wonderful to look at the stars from there?"

Laura got out of the carriage and gazed at the institute's red-orange exterior, its deep colonnade supported by thick columns topped with Ionic capitals. Groups of male students, in long flowing robes and carrying satchels filled with books and quills, moved across the stone courtyard.

Laura and her father moved to a large doorway and entered the loggia. The entry room was impressive. Laura took in the glass-faced bookshelves filled with artifacts—skeletons of small mammals, books, scientific instruments, and geologic specimens. She gazed up at the painted frescoes that lined the upper areas of the walls.

"Papà, look, it's Odysseus and his adventures."

"As I understand it, the Cardinal Giovanni Poggi, who first owned this palazzo, was inspired by the story of the Greek god . . . ."

A voice from behind them finished the thought. "And when Count Marsili bought the palazzo, he too found it applicable to scientists' adventures, all full of curiosity and strength." Monsignor Lambertini joined them in admiring the frescoes. "Pellegrino Tibaldi painted them. You can see that each panel is one of the adventures where Odysseus outsmarts or outlasts an opponent."

Laura saw Count Marsili enter the doors. She dipped into a curtsy.

The count nodded to the two men and ignored Laura. "I'm off to a meeting with the Academic Council. Pray that they will cease to argue with me about accepting new curriculums. We must keep up with the French and English." He nodded to Signor Bassi. "You've been a generous donor. Perhaps you might consider hosting one of the salons?"

"It would be my honor, Count Marsili," said Signor Bassi.

Laura's heart beat faster. If a salon was held at the Bassi home, she would have a chance to listen to the lecturer and the discussions.

Marsili turned to Lambertini. "Monsignor, you leave for the Vatican today?"

Lambertini nodded. "In an hour."

Marsili bowed to the men and moved off.

Laura realized she had been ignored again. She frowned, concluding that the count must not find her interesting enough to acknowledge. But she lifted her shoulders and shook off the feeling. Nothing was going to dampen her happiness at being at the university.

Lambertini motioned to a door that led to the classroom area, and Laura and Signor Bassi strode next to him and listened to his tour.

"Many of the larger rooms of the palazzo are now lecture halls," he explained. "Others have been designated as laboratory space. There are studies in navigation, chemistry, military history, geography, astronomy, physics, optics, anatomy, and natural sciences."

They passed the open doors of laboratories and Laura saw male students at long tables, looking into microscopes. There were small cages filled with frogs, snakes, and mice. Across the hall was an open classroom door, Laura saw a mathematical problem written on a painted board. They entered a lecture room that had once been the ballroom.

"We'll sit here, in the back," said Lambertini, "so as to not disturb the students."

Risers were set into three sides of the room; on each level were benches with thin wooden tables in front of them. Students were settling in, taking inkwells, quills, and vellum from their leather satchels. In the center of the room was a large table flanked by a dozen chairs, reserved for professors. A dais was set at the far end, ready for the lecturer. A glass pitcher of watered wine was set on one side of the lectern.

Just then, three aged men dressed in deep burgundy velvet robes and gray wigs, their feet moving slowly, entered the room and took their seats at the long table.

"Who are they?"

"Members of the Academic Council," Lambertini spoke in a low voice. "They have been professors at the university for decades."

The door near the dais opened, and the lecturer entered. He wore a full, flowing black robe and a white wig. He quickly took his place behind the lectern and planted a pair of glasses on his nose.

"Today, students, we will start our understanding of the thermoscope."

Laura leaned forward as he nodded for the assistants to lift the cloth off a large rectangular board. On the board, thin glass tubes with glass bulbs at their ends were attached to hooks. Laura could see dots painted on the thin glass tubes, all black except for the white top line.

The lecturer continued, "Galileo often gets credit as the first to have designed an instrument that could show temperature change. However, history reports of a more primitive instrument designed during the Hellenic periods. It looked like this . . . ."

An assistant lifted the cloth off another hidden object, revealing a vase filled halfway with water. A thin glass tube topped with a glass bulb stood in the vase.

"The liquid inside the tube will rise and fall with a change of temperature," said the lecturer. "When there is heat, the air in the upper bulb will expand, forcing the water level down. When it is cooler, the air in the upper bulb will contract and the water level will rise."

Laura was fascinated.

The lecturer went on. "In 1701, the Danish scientist Romer added numbers—to show where the temperature reached a freezing effect and a boiling effect. Today, we will discuss the work of Dottore Daniel Gabriel Fahrenheit, working in The Hague, and his use of mercury in a thermoscope. What term do we use for a thermoscope today?"

A student raised his hand and stood. "A thermometer."

"Correct," said the lecturer. "Firstly, we'll discuss where this mercury is obtained and note that it is the only metal that is liquid at normal temperatures and pressure."

Laura was struck by the realization that all discoveries contributed to and built on one another. It was exciting to know what instruments were available now and how to use them, but they became doubly interesting when she knew of their evolution.

Monsignor Lambertini leaned over to whisper to Signor Bassi. "It is time for me to leave for Rome."

Laura wanted to stay and hear the rest of the lecture, but

she knew she had to follow Lambertini and her father out of the classroom. Moments later, they were thanking the monsignor for the tour. He smiled.

"So, now you have been in the institute, Signorina Laura. Was that satisfactory?"

"No, monsignor."

Signor Bassi was startled. "Laura, *prego*."

Laura made herself clear. "It was wonderful. But you asked if I was satisfied and I am not—because I want to be here every day."

"Ah." Monsignor Lambertini nodded.

"*Ma questo è stato un grande regalo. Mille grazie.*" Laura curtsied. "It is a great gift you have given me."

Several months later, the leaves on the trees were a brilliant orange and the Mucchis' rose-colored palazzo glowed in the autumn sunlight. Signora Mucchi had arranged for dancing lessons to be held for the girls in the palazzo's ballroom and Laura was excited to see Eugenia to share with her the new Greek words she'd learned. She wanted to tell her about how Aristotle and other Greeks held dramas in amphitheatres and how there were grand games of sports called the Olympics. Laura, stepping carefully in her first pair of heeled shoes, held her mother's elbow as they exited their carriage and stepped onto the courtyard of the Mucchi palazzo.

"*Buongiorno!*" the daughters of Bologna's noble families called to one another as they alighted with their mothers from the carriages. New hats were admired, new jewelry was appreciated, and the mothers shared wonderment that their daughters were now of an age to be considering promises of betrothal.

"They're barely twelve years old," Signora Bassi commented. She pulled her shawl more tightly around her shoulders; the chill in her bones still persisted.

"I was married at thirteen," the sour Signora Belnonte divulged, patting her high-necked mantua and string of pearls. "My first confinement was at fourteen and three other children followed quickly. Plans must be made."

Signora Mucchi, her wide, shimmering silk skirts rustling, walked next to Signora Bassi as the mothers moved to the parlor. "Eugenia has told me that Laura is being tutored."

Signora Bassi was aware of a criticizing tone. "In subjects that are proper. Laura, as you know, is very curious."

Signora Mucchi sniffed. "And you approve?"

"Signor Bassi finds it appropriate." Signora Bassi felt she should defend Laura's tutelage, but she did not want to displease Signora Mucchi.

Signora Mucchi emitted a long sigh. "A father may not understand how difficult it is to make a matrimonial match."

"We hope for happiness for Laura."

Signora Mucchi tsked, her tongue clicking crisply against the back of her front teeth. "Of course, I forgot. You and your husband are not from the old families of Bologna, so how could you understand the society here?" She lowered her voice and leaned in close to Signora Bassi. "We've already had inquiries about Eugenia, of course. The Mucchi family is generations-old and respected, well-connected." She smiled, pleased. "My task, most likely, will be sorting through suitors."

"Of course. Eugenia is lovely," Signora Bassi nodded.

"And Laura is . . . different. A man can stand out, be admired for accomplishments. That is not a woman's place. So, you see why I say a mother must always look ahead." Signora Mucchi quickened her pace and swept into the parlor, announcing, "Today, *mia amicas*, a game of Scopa. Let us ready ourselves for card play."

Signora Bassi took her designated place at a card table. The words of her hostess stung—for Signora Bassi had recognized the underlying truths. Bologna's society was tiered and uncompromising. And, more importantly, a mother does want the best for her daughter.

In the wide, tapestry-filled hallway, Laura and Eugenia walked, their arms wrapped around each other's waists.

"My mother says that these heeled shoes will give us finer posture," said Eugenia.

"They slow me down," Laura complained. "But my mother says running is not acceptable for 'a young lady.'"

They snorted with glee. It was a new term for them to contemplate.

Eugenia twirled. "Being a 'young lady' might be wonderful, going to the theatre and concerts and parties. Flirting."

"Shall I teach you how to flirt in Greek?" Laura teased.

Eugenia's eyes twinkled. "*Sì*, that will make me very special."

They could hear the excited voices of the other girls behind them. "Wait for us!" The girls caught up with them, all nervous about the dance mistress. "We've heard she demands perfection."

"Signorinas!" A shrill voice streaked through the air as the ballroom doors opened.

Signora Aldona, wielding a thick, twisted cane with an ivory handle, stood before them. She was big-boned and wore a widow's black dress. Her dark hair, streaked with gray, was pulled back tightly, straining her scalp.

Eugenia leaned into Laura. "Her mouth turns down so far, the edges of her lips touch her chin."

"Her first chin," Laura giggled. "She has three or four of them."

Signora Aldona watched as the girls formed a line in the elegant room. Then she paced, assessing the party dresses and high-heeled shoes. Finally, she nodded.

"We'll start with the allemande, the dance that has swept Europe. It originated in Germany, but when the King of France took an interest, it became the mode of Europe. It must be in your repertoire. Imagine catching the eye of the new king, Louis XV—who has yet to take a bride!"

Eugenia's eyes were bright. "Let's pretend we're dancing in the king's ballroom."

Signora Aldona announced, "Every movement is an opportunity to catch an eye!"

Each girl ventured a shallow curtsy, then hopped to the left and to the right, turned her head, and dipped a shoulder to the left as Signora Aldona thrust the cane into the floor, creating a sturdy, rhythmic *thwump*. "Arch the foot as you present it. The hem of your dress is raised one inch. Only one inch of stocking! Decorum is expected."

Laura, standing next to Eugenia, wobbled in her high-heeled shoe. "I have to concentrate on staying upright."

Signor Aldona's strident voice penetrated. "My son will play the spinet and provide the music! Let's start the promenade!"

Her bored and pimply son, only a few years older than the girls, played an uninspired rendition of a Baroque dance suite.

Signora Aldona raised her cane in the air. "The allemande is the beginning, signorinas. Then we learn the gavotte and the gigue. Under my tutelage, you will impress! Now, a full turn— and back to the beginning steps!"

Laura turned the wrong way and her ankle twisted as she

tried to adjust her direction. She strove for balance, trying not to put weight on her throbbing foot, and her heel slipped on the varnished floor.

"Ah!" She landed on her backside, her stiff petticoats lifting her dress upward and exposing her hastily tied stockings.

The music stopped. A silence fell as all waited for Signora Aldona's reaction. Laura heard the *thwump thwump* of the stick.

Signora Aldona strode over to her. "Name?"

"Laura Maria Caterina Bassi." Laura's voice was small.

"You must listen to my instructions and concentrate." Signora Aldona was not pleased. "Are you a hopeless girl? You will not 'catch an eye' being hopeless!"

Tears of embarrassment came to Laura's eyes. Several of the girls tittered as Eugenia helped her friend onto her feet.

Laura, nursing her ankle, sat on a hard-backed chair for the rest of the dancing lesson. She wished she had tucked the handkerchief Nucca had wanted to give to her into the sleeve of her dress because she wanted to dab her runny nose. Her ankle felt as if it were on fire. She watched Eugenia and the other girls move across the floor. She thought of the words of Aristotle: "Pleasure in the job brings perfection in the work." She saw how much Eugenia enjoyed dancing and that surely her friend would be good at it. Laura sighed, wishing she was at home with her books, where she was happy.

Outside the long windows, she saw dark clouds gathering. She heard a rumble of thunder and perked up—had there been a streak of lightning that preceded the sound? She wished she could have witnessed the flash. The music continued, but Laura was no longer thinking about it. She was waiting, wondering: Would there be a storm tonight that would stir the air? Create an energy that, to her, was breathtaking? She had so many questions.

What moved the sky to these sensational shows? What was in the air that seemed to ignite? She hoped she would get answers to her questions one day.

Chapter Five

During the next year, Laura continued to master the Greek language and added German to her studies. The number of notebooks full of questions grew as she devoured the pamphlets her father brought home from the monthly salons. In the winter, she bothered Cook, conducting simple experiments in the kitchen. She set up jars in the windows to study evaporation of various liquids. She asked Cook if she could cut up and examine the organ meats delivered by the butcher. Early in the spring, Laura and her father installed a sundial in the garden. She put a fabric flag on a post and used a compass to take notes on the direction of the winds, and also gathered caterpillars, fed them, and watched the butterflies emerge from the cocoons. She and Nucca moved her father's telescope to the veranda so that she could better study the stars at night and make notations on constellations.

To her mother's consternation, Laura made excuses so as to not attend the dance lessons held at the Mucchi palazzo.

Signora Bassi was anxious. "Husband, there are dances and picnics in the parks. Musical concerts. Parties to announce the latest betrothals. Laura is often not invited."

"There is no cause for worry, Rosa Maria. Our Laura is happy. That's all that counts," said Signor Bassi.

Spring arrived and Signora Mucchi was at the Bassi home to settle plans for a summer social event at the city's exquisite botanical gardens. As the mothers conferred, Laura showed Eugenia her simple experiments in the Bassi garden. Then they entered the back door of the kitchen and looked at Laura's jars filled with various liquids, animal organs, and fruits.

"I'm experimenting with controlled fermentation and the development of yeast."

Eugenia tittered. "I don't know anything about those things."

"In a way, you do. Wine is made with fermentation. And bread with yeast. Those are just two things. Do you want to help with my next experiment?"

Eugenia crinkled her nose. "I don't want to cut open a liver or a lamb's heart."

"This experiment is about gravity."

"What is that?"

Laura gathered a small loaf of bread, a melon, and a bunch of grapes from the long kitchen workspace. She put them on the kitchen scale and notated their weight in her notebook.

"It's around us everywhere. It's why you and I don't float in the air. It's why plates stay on the table, why horses can pull carriages, why fruit falls from trees. It's why our dresses don't rise above our heads."

Eugenia's eyes grew wide. "Then I'm glad it exists." Spending time with Laura was always fun.

Laura put her notebook and the food items into a basket. "Sir Isaac Newton, an Englishman, has done interesting experiments and writings on it." Laura led Eugenia to the carriage house, whispering conspiratorially. "The groomsmen are walking the horses. So we'll have the place to ourselves."

Laura peeked through the door—the stables were, indeed, empty. The girls slipped inside.

Eugenia took in the packed earth floor and sniffed at the air, unused to the scent of the stables. "Did I tell you Count Cabell is accompanying my family to the opera tonight so that I may acquaint myself with him? He's a widower, more than four decades old."

"That's old," said Laura.

"And he has three daughters near our age. But Mamma may allow him to court me, for he has a grand palazzo, extensive properties along the Reno River, and five fine carriages." She saw Laura was climbing the thick ladder into the hayloft. "Where are you going?"

"We have to get up high." Laura reached the top of the ladder and stepped on the hayloft.

Eugenia shook her head, afraid to climb. "I'll stay down here."

Laura nodded. "Good idea—then you can see the results more clearly."

Laura, now more than twelve feet above Eugenia, held up the basket. "I've weighed this loaf of bread, this melon, and the grapes. They all have different weights. I'm going to drop them all at the same time and you tell me which hits the ground first."

"The melon will, won't it? It's the heaviest."

"Aristotle thought that, but it was just a theory. He never experimented and that's what determines the proof of an idea. Isaac Newton wrote that, when studying gravity, there are things to take into consideration. Like the mass of an object."

"The mass?"

"Mass is the density of matter in an object."

Eugenia wanted to ask about the terms "density" and "matter," but then thought she'd just listen to Laura and hope that things became clearer.

Laura continued, "Newton wrote that objects react to gravity in different ways, taking into consideration the inertial mass and acceleration and something called 'resistance.' But if all things are equal, weight alone should not win out."

"But it must." Eugenia's brow furrowed and she put her hands on her hips. "I still think the melon will hit first."

Laura held the objects high and leaned over the open edge of the hayloft. "Let's find out."

"Be careful!" Eugenia cried.

"Go!"

Laura dropped the items and the girls watched the descent.

"Don't take your eyes off them!" Laura called.

There was a single sound as the melon, bread, and grapes hit the stone floor at the same time.

Laura nearly crowed. "My first simple proof! I see for myself that Newton's assertions are correct!" A grin spread across her face as she started down the ladder, the empty basket hooked over her arm. "Physics is part of almost everything—how things move, how they sound, how everything is built." Laura looked over her shoulder down at Eugenia, excited to share her thoughts. Her leather-soled shoe slipped on a rung of the ladder.

"Laura, be careful!"

Laura, off-balance, one leg hanging in the air, strained to keep hold of the rail, but the basket swung and pulled her weight in another direction. Her fingers slipped. She couldn't hold on, and she lost hold of the side rail.

"Ooohhh!"

Laura felt the whoosh of air against her face, the movement of her heavy petticoats, the weight of her body falling through the air.

Eugenia squeaked with alarm. "No! No!" She got to her friend just when Laura landed in a thick, tall pile of hay. "Are you hurt?" Eugenia climbed into the loose hay.

Laura did not move; her gaze was up toward the rafters. For a moment, she felt suspended in time, not aware of breathing. Birds fluttered and squawked. Then she shook her head and laughed.

"Not hurt." She reached for Eugenia's hand. "I wonder if I would have hit the ground in tandem with the melon if I'd dropped from the hayloft at the same time."

"Oh dear." It was Signora Bassi. She was standing in the open double doors of the carriage house.

"Eugenia!" Signora Mucchi's imperious voice cut through the air. She was standing close behind Laura's mother.

The two girls, covered in hay, turned to their mothers.

"Look at you!" Signora Mucchi said, furiously pulling hay from Eugenia's hair and whisking the stiff yellow strands from her daughter's dress. "You're a mess." She sniffed. "It smells in here."

"Like horses, Mamma," Eugenia said. "Carriage houses smell like horses."

"And with this hay, you will smell, too," Signora Mucchi groaned.

"I was helping Laura with an experiment."

"You will never do that again. I'll hear no more about it." Signora Mucchi's eyes shot over to the disheveled Laura, her lips drawn in a thin line. Then she grabbed Eugenia's hand and led her quickly out of the carriage house.

Signora Bassi opened her mouth to apologize, but Signora Mucchi held up her hand. "I want to hear no more about it."

Later that day, the sun was setting and the sky shone in soft pinks and lavenders. Laura sat at the small table in her room, quill and pen in hand. She wrote:

Dear Sir Newton,

I live in Bologna, Italy. I am almost thirteen years old. Today I set a very simple experiment that illuminated for me one of your precepts on gravity. I have many questions. Where is gravity formed? Are the changing tides in the ocean a proof of gravity? What keeps the sun—and birds—and other things from falling from the sky? I hope to be a scientist one day, that is why I ask so many questions. Mille grazie—in quest of all Enlightenment.

Signed: Laura Maria Caterina Bassi

In addition: I have been told you have made sundials. I too have built one in my garden.

She folded the letter and placed it in an envelope. She would ask her father to post it, and hoped it would reach England.

Laura moved to the window seat and watched the sun descend behind the horizon. She looked at the clock, mumbled to herself as she marked the time on her calendar, and wrote in her notebook: *First of May. Hours of sunlight increasing. Nearly two minutes more sun than yesterday. Summer will be here soon.* She looked out into the gardens. She was surprised to see Dottore Tacconi, wearing his blue tricorn hat, a burgundy waistcoat, and crisp ruffled shirt, striding up to the villa. Did they have a lesson? If so, how could she have forgotten?

She grabbed her book of poetry and moved quickly down the stairs. Nucca was standing in the hallway, and the library doors were closed.

Nucca put her fingers to her lips, then whispered, "He asked to see only your parents."

Laura and Nucca put their ears to the door. They heard Tacconi speaking.

"It is with great regret that I inform you of discussions in some of the highest social circles of Bologna . . . concerning your daughter."

Laura heard her mother gasp. Her mother disliked displeasing anyone.

"Go on, Dottore Tacconi." Her father's voice sounded cold.

Tacconi continued, "I've spoken to your daughter multiple times about staying to subjects that are acceptable for a young lady. But she is headstrong. Which seems to have led to an incident in a hayloft. As your daughter's tutor, I've been vocal about curbing her interests in science and mathematics. After all, what good could they ever do her?"

Laura's stomach formed knots; she had to concentrate on slowing her breathing. Fear filled her body. The learning that gave her joy every day—was that about to be taken away?

An instinct for self-protection surged through her—and she raised her hand and rapped loudly on the library door. Nucca clucked, alarmed. Laura, breathing deeply because her chest felt so tight, slid the door open and stepped into the room. Signor Bassi held up his hand and seemed ready to ask Laura to leave.

Laura's jaw tightened, but she spoke softly. "Papà. Mamma. This conversation seems to concern me. I should be part of any decision that affects me."

Tacconi's pointed chin rose in the air. "There are some matters determined for your own well-being, Signorina Laura. Your parents will come to a decision."

Laura held her father's gaze. Would he deny her? "*Prego*, Papà. Please."

"Very well," said Signor Bassi. "Daughter, you may stay."

Tacconi tried to hide a scowl. It was accepted that daughters were to be told of their futures, that they did not participate in decisions, and to him, Signor Bassi was too lenient.

He shrugged and explained to Laura, "I've pointed out that you, young signorina, are interested in the study of too many things and that it is advisable for us to stay clear of certain subjects. That you should follow my instructions and not venture into studies of your own."

A determined, focused calmness came over Laura. She knew, in every fiber of her being, that this moment was very important. She kept her voice level.

"I've researched fine thinkers of the past. Especially those who are women."

Tacconi dismissed her statement. "There are no females in our ranks."

Laura folded her hands to still a nervous tremor. "I would like to bring up the example of Elena Lucrezia Cornaro Piscopia of Venice. She earned a laurea in philosophy—nearly fifty years ago—and became a mathematics professor at the University of Padua."

Tacconi waved his hand as if this information was not applicable. "*Sì*, she entered the Benedictine Oblate order and never married." He leaned toward Signora Bassi. "Surely, you do hope Laura will marry? Give you grandchildren?"

Signora Bassi pulled her shawl closer and looked at her husband. She had always hoped for the happiness of a good husband for Laura.

Laura placed her hand on a table for support, standing as tall as she could. "There have been other women. There is Juliana Morell of Spain, one hundred years ago. Her study of ethics earned her a doctorate in law."

Tacconi was about to interrupt, but Laura continued, looking at her father. "She believed laws concerning the education of woman should be changed. And I agree." She forged on. "And Sister Juana, much more recently, in the New World—I believe in Spain's lands that are called Mexico. She wrote of a woman's ability to be a scholar and create ideas. She advocated for women not to be held back. And Bologna's own Saint Caterina. She thought education—of both male and female—was important. And took it upon herself to be true to her beliefs. I've been honored with her name, and all in our city respect her."

Tacconi sighed. "All these women chose education over family duties—such as bearing children and serving a husband. They lived in convents."

"A convent?" Signora Bassi did not want to think of her daughter making that choice.

Laura pressed on. "Dottore, there is also Elisabeth of Bohemia. She corresponded with Descartes about the importance of the soul in relation to the body. She was considered an excellent mathematician and philosopher. She was not a nun."

Laura's mother softly asked, "Did Elisabeth of Bohemia marry?"

"No, Mamma," Laura said. "She was a Protestant ruler and her advisors wanted her to marry a Catholic. She followed her heart and refused. But that has nothing to do with her learning." Laura continued, building her case. "Queen Christina of Sweden reigned for thirty years in the last century; she was a patron of education—"

"She was controversial and there is undesirable gossip surrounding her," Tacconi interjected.

"But she made education—for all—a priority in Sweden." Laura's voice rose just enough to gain the attention again. "And the Grand Duchess of Tuscany—in the same era in Florence—she was educated in many things." She looked to her mother. "She was married, Mamma, to the great Ferdinando de' Medici. Galileo wrote of his admiration for her. These were women in power who sought out the most advanced thinkers of their time. They helped fund experiments . . . often put food on scientists' tables so that they might have the energy and time to think."

Tacconi struck a point. "Those women were protected by their royal standings." He turned to Laura's parents. "Signorina Laura is not of royal heritage, not even noble—"

Laura interrupted, "There are the stories of the women Bettisia Gozzadini and Novella d'Andrea. In the thirteenth and fourteenth centuries, they were at the University of Bologna—"

Tacconi raised his hand to gain attention. "The tale of Bettisia Gozzadini is this: She disguised herself as a man. When she was discovered, she was allowed on the university campus only if she wore a veil over her face—and she was only allowed this because of her family's social standing. Novella d'Andrea's father taught canon law at the university, and when he was ill, he sent his daughter to do his lectures. However, she spoke through a curtain and was not visible to the male students."

Laura kept her voice steady. "Which brings up this marked question: Should any person who desires knowledge be judged and found lacking by anyone? Should a woman be denied only because she is a woman? God made males and females."

Signora Bassi glanced at her husband and spoke nearly at a whisper. "Some things are best attributed to the will of God. He has determined our world. We cannot question Him."

"Oh Mamma." Laura moved to her mother and took her hands. "I believe God does not care which person—which gender—wonders about the makings of world. God has given me the desire to understand. And with each new bit of knowledge that I gain, I honor Him more."

Tacconi repeated his argument. "We are not the ones to rewrite rules. There are roles in society that we must accept."

Laura's voice was firm. "Would all men be content to embroider and take tea and attend to a house each day? Why must all woman be content doing so? Sir Newton wrote, 'What we know is a drop, what we don't know is an ocean.' I find that to be the truth, and I, Laura Bassi, want to wade in the ocean. And, I venture, I'm not the only female in Bologna with aspirations of knowing more of the deep waters of knowledge, who feels frustration in the role they're expected to accept. I think it is not me that should change, but society."

Tacconi stood, rising to his full height. "Everyone has their place, as it should be."

Laura, a foot shorter, faced him directly. "Doesn't everything change, Dottore Tacconi? Our bodies, our thoughts, amounts of knowledge, the seasons, day to night—even fashion? The world and society are in constant change."

Tacconi looked to Signor Bassi, hoping he would still the debate.

But Laura continued, "I point to the words that you, Dottore, asked that I attach to my memory. Thoughts of philosophers, meant to guide us. Descartes writes, 'To be a real seeker of truth, it is necessary to at least once in your life doubt as far as possible, all things.' He did not say that only to men. What about Descartes' words 'I think, therefore I am.' Women think. They *are*." She felt her emotions well up, but said with determination. "I *am*. And we live in the Age of Enlightenment, the Age of Reason. Therefore, it is time to see how reasonable it is that women desire more."

There was a silence. Tacconi had no ready comeback.

A smile tugged at Signor Bassi's lips. He felt pride in Laura's ability to argue her opinions. He folded his hands across his chest.

"I came from a small village and I had a desire to know—to be—someone beyond others' expectations. As a man, I could find my way; my gender was not considered a hindrance." He looked to Tacconi. "You're suggesting we curtail our daughter's felicity—her joy of learning—to please those who do not choose to understand a thirst for knowledge—or to see who my daughter truly is."

"But Signor Bassi." Tacconi would not relent. "There are noble ladies, leaders of our society, who have asked me to keep watch on your daughter's interests."

Signor Bassi's voice became icy. "Dottore. Laura's mother and I have not hired you for that purpose. Watching over our daughter is entirely in *our* purview." Signor Bassi stood. "I've decided that my wife and I will support Laura's education in all that she finds of interest."

Signora Bassi leaned toward her husband, worried. "Giuseppe?"

"Wife, she's our child," said Signor Bassi. "How can we deny her?"

Signora Bassi put her hand to her lips. She would not disagree publicly with her husband. But she worried about her daughter being considered too odd, too unsuitable for society.

Laura's father eyed Tacconi. "We see no reason why Laura should shirk certain subjects. But of course, Dottore, if you feel you are not up to the task, I'll accept your desire to end your instruction here."

Tacconi was stunned. He'd come to rely on the fees that Signor Bassi paid regularly. He enjoyed his new hats, perfumes, and ruffled shirts.

"There's no reason for a hasty decision."

Signor Bassi stood. "But, as you find some topics unsuitable, we will look for other tutors."

Laura shouted with excitement. "Papà, would that mean I could schedule a tutor almost daily? Boys at the university school study in this manner. It would be as if I were doing the same."

Tacconi quickly made his way out of the Bassi home. He was not happy with how things played out, but he realized he had learned a hard lesson: Don't underestimate Laura Maria Caterina Bassi.

Chapter Six

Over the next two years, Signor Bassi sought out tutors to add their expertise to Laura's education. A thin and frail botanist, Dottore Greci, instructed Laura in the classification and physiology of plants in his quiet, whispery voice. He also instructed in theology, in both the Old and the New Testaments. Astronomy was covered by the very strict Dottore Flano, whose unmanageable white-blond hair reminded Laura of clouds. He told her he was against wigs, for they were too hot and often provided nests for bugs. Did she mind? She laughed and said wigs had always seemed impractical to her. They agreed that the history of the Greeks and Romans should be part of the assignments, for many of the constellations bore the names of ancient heroes. Sporadic tutelage in geology and poetry was covered by a sturdy Dottore Rios; his rough hands and fingernails were often filled with dust, for he was involved in excavations near Rome—but he enjoyed Signor Bassi's fortified wines and

Laura's inquisitiveness when he visited the Bassi home. Tacconi continued with ethics, logic, and languages.

The search for someone to tutor Laura in science and mathematics had been difficult. Laura spent hours with pamphlets and books, working on concepts and problems.

Signora Bassi was worried that Laura spent too many hours reading by candlelight. "You don't want to squint, *mia cara*." Laura would blow out the candle to please her and then relight it when she knew her mother was asleep.

Most esteemed Monsignor Lambertini,

There is such exciting news here at the Bassi villa. I now have multiple tutors. I often think of my visit to the university, and when I study astronomy, wish I could climb into the institute's Specola Tower to be closer to the stars—and to also look through the most powerful telescopes. I like the words of William Shakespeare: "It is not in the stars to hold our destiny, but in ourselves." I do agree with him, and isn't he a wonderful poet?

Laura Maria Caterina Bassi
Bologna

It was midsummer and the family settled at the dining table to enjoy the bounty of Emilia-Romagna. There were fresh cheeses and olives, roasted chicken, beans, and plump, juicy, sweet tomatoes. Laura cut into a thick tomato slice.

"Dottore Greci told me the *pomodoro* was first found in South America. And brought to Italy two hundred years ago.

This hot summer has brought an excellent crop—did you know the heat is more important to pomodoro than the sun?"

Signora Bassi was used to gaining tidbits of information from Laura's tutelage. "Perhaps we should move our garden to the warmer side of the stables."

Signor Bassi nodded. "I will arrange." He savored the tomato, and then looked at Laura. "I have news."

Laura wondered about his mysterious high spirits. "What is it, Papà?"

"Because our new pope, Benedict XIII, is focusing on cleaning up the corruption in the Vatican, he will not commit increased funding to the university. That means that some of Bologna's most learned academics are now seeking extra income. And a pioneer in infinitesimal calculus, Dottore Gabriel Manfredi, has honored me with a response to my query about tutoring."

"Calculus! Oh , Papà, what did he say?"

"The mathematician will meet with you and determine if you might be a deserving pupil. Will tomorrow morning suit?"

Laura put her hands to her chest; she felt her heart beating fast. She was already planning. She would read all night; she'd go through all her notebooks and fashion questions with hopes to assure this tutor that she would be worthy of his time.

Laura's mother shook her head. "That will be impossible. It's the day of Eugenia's betrothal party."

Laura's bubble of anticipation burst. Eugenia had sent her a special note—she wanted to make sure Laura would be at the celebration. Laura couldn't disappoint her only friend. But there had to be a way.

"Mamma, Dottore Manfredi is coming in the morning—

just to see if he will accept me as a pupil. After I meet with the professor, I'll have time to get ready for the afternoon party."

Signora Bassi looked to her husband for his support, but he was busy cutting his chicken. "Giuseppe?"

He glanced up, his eyes also beseeching. "I did go to great trouble to arrange this, Rosa Maria."

Signora Bassi sighed. She knew her husband had no idea of the time and energy needed to get every ruffle, bow, petticoat, and curl in place.

"*Prego*, Mamma," Laura pleaded. "If I postpone now, Dottore Manfredi may never give me another chance."

Dottore Gabriele Manfredi arrived with bulging pockets and a large satchel of books slung over his thick shoulder. Laura had been waiting anxiously, looking out the parlor window. She watched as he approached and stopped to look over the garden. She noticed his short, heavy legs supported a very round torso. She was fascinated by his ball-shaped head, his askew horsehair wig, and his pudgy, plump fingers trying to right his collar and eyeglasses. This was a pioneer of infinitesimal calculus? She quickly moved toward the front door.

Nucca was there. "It's proper for me to answer the door, as you know, Signorina Laura."

"He mustn't wait, not even one second," Laura said. Her mouth was dry; her heart felt as if it were in her throat.

Signor Bassi, carrying papers he'd been working on in the library, joined them in the hallway. "He is here?"

Laura nodded.

Signora Bassi moved down the stairs, followed by one of the new young housemaids, Deirdre. She was near Laura's age and had a mousey face that always looked sullen and pinched.

But this morning her nose was high, for Signora Bassi had chosen her to help with the toilettes for the party because she'd proven herself good with last-minute needs of needle and thread. Deirdre held silk ribbons, the color of cranberries, in her hand.

Signora Bassi pointed to them. "Laura, Deirdre has suggested that these will match the ornament on your shoe and I venture she may be correct."

Laura could not concentrate on ribbons. "The science and math tutor is here, Mamma. I prefer you to decide."

A sharp double knock on the door resounded.

Signora Bassi saw she could expect no decision. "Very well." She and Deirdre moved back upstairs.

Laura turned to Nucca and pleaded, "Now, Nucca. *Prego.* Now."

Nucca opened the door.

Manfredi bowed. "Glorious day. Temperatures are pleasing. I think I smell roasting turnips, onions, and rosemary from your back kitchen, which also adds to a day's enjoyment." He took a peach from his pocket and handed it to Signor Bassi. "From the humble Manfredi gardens."

Signor Bassi accepted the gift. "Most gracious."

The energy of the mathematician filled the foyer. His large brown eyes twinkled when he took in Laura. "You must be the family scholar. Shall we see how we get on together?"

Laura curtsied. "I've wanted to study advanced calculus since I was six years old."

Manfredi laughed. "When I was six I wanted to be a gladiator."

Signor Bassi led the way into the parlor and excused himself. "I'll be across the hall, Dottore, in my library."

Laura quickly moved to the table she used in her lessons. Her quill, pen, and vellum were at the ready. She swallowed hard. She knew she was about to be judged.

Manfredi placed his satchel on a side table. He took a linen bag from his vest pocket.

"Lovely and luscious Medjool dates from Africa—Morocco, to be exact. The royals of Spain claim most for themselves." He chuckled. "But if you know the right people, it's possible to enjoy them. They're worth every *scudo*." He patted his round belly. "I find when I have deep thinking to do, sustenance is always a helpmate." He popped a date into his mouth. "What mathematics and science do you desire to explore, signorina?"

Laura's heart soared. She lifted a notebook from the parlor table and read from her list. "I would like to study the works of Francis Bacon. And the mathematics of George Berkeley and Christiaan Huygens, and of Gottfried Liebniz. I would like to understand the origin of lightning and thunder—I've always wanted to know that. And I also want to know classical mechanics—and all Enlightenment ideas that will help shepherd us into what is being called the Industrial Revolution."

Manfredi straightened the wig that slid on his bald pate. "That's a long list."

"I think that by knowing the ideas of others, I can agree or disagree and come to my own thinking."

Manfredi chuckled. "You're willing to differ with known experts?"

"Sir Francis Bacon wrote that it was not possible to discover the deeper parts of any science if one stands at one level and simply agrees. He was adamant that questioning leads to an ascending process, to a higher level of science. The Enlightenment is also based on these principles."

Manfredi popped another date into his mouth. "I happen to agree."

"But most of all," Laura continued, "I want to know more about Sir Isaac Newton. I've admired his work on gravity and long to understand it more completely. And my father recently brought home new pamphlets on Newton's thoughts on light and how it moves and reflects. He calls it 'optics.'"

"Which language?"

"I read pamphlets written in Latin. And French."

"German? Greek?"

"I am nearly fluent," Laura told him, wishing she could say she had mastered the languages.

"English?"

"No," Laura admitted, her voice small.

"It's true that many works in science and mathematics are written in Latin, so they can reach a wide academic audience. Newton has done this, but has now started writing in English. Clearly times are changing. And I feel it's better to study work in the native tongue."

Laura nodded. Would her lacking be held against her?

Manfredi chewed on the date. He spoke carefully. "Newton is considered controversial. Some in science do not support his findings on optics—what Newton calls a 'spectrum.'"

Laura was confused. "Hasn't he proven himself a fine thinker? He was knighted. He is 'Sir' Newton."

"The English queen of the time was impressed with his work on the laws of motion, the most influential work in physics. That was nearly twenty years ago. And since then, he's proven himself unpredictable and reclusive. I've heard there is darkness in him, a troubling condition where he, at times, feels unable to deal with society. Because he was not born into the noble class, he has no support from that sector. And because he's not of holy orders, he doesn't have that group to support him. His finances now, at age seventy, are often precarious, so he cannot fall back on wealth. These facts cause his position at Trinity College in Ireland and memberships in institutions in England to be precarious."

Laura frowned and spoke quietly. "There are times I know what that feels like—to be out of step with society."

Manfredi was taken aback, now seeing Laura's vulnerability. Yes, he thought to himself, a young woman wanting an education would be seen as an oddity. "It's often the people out of step in their youth who grow into themselves in extraordinary ways." His voice was soothing. He offered Laura the linen bag. "Medjool date? I suggest the sweetness will please."

Laura accepted a large date and took a dainty bite of it. "And the chewy texture is fine, too." She took another bite, enjoying the taste. "It's a delicacy."

"The date palms in the desert are a very interesting species, growing in sweltering temperatures barely manageable for Europeans. A botanist spoke last night at the university of the increased efforts of African farmers to aid in the pollen transfer between trees, and the use of rather primitive but helpful mechanicals to increase production."

Laura felt an ache, a deep desire for this lesson never to end. How wonderful it was to talk about science and its practical uses.

Manfredi patted his round belly. "Back to your question on optics. One of Newton's earliest experiments in this area was . . . shocking. The details may be too indelicate for you."

"If it's science, I'll not find it indelicate."

Manfredi did not believe science was indelicate either. "Very well. This falls within extreme self-experimentation and I do not condone it."

"Understood." Laura's interest was even more piqued.

"Newton wondered about seeing colored spots in front of his eyes, at certain times in certain situations of exertion or while rubbing his eyes, or even sneezing. He had listened to others recount similar experiences. He wondered—were colors created within the eye itself? He performed less intrusive experiments, but found no satisfaction. He came up with the idea of sticking a thin needle into his own eye—forcing the needle deep enough to reach the bone at the back of his eyeball. He moved the needle to different targets—wondering if he might find a point that produced color."

Laura was stunned; the image was intense. "That's too much of a risk." Curiosity got the better of her. "What were his conclusions?"

"Newton documented his results in his notebooks. He saw spots of dark and light. He calls them phosphenes—the *phos* for the Greek word for 'light,' and *phene*, the Greek work for 'show.' But no colors. Therefore, he concluded, the eye itself was not the producer of color."

Laura leaned forward. "He went on to look for color's source?"

"In a tamer experiment, on a sunny day in his room at Cambridge University, he closed the shutters to darken the space. He made a small hole in the shutter to allow only a slim beam of light to enter. He held a glass prism into the light and found—refracted through the prism—colors. 'Like a rainbow,' Newton wrote, and he identified seven colors. He asked himself—are these colors actually part of sunlight? He took another prism and put it upside down to the first prism to refract—change the direction—of the light. This caused the colored particles of light to merge and become singularly white again."

"He thinks the white of sunlight is actually formed with a combination of colors?" Laura sat back, trying to understand.

Manfredi liked how Laura's mind moved from insights to questions. "Newton's belief is that color is a property of light particles, not an object itself." He shrugged. "Others do not see it his way. One reason for their disagreement is the materials he used in the experiment: A prism is considered to be a toy, not an instrument of science. They asked if Newton's experiment could be taken seriously if he was using a toy."

"But if it works, if it suits . . . ."

Manfredi continued. "In addition, another Englishman, Robert Hooke, at the same time, theorized that light consisted of waves, not particles as Newton suggested. A Dutchman that you mentioned, Christiaan Huygens, also favored the idea of diffraction—a spreading out of light—and it moving in longitudinal wavelets."

"Could each of them be right?" Laura asked.

Manfredi picked at a bit of a date stuck to one of his small teeth. "Science, in the future, will certainly determine the veracity of all theories. We shall have more experiments with more advanced instruments—once those instruments are invented."

"Inventing instruments to test theories is also of interest to me, Dottore Manfredi."

Manfredi chuckled. "*Sì*, I can tell you have many interests." He took in Laura's bright face. Then he added, softly, "'Judge a man by his questions rather than his answers.' Do you know who wrote that?"

Laura shook her head.

"Voltaire. A Frenchman. And you ask excellent questions, signorina."

There was a rap on the doorframe. Deirdre, her pink-rimmed

eyes on the floor, announced in a strong, flat voice, "*Scusami.* The signora of the house requests her daughter."

Laura's face fell. The time had gone by too quickly.

Manfredi stood. "Your social engagement is taking priority."

"Dottore," Laura blurted, "I would much rather be here with you, talking of science."

A deep dimple folded into place on Manfredi's cheeks. His voice was kind. "I, too, enjoy discussion on mathematics and sciences more than almost anything. An apt pupil makes it even more enjoyable. I could return next week at the same time, if it suits."

Laura's spirits soared. "*Sì. Sì*, Dottore. *Bene.*" She curtsied.

Manfredi took out a book on mathematics from his satchel. "To add to your library, my own book on the subject of calculus. Inspired by the work of Newton. You will see I am also an admirer."

"*Grazie*," Laura said. She held the book close to her as if it were a lifeline.

He slung the strap of his satchel onto his round shoulder. "And I'll take it upon myself to teach you English."

Laura couldn't keep the tears of joy from spilling from her eyes. Could this be really happening?

Chapter Seven

With Nucca's help, Laura rushed to dress, donning the layers of petticoats, her chemise, and corset, and finally slipping on shoes that Eugenia had insisted she wear. She descended the stairs of the villa and out into the courtyard. She held onto her hat, for there was an energetic dry breeze, and quickly joined her parents in the carriage. She reached for the handle to close the carriage door and received a shocking tingle.

"What is that charge, Papà? Metal doesn't always send a spark. Why does sometimes it happen and others not?"

"There is no explanation I know of, my daughter." Signor Bassi rested his hat on top of his best wig.

"It's like the metal is sending a shock to me." Laura thought for a moment. "Or from me to it."

Signora Bassi patted her coiffure, her mind on the party ahead. "It's good our hair is curled tightly for the air has no humidity. We do not want falling tendrils."

Laura considered her mother's observation. Could the dry

air be part of the cause of the spark? She pulled on her elbow-length gloves and touched the metal door handle again. There was no reaction.

"It doesn't happen when I wear gloves," she mused.

Her mother's mind was focused on the party. "Eugenia, at age fifteen, is the first of your friends to be married. There will be many following her lead."

Laura thought of the last time she'd visited Eugenia, just last week. Eugenia had shown her the French gowns and garments of her trousseau. "Louis XV has moved his court to the Palace of Versailles," Eugenia had told her. "He's about to be married to a Polish princess and has asked for new, wonderful fashions. Like these. Oh—and I've heard the French king likes science, Laura."

"Really?"

"He has hired a Swedish botanist to work in the Versailles gardens. And an astronomer. And he collects clocks and scientific instruments." She held up a pair of shoes. "See how the heel is not straight? It's called a 'Baby Louis heel.' It curves inward and then flares out again so it makes the foot look even more dainty. On my betrothal night, I'll wear a pair in golden suede with lace and pearls on the toes. Count Cabell wants me to be a leader in fashion. I cannot disappoint." She handed Laura a pair of shoes. "And you, *mia amica*, must wear these. Try them on."

Laura had placed the French shoes on her feet. There was a burst of blue chiffon in the shape of a rose on its toe.

Eugenia had been thrilled. "I think we could dance at Versailles and fit right in."

"My tutor tells me that many in France are unhappy," Laura had replied. "The poor do not have enough to eat and the king pays no attention. The French Catholics have even asked the pope for money."

Eugenia had not wanted to be serious. "Count Cabell tells me a woman should not worry about politics." She took Laura's hand. "My friend, you must concentrate on finding a suitable suitor. Mamma says a woman who never marries is always an extra at supper parties and she is looked on with pity. We are fifteen now. You must be diligent in finding a match."

Laura hadn't wanted to tell Eugenia that she wished to spend all of her time on her studies. Laura knew her friend would not understand.

The ballroom of the Mucchi palazzo was crowded. Nobles, bishops, bankers, estate owners, and others who were part of the top echelon of Bologna's society were dressed in their finest, all proud to be invited to this social event.

Laura stood with her mother in the receiving line, waiting to be welcomed by Eugenia, her parents, and Count Cabell.

Signora Bassi whispered to Laura, "Our new maid knows nothing of this new face paint."

Eugenia and her mother were decked in French gowns, their faces adorned with white creams and powders and dustings of pastel powder on their eyelids. One of Eugenia's cheeks also featured an added beauty mark in the shape of a heart.

"Eugenia told me the French adopted the face paint for the king, for he doesn't like his smallpox scars. It covers up remnants of the speckles and other blemishes." She hooked her arm into her mother's. "But there's no need to worry; there are others that have dared to not look like ghosts."

It was true, only half of the ladies had adopted the powdered face—but all of the brocaded gowns were wide and sumptuous and influenced by the court of France.

Laura felt Eugenia's hand on her arm. "It's now very real. It seems I'll have a life just like my mother's. Remember how we used to talk about my dreams of traveling, of seeing the world. I'll never do that, for Count Cabell is insistent that I do my best to give him a son." Eugenia leaned in, her voice tight with worry. "We'll still be friends, won't we?"

Laura kissed Eugenia on the cheek. The face powder felt odd on her lips. "Always friends," she promised.

Signora Mucchi was welcoming the next in line. Laura and her mother moved on and joined Signor Bassi, Father Stegani, and her cousin Carlo.

"Let's walk, cousin." Carlo offered his arm to Laura and led her through the ballroom. "I must see everyone who is here."

Laura wanted to talk to him about his studies at the university; he was now enrolled in the areas of politics and law. But Carlo was looking for a young woman who had caught his imagination: "She is luminescent; her hair glows like the sun." Laura teased him that she'd never seen him so distracted.

He nodded toward the fine gowns of the women, to their intricate, piled-high hairstyles. "But how is a husband to afford all this? Do you know, cousin, that the cost of each hairpiece—be it human hair or that of an animal—exceeds what a shopkeeper's assistant in Bologna is paid in two years? And the jewelry—ships could be bought and thrice sailed to China with just one of the diamond necklaces here tonight." His gaze took in her gown, her simple hair wound with the cranberry-colored ribbons. "You look pretty tonight. Without powder. The color of the pink rose suits you."

"Mamma hopes so."

Carlo patted her arm. "I know your mother is hoping for a

betrothal for you." He finally spotted the young woman. "There she is."

Laura saw where he was looking. "But that is Signorina Genevieve Belnonte. Her mother will not allow you to speak to her. We're not from the right families."

Carlo groaned. "But we're connected because of your father's job as a city chancellor. And your friendship with Eugenia." He saw that the musicians were getting ready to play. "I'll get you a dance card."

"I won't need a dance card, cousin. I am not skilled . . . ."

Carlo was not listening. He deposited her next to a young woman standing with an elderly, straight-backed woman and told a confident lie. "My cousin, Signorina Laura Bassi. She's told me she admires your curls and would love to know the name of your hair-maker." Carlo patted Laura's arm. "I'll be right back."

Laura, uncomfortable, stood with the ladies. The older one turned to her. Laura's heart fell as she recognized Signora Aldona, the dance mistress, glowering at her.

"Have we met?"

Laura gulped and fibbed. "I don't believe so."

Signora Aldona sniffed suspiciously, but returned to her detailed recitation on the quality and strength of purchased hair.

Laura's attention strayed as a group of university students moved to the nearby table weighed down with Italian macarons, truffles, and creams. She heard the freckled Vincenzo Cruce's sardonic voice.

"Go ahead, Alesso," he dared his square-faced peer. "Rub the amber stone with your handkerchief—let's see the trick of electricus. See how many feathers from ladies' hairpieces you can attract to your stone."

Laura was intrigued. What was that word *electricus*?

A young noble, his head held high, his trim figure perfectly outfitted in a black velvet waistcoat and a lemon-colored brocade vest, joined the students. Laura recognized him as the eldest son of the Galeazzi family—a family that often sat in the front pews at the Basilica di San Petronio.

Cruce ingratiated himself. "Domenico Galeazzi, the esteemed pupil, about to complete your laurea. We'll soon have to call you 'Dottore.'"

"First I must pass my defenses," Galeazzi said humbly.

"You will certainly triumph," Cruce flattered. "How many subjects have you left?"

Laura took a step closer. She wanted to hear more about how to earn a laurea.

Galeazzi was speaking. "There will be eleven total. Three years ago, I passed chemistry, geometry, and biology. In the next year, I covered my languages, rhetoric, and logic. Last year it was theology and grammar and philosophy. I've yet to complete medicine—with particular focus on anatomy and internal organs. That's where I'll concentrate my work—as a surgeon."

"One day we may all need you." Cruce lifted a glass of prosecco off the tray of a passing servant. "Ah, the sparkling wine from Trieste. It bubbles on the tongue and is good for the stomach."

Galeazzi noticed the amber stone in Alesso's hand. "Ah. Hardened tree sap. Electrum. Isn't that what the amber is called in Latin? Electricus is one of the newest fields."

There was that word again. *Electricus.* She longed to move into the conversation, but she saw that Cruce had noticed her— and his eyes were not kind. She looked away.

Galeazzi accepted a glass of prosecco from a servant and continued. "I would start with the work by William Gilbert; he was Queen Elizabeth's personal physician a hundred years ago. His investigation was limited but he did theorize electricus could be all around us, perhaps in the air. And related to the magnetism found in certain metals. Perhaps one day it could be used in medicine."

Cruce spoke out of the side of his mouth. "What do you envision? That we will swallow amber and cure all ails?"

Alesso guffawed, then choked on a grape that was lodged in his throat. Galeazzi quickly slammed Alesso's back with his hand. The grape shot out and rolled onto the floor and disappeared under the gown of an unsuspecting guest.

Cruce sneered, "You must chew, Alesso."

Laura spoke without thinking, taking a step closer to the men. "I've read a pamphlet on the work of Gilbert called *De Magnete*. In it, he does not mention electricus, but your conversation has made me wonder again about the unexpected, slight pricking shock that can be felt sometimes when touching a metal door handle. Or amber—such as you have there. It's almost like a result of a crackling in the air."

There was an awkward silence. And then Galeazzi, gallant, bowed.

"We haven't been introduced, signorina."

"I am Laura Bassi."

Cruce coolly filled in the provenance. "Daughter of Giuseppe Bassi, one of our city's officials."

"I know of the spark you mention," said Galeazzi. "There's a South American knifefish, over six feet long. It looks similar to an eel, but it's an air breather, and must surface nearly every ten minutes. It uses a spark of energy to stun its prey. Humans, touching one of these creatures, can feel a shock through their body. Of course, we don't understand it. Yet."

Cruce wanted the attention back on himself. "Perhaps a closer read of Gilbert, in the original language." He turned to Laura, challenging. "Do you read in the English language, signorina?"

Laura's brow furrowed. "Not yet."

Cruce pontificated. "I am a proponent of studying in the native language of each academic."

Laura nodded. "My new tutor, Dottore Manfredi, mentioned today that this may become the standard."

"Ah. *Sì*. I've heard your father has hired the best tutors." Cruce clucked. "Seems wasting them on a female is silly and unnecessary."

Laura flushed. Galeazzi cleared his throat, surprised by Cruce's rudeness. The musicians began to play.

Cruce, taking his leave, did not bother to bow in Laura's direction. "Alesso, let's find suitable dancing partners." Cruce moved off, Alesso following.

Galeazzi stole a quick look at Laura. "Cruce has a harsh edge and can take sad pleasure in offense. But it shouldn't ruin an evening. I hope."

The music filled the room. The moment was awkward. It was considered a social gaffe for a young woman to be left on her own and she did not want Galeazzi to feel any responsibility. Laura glanced behind her and realized Signora Aldona and the ladies were no longer there. Her parents were across the room.

She nearly cried out in relief when she saw Carlo approaching. "Ah, there is my cousin."

"Excellent," said Galeazzi. "And I must go to find my wife. She enjoys the dance."

Laura quickly curtsied, and hurried to join Carlo.

He waved her dance card in the air, then noticed her reddened face. "Has something gone wrong?"

Laura shook her head. She didn't want to talk of her embarrassment. But she felt deflated. She wondered about her desire for conversations and company—a whole life—that did not want her. Would she always feel on the outside?

Carlo's eyes were again on Genevieve Belanonte. He leaned into Laura. "The beautiful one is away from her mother. This is my chance."

Laura panicked. Was he going to leave her again? But Carlo had reached out and stopped a tall young man. "Ah, my fellow student. Before my brilliant cousin's dance card fills, shall I put you down for the next dance? I believe it is the allemande." Carlo scribbled the young man's name onto Laura's card.

Laura was mortified. "Carlo, I do not . . . ."

The student bowed gallantly. His coat was not ostentatious and he did not wear a wig; his dark, thick hair was pulled neatly back into a tail and tied with a crisp black ribbon. "If I'm not too undeserving of Signorina Bassi's time. We share some of the same tutors."

Carlo patted his fellow student on the shoulder. "You're in medicine—correct? A junior in Galeazzi's group. This is good timing; the musicians are about to begin." Carlo hurried off.

Laura was left standing with the stranger. "I'm sorry, I've not mastered the task of dance. If you would escort me to my parents . . . ."

He had a touch of a country accent. "Mhm. The task of

dancing. It is a task, isn't it? Although I do find it interesting when I approach it as a mathematical equation."

"Dance as mathematics?"

"A series of squares, triangles, and circles made with one's legs and feet and hands—if combined properly, they might look pleasing. My past experiments have been unsuccessful, but I'm willing to continue the endeavor."

Laura liked his humorous self-deprecation. She glanced at him again. She noticed he was a foot taller than her and that his worn shoes were buffed to a shine.

The musicians began to play Bach's Partita in B Minor.

The student's voice rose in excitement. "Bach. Perfect. Did you know the German experimented with math in his music?"

Laura was intrigued. "What was Herr Bach's experiment?"

He nodded toward the dance floor and offered his hand. "Shall we talk as we promenade around the perimeter?" He smiled. "That will not tax our dancing skills."

Laura hesitated, but then acquiesced; she wanted to continue the conversation. She placed her small, gloved hand on his. She felt a slight spark—it felt entirely different from that of touching the metal door handle, but there it was. What was this feeling?

"You know of the Greek Pythagoras?" He led her around the outer circle of the dance floor.

Laura nodded. "The ancient. I know of his work on the right triangle—that the square of the hypotenuse is equal to the sum of the squares of the other two sides."

"You've had a chance to read about Pythagorean tuning?"

Laura nodded. "Frequency ratios. Scales constructed with perfect fifths."

"It happened that Bach read of Pythagoras's experiments

with sound—starting with the story of the blacksmith wielding his hammer and changing the distance to the object being struck and also changing the weights of the hammers. Both of these variations caused the sound to resonate in different tones."

Across the room, Signora Bassi noticed Laura on the arm of a young man. She strained to identify her daughter's partner, but the tall hairpieces and feather fans of the ladies got in her way. Excited, she moved to join her husband and whispered to him. They both looked across the ballroom, hoping to catch a glimpse of Laura.

The medical student guided Laura around the wide skirts of the dancing ladies. He continued, "What caught Bach's imagination was how Pythagoras imagined strings that stretched between planets in the sky. He imagined if these strings were plucked—depending on their distance from one another—sounds would be generated in different octaves and create a magnificent harmony."

Laura made the connection. "And that's why Bach called his composition the 'Music of the Spheres.'" She smiled. "*Grazie.* That's a wonderful thing to know."

The musicians came to the end of the dance suite. The dancers on the floor curtsied and bowed to each other. Laura and the young man were near a set of the open doors that led to the ballroom's balconies. The Mucchi gardens were glowing in the dusky sunset. There were iron posts topped with candelabras. Servants walked the lawns with torches to light the candles, creating spots of moving light as the sun set for the day. Laura smiled. Light in the darkness was always a magical sight for her.

"Imagine the music that might be created by lightning . . . and other mysteries of the air," she said. "Have you read of 'electricus'?"

"Only in minor pamphlets," he said. "But of course, it will be on my list of studies." For some reason, he did not want to disappoint Signorina Bassi.

Laura looked up to the stars. "Mine too. It has caught my interest."

Eugenia, on Count Cabell's arm, joined them. "Laura, the young ladies are retreating to the parlor for a refreshing moment." She held her hand out to Laura. "I want you with me."

Before Laura could acknowledge the young man, Eugenia pulled her away.

"Giovanni Veratti," said the approaching Vincenzo Cruce. "My sympathies. You must be glad to be relieved of your dancing partner, the peculiar Laura Bassi."

Veratti turned to Cruce, his voice level. "Vincenzo, I was honored and invigorated by her excellent conversation." He nodded politely and walked off.

Cruce's mouth turned downward. He muttered to Alesso. "He's only here because he's in Galeazzi's medical studies group. He's no one in Bologna."

An hour later, the guests of the betrothal party took their leave of the Mucchi palazzo. Laura followed her mother and father into their carriage, ruminating over the odd evening. She had been glad to see Eugenia as the center of attention, but knew that her friend's choices were now curtailed—that it was expected she would do as her husband wished. Laura wondered if she could ever make such a promise. She had also been energized by the conversation with the students, but hurt at Cruce's slights. And she had come to know the origins of Bach's "Music of the Spheres."

Signora Bassi fell into step beside her. "You were dancing?"

Laura shook her head. "No, Mamma."

"But I thought I saw you on the arm of—"

"I only promenaded. Carlo introduced me to a fellow student."

As they entered the carriage, Signor Bassi added his curiosity. "And the name of your promenade partner? His family?"

Laura moved onto her seat. She realized she did not know the young man's name. "I don't know."

She looked out the window of the moving carriage as they entered a park. Moving through a line of thick trees that hugged the narrow road, Laura saw light flitting through the air.

"Look. Fireflies. It's the season. What do you think it is that gives them their light?"

Signora Bassi sighed, disappointed. It seemed Laura's dancing partner had not made an impression.

Chapter Eight

"Giuseppe, do you think this is wise?" Signora Bassi fussed over the placement of a vase of ivy sprigs.

She glanced at Nucca, who was polishing the furniture for the third time that day. Laura was placing copies of the latest pamphlet, written by tonight's guest lecturer, Professore Russo, on the credenza.

"Our parlor is not as grand as one in the Mucchi palazzo or that of Count Marsili," Signor Bassi said, "but it's large enough. We'll be able to seat all." He poured himself a glass of fortified wine and raised it into the air. "Salons—the place for new thinking."

"It will be wonderful, Mamma," Laura said. "There'll be a presentation on Sir Isaac Newton's third law of motion and then discussion and questions. Isn't that right, Papà?"

Deirdre hurried in and gave a bumbling curtsy. "Carriages are arriving."

Nucca clucked, tucking the dusting cloth into her pocket.

"I have to get my notebook," Laura muttered and hurried up the stairs. She wanted to time her entrance perfectly. She and her father had placed a chair in the corner by the door and set a "Reserved" sign on its seat. The plan was for her to slip into the parlor just as the lecturer began, so that no one would notice her.

In her bedroom, Laura took a moment to settle. For the past months, she had worked hard in her sessions with her tutors. Dottore Tacconi assigned readings in logic and ethics and grilled her in languages. Frail Dottore Greci added biology to his teachings in botany, while the more unconventional Dottore Rios and Dottore Flano added more work in geology, astronomy, and poetry, for they had found Laura's curiosity insatiable. The round Dottore Manfredi arrived twice a week; they studied calculus, mechanical sciences, optics, and hydraulics.

She pressed her hands together to settle her nerves. Her tutors would be here tonight, but they did not know Laura had convinced her father to let her attend. "I'll sit quietly, Papà, and just listen," she had promised.

She looked out the window and down into the courtyard. Count Marsili was getting out of his carriage, followed by a hunched man in a matted wig. Laura recognized him as Dottore Salti, the head of the Academic Council. She'd heard his classes in sciences were rigorous and demanding and that he could be impatient and sometimes cruel. Others were arriving on horseback. She recognized more members of the institute's Academic Council along with nobles and businessmen. Wigless students from the university were arriving on foot, breathing in the last of the crisp winter air; they carried notebooks under their arms. Vincenzo Cruce was among them, walking with the medical student Domenico Galeazzi. Her heart beat a bit faster. She hoped

Cruce wouldn't single her out. This was a special night for her father, and her mother worried about anything going amiss.

Laura heard her father announcing the beginning of the salon. She moved down the stairs. The hallway was empty. The parlor door was open and she could see the empty chair placed in a corner. Laura took a deep breath, slipped inside, and took her seat.

More than thirty men filled the chairs facing one end of the parlor. She could see Tacconi sitting in one of the front seats, his back straight, wearing a platinum blond wig of the latest fashion. She was glad to see that Cruce and his group were rows in front of her; surely they would have no reason to turn to see her. She glanced to the side and saw Dottore Manfredi watching her. When their eyes met, he nodded, surprised by her presence.

The lecturer, Professore Russo from the institute, moved to the front of the room. "Let us celebrate that our esteemed cleric, Prospero Lambertini, has been raised to the status of cardinal."

A round of applause and calls of "*Evviva! Evviva!*" filled the room.

Russo continued, waving a letter in the air. "Cardinal Lambertini sends his regards, and regrets that—under the leadership of Benedict XIII—there will be no increase of funds to the university."

The men groaned.

Russo continued, "So, as we are ignored by Benedict, we must remember the importance of our salons. We must continue to examine science in order to advance it. A discussion of Newton's Law of Motion is on the table tonight, for in broad terms the laws give us the base for the study of classical mechanics.

Newton's third law of motion states that for every action—or force—in nature, there are consequences. Equal and opposite reactions. I might shake your hand; my fingers clutch against your skin and your skin compresses and expands—your body has a reaction. I might place a brick on my head and the extra weight will force my body more downward. But the earth below my body is also exerting a force upward, and thus, chances are I'll stay upright. Two forces working against each other. Newton's third law takes into account the symmetry in nature: that forces always occur in pairs. Action-reaction. And classic mechanics has great reliance on this."

Laura noticed one student standing in the far corner of the room. His suit was made of wool; it was tidy and clean, but clearly well-worn. He was tall and lean, his long hair pulled back with a ribbon. Laura realized it was the student who had led her in a promenade at Eugenia's betrothal party. He looked in her direction and nodded his head. She tried to remember his name. Had she ever learned it?

The lecturer continued. "Now, what are the factors to be taken into account? Let us say a farmer has two carts. One large cart is filled with hay; the other cart has two sturdy horses attached. The driver attaches the cart with the horses to the cart with the hay. Let's say the total mass of the cart with the hay is three times the mass of the driver's cart. What are the elements to be taken into consideration when predicting the motion of these connected carts?"

Galeazzi stood. "Weight. Mass. Speed."

Another student stood. "The new mechanical weaving machines make use of this principle. As do the newly designed pianos."

Galeazzi added, "And steam engines."

"Other examples?" Professore Russo asked.

Laura stood, forgetting her plan to remain unnoticed. "Sybilla Masters—a woman who lives far overseas in England's American colonies—has invented a machine she calls a corn mill. It grinds corn so that people don't have to grind it between two millstones or pound it with wooden posts. The design took into account Newton's principles. The machine saves time and energy and adds in efficiency."

There was a silence. Men turned, eyeing Laura.

Marsili stood. "And you are?"

Signor Bassi got to his feet. "You've met her before, Count Marsili. For those who have yet to meet her—my daughter, Laura Bassi."

Cruce groaned, giving an exasperated look to the other students around him.

The lecturer, Russo, looked toward Laura; he saw a slight girl with loosely styled blonde hair dressed in a soft blue gown not cut in the French fashion. He glanced at the displeased Dottore Salti, who had not turned to look at Laura.

The young man who had been Laura's promenade partner stepped forward and filled the silence. "I've seen drawings of this corn mill. Ingenious design."

Laura, now realizing she had actually entered the conversation, flushed. But she did not back down. "It is exceptional. Sybilla Masters has also invented a machine to weave straw and palmetto leaves from the West Indies to make hats and baskets. It is a fine example of Newton's principles in action. There is a drawing of it in a British pamphlet, for she traveled all the way to England to gain the patent. King George of England signed the patent—the first one ever awarded to anyone in the colonies of America—but it was given in her husband's name, not hers."

Professore Russo explained, "Because women aren't allowed to hold patents, as we know. Let's move on from corn mills and return to our discussion."

Laura sat down. She hoped her father would not be put out that she had spoken, but he did not meet her gaze.

A young professor with a long thin nose and reedy voice stood and presented his opinion. "I suggest we not bow at the altar of Newton. Aristotle, in the years before Christ, wrote that the natural state of an object was to be at rest. Newton's ideas on inertia did not spring from nothing."

"Aristotle was not a scientist," Galeazzi pointed out.

The young professor continued, his voice grating. "But he was one of the extraordinary thinkers of his time and thought on many topics. Aristotle wrote that the natural state of an object was not to change its motion. Newton's first law is clearly based on Aristotle's writing, and it might be fair to say that his second law, regarding acceleration, is simply a rewording of the first."

Cruce stood. "If that is the case, credit should be assigned where applicable. Newton's reputation is filled with oddities. He's often not welcome in Britain's Academy for he has breakdowns, he is unstable, he is . . . odd."

Laura stood quickly, wanting to defend. "No matter his frailties, Newton has contributed greatly to science."

Professor Russo could not disagree. "Undeniably true, signorina. Cruce, you know that the personality of the scientist is not of consequence here."

Cruce scowled and sat down.

Galeazzi stood. "I would venture this observation: Does it really matter which law is recognized when the first and second laws would be a correct answer for most questions on motion?

We could say the first law is a consequence of the second. Simply put, one could say this: If there is no force, there is no change."

Marsili stood. "The term 'law' itself could be brought to question." He laughed. "These are not legal laws and we must remember that all ideas in science are in constant flux."

Laura stood, straightening to gain her fullest height. "*Perdono, una domanda*." She looked at the notes she'd scribbled in her notebook. "My question is this: Could Newton's first law be seen as a limiting agent of the second law? As an independent observation? Perhaps by understanding what the physicist meant by the word 'force,' this could be determined. In addition, as we see in the well-detailed and enlightening pamphlet our lecturer Professore Russo provided . . . ." She looked up and saw Russo preen at the compliment, then continued, "Sir Newton used geometric equations, and I would ask if anyone thinks that it would be a fine experiment to look at his early work with the later calculus—a mathematic form Newton helped construct. Would that, perhaps, make understanding of three separate 'laws' clearer?"

There was an awkward silence. It was a notion no one had yet considered.

Marsili stood. "Excellent observation. This can lead us to more topics for discussion." He looked over the group. "Galeazzi, your response?"

Laura sat and opened her notebook and took out the short graphite *penicillus* she had tucked into her sleeve. As Galeazzi and others discussed questions and variations of thinking on Newton's work, diverse observations were illuminated. Laura quickly wrote them down so that she could discuss them later with her tutors.

Laura's recent dance partner, in the opposite corner of the room, folded his arms and enjoyed the sight of her, enthused and bent over her notebook. Her tutors had spoken highly of Laura Bassi, and it was clear her reputation was earned. He hoped that the gift he'd brought to give to her—the small booklet now nestled in the inside pocket of his coat—would be appreciated. He planned to approach her at the end of the evening and properly introduce himself.

An hour later, Professore Russo called the salon to a close. Several medical students arranged to continue the conversation at one of Bologna's cafés. The young professor called out, "Veratti, are you coming?"

"I'll join you later," Laura's admirer replied. He moved to cross the room, but was waylaid by others as they gossiped before their departures. Veratti could only watch as Laura quietly slipped out of the parlor, crossed the hall to the library, and shut the door.

Away from the men, Laura moved to sit by the fire. She felt as if she were walking on air. The excitement of the intellectual discussion was still lightening her thoughts. She reached for vellum, then dipped a quill into the inkpot and began to write. She had come to a decision and she wanted to get the details on paper as quickly as she could.

Across the hallway in the parlor, the last of the fortified wine had been drunk. Men headed into the moonlit night to their carriages and waiting horses. Laura could hear Count Marsili's booming voice talking to her father. "Where is this daughter of yours?"

Laura, suddenly unnerved, quickly put the quill down. The library door opened. She curtsied as Marsili and her father entered the room. Was she about to be chastised?

"The evening was going along expected lines, signorina," Marsili said, "until your observations and questions sparked new discussion. Your father tells me you have tutors."

"Because I'm not allowed to study at your institute," she said simply, stating the truth.

Signor Bassi paled. It was not seemly to appear to criticize. "Laura, *prego*."

Marsili's eyes narrowed. "The institute is not 'mine.' *Sì*, I've ceded my property to the university, but it is left to the Academic Council to make the rules."

"I do not wish to be overly assertive, Count Marsili," Laura explained softly, "or to distress my papà." She could see her father was fiddling with his silk waistcoat's brass buttons, as he always did when he was nervous. "But I remember hearing you, Count Marsili, when I was five years old, speaking at a salon held at the Mucchi palazzo. You said, 'Without dreams, humankind will not move forward.'"

"I believe that," Marsili agreed.

Laura ventured softly, "Dreams do not belong only to men, signore."

Marsili heard the quiet intensity of her words. He hesitated, then nodded, signaling his departure.

"A compelling evening, Signor Bassi. I'll find my way out." He strode out of the room.

Signor Bassi looked to Laura. She didn't know if he would censure her, but she wanted to defend herself.

"Papà, I only speak from my heart. Perhaps there are people who disagree with the status quo, and if so, I wonder why they blame the rules on others and take no action to change them."

"Count Marsili told you, the Academic Council is in charge."

"But his influence is great. And his silence on the matter of keeping women out of the university speaks volumes."

Before her father could respond, Dottore Manfredi peeked into the library. "Your tutors wish to congratulate you."

The tutors entered and closed the door behind them.

Laura did not see Veratti lingering in the foyer, but Nucca took notice. "Can I help you, signore?" Nucca said.

Veratti, startled, reached inside his coat to take out a thin booklet. "I was hoping to give this to Signorina Bassi."

Nucca, eyes on him, reached for the booklet. "I'll see that she gets it."

Veratti handed over his gift. "It is on the new findings on the topic of electricus."

Nucca nodded. "*Buona notte,* signore."

Veratti, disappointed at the clear dismissal, bowed his thanks and moved out of the villa. He headed across the courtyard thinking that perhaps Signorina Laura might send him a note of thanks. That might open the door to another visit. He could only hope.

Nucca placed the booklet on the foyer's credenza just as Deirdre, with a tray full of glasses and half-filled carafes of wine, moved out of the parlor. She tripped on the edge of the rug; wine flew through the air and the red liquid landed on the booklet, saturating it. Nucca clucked, wiping it as best she could—and put it to the side.

In the library, the tutors and Signor Bassi toasted Laura. "Very much a surprise, but not an embarrassment, signorina," Tacconi declared.

Dottore Flano, his thin white-blond hair shimmering in the candlelight, helped himself to a glass of wine. "You did honor to our tutelage. Good points."

Laura faced her team of tutors. "*Grazie*. I would like to speak to you all, if you have the time, and tell you of my plan."

Tacconi took a seat. He stretched his long legs out in front of him and pulled at the cuffs of his expensive bombazine silk waistcoat. "What is it?"

Laura took a deep breath. "I haven't discussed this with my father—this comes from me entirely. This evening has solidified my intention to fulfill a dream that began in my first tutoring session with Dottore Tacconi."

"Me?" Tacconi straightened, always afraid of being blamed.

Dottore Manfredi reached for the nut dish and placed an almond in his mouth. "Ah, let us hear of Tacconi's inspiration."

"What is this goal, daughter?" Signor Bassi asked.

Laura took a place in front of the fire. She looked at each man solemnly. "I want to earn a laurea at the University of Bologna."

The men were startled.

"What?" Tacconi said. "Impossible."

Laura continued. "In order to do that, I must be able to defend my knowledge on many topics, distinguish myself as a polymath. I hope that you, my esteemed tutors, will help prepare me."

Manfredi spoke gently, "Women are privately tutored. There is no reason to concern yourself with gaining a laurea."

"But there are reasons," Laura quietly argued. "First, it is the only way to truly be accepted in the larger community of scientists in Bologna. Second, I desire the challenge and I do not believe I should be denied the opportunity."

"May I also point out that you are not an official student." The geologist Dottore Rios rubbed his craggy face with his hardened, rough hands and said gently, "Only students of the university are allowed to mount defenses to earn a laurea."

Dottore Greci agreed. "Signorina, in addition, the Vatican would not be in favor. Benedict XIII's interpretation of the Bible supports the idea that the woman's place is in the home, with a man as her master."

"Dottore Greci," Laura said, "I know you are more forward-thinking."

Greci shrugged. "But that does not change the reality."

Tacconi sniffed. "The society of Bologna would frown."

Dottore Flano sipped his wine. "And the task itself is difficult. Many men, long-standing students of the university, try and fail to gain a laurea."

Laura's jawline tightened. "Will you help me prepare as I find my way?"

As the men digested this news, Laura opened a binder and took out what she had written. "I'll be eighteen soon; it's time. I have just written a letter—stating my intentions and asking for instructions to make a proper application. I've addressed it to Dottore Salti, the head of the Academic Council."

No one spoke. No one reached for the letter.

Dottore Manfredi dipped his quill into the inkpot. "Before sending your inquiry, let us consider the great difficulty you are considering." He was writing a list on a piece of paper. "You must show mastery of at least a dozen subjects. Latin must be one, for all the presentations must be made in that language. Topics could include logic, ethics, rhetoric, philosophy, and grammar. And theology—a deep knowledge of the Bible impresses. Multiple languages. If it is in the disciplines of science that you wish to make your mark, you will need to present and defend mathematics, geometry, and calculus as well as five or six other sciences; choose from among chemistry, hydraulics, mechanics, physics, botany, astronomy, anatomy, biology, and medicine. Each presentation will tax your time and energy; each defense, where questions will be hurled to confuse and point out weaknesses, will be grueling." He pushed the piece of paper across the table to Laura. "Is this what you really want to do?"

Part Two

1728–1731

Chapter Nine

The next day, Laura waited in the parlor for Dottore Manfredi's scheduled arrival. She was ready with questions on her latest calculus problems. She listened for his footsteps, but all she could hear were the sounds of the home—her father in his library, her mother discussing the dinner menu with Nucca in the breakfast room, the cook gathering fresh eggs from the chickens in the back garden. Dottore Manfredi was never late. Had he decided he would not aid her in her quest? Did he not believe in her? Did he think her plan was foolhardy? Her hopes unattainable?

Laura wrapped a shawl around her shoulders and moved to the large carriage house. She pushed aside the wide sliding doors that led to the stables. There she stroked the long noses of the family's horses, Zeus and Hero, and offered a carrot to the mare, Artemis. She was filled with worry. What if her tutors discontinued their time with her? It would make her preparation for a laurea all the harder.

"Signorina Laura?"

She turned to see the rotund Dottore Manfredi.

"I have news," he said.

"What is it?" Laura steeled herself. She had come to rely on Manfredi's expertise; she even thought they were kindred souls in the pursuit of knowledge. She did not want to lose that.

Manfredi took a bulletin from his pocket and unfolded it. "I regret my tardiness, but I waited to receive a copy of an announcement in the *London Gazette*. News has just reached Bologna." He handed her the flyer. "Sir Isaac Newton has left this earth. He has succumbed to death."

Laura collapsed on a nearby stool. Newton was bigger than life to her, a man whose writings had inspired many people, whose ideas had changed science, had changed how she thought about the workings of the universe. He was a giant among scholars and thinkers. How could the world be denied his presence?

"What happened, Dottore?"

"It's reported that Newton experienced a sudden, sharp pain in his lower torso. No one is sure if it's related to the stomach or another organ, or even—maybe—if it was related to his bones. Whatever it was, the pain was severe and Newton fell into an unconscious state. The great man never opened his eyes again." Manfredi took a long moment. "He rests in state at London's Westminster Abbey. No scientist has ever received such an honor and the *Gazette* reports that many have lined up to pay their respects. The poet, Alexander Pope, has written this . . . ." He pointed to a short poem reprinted on the bulletin.

Laura read aloud: "*Nature, and Nature's Laws, lay hid by Night. And then God said, 'Let Newton be! And All was Light.*" She had tears in her eyes. "Sir Isaac Newton is surely in heaven.

I know he's happy speaking with God, but I'm most envious. I wanted to meet him at least once in my life."

Manfredi nodded. "*Sì*, we've lost an exceptional thinker."

"Thank you for bringing the news." She confessed, "When you were untimely, I thought perhaps you'd decided my ambition displeased you."

Manfredi rested his thick fingers on his belly and shook his head. "Nothing could keep me away. I expect you to continue to honor Newton by moving forward. Perhaps you will be his champion, signorina; solidify his legacy here in Bologna."

A week later, Laura sat on her window seat in her room and looked out into the dark sky. The moon was half full, mostly covered with thin clouds. A wind had whipped up and dust from the streets swirled upward, filling the air. Laura placed her hand on the cold glass of the window. She muttered a prayer, thanking God for all that Newton had given to the world.

She paraphrased one of his statements, wishing again she could have met the man. "I, too, Sir Newton, find that I am like a child on the beach, hoping that the vast oceans of undiscovered truths will show themselves to me."

And then, there it was. A flash of lightning, exclaiming its presence in a short burst. It crackled, pulsed for a moment, and then was gone.

Laura sighed and smiled, imagining this to be a sign. "Is that your answer to me? To end my sorrow and move forward?"

She reached for the small booklet she kept on the nearby table; its title was *Electricus*. She looked again at the inscription, indecipherable because watered wine had fallen on the ink and the signature had been swept into unreadable swirls. She did not know who had left her this booklet, but she treasured it.

Inside was information about the first discoveries pertaining to this elusive electricus. There was a chapter on William Gilbert's experiments with compasses and metals that reacted in magnetic ways. Also, Gilbert's contention that magnetism and electricus might, in fact, be totally unrelated, for electricus was diminished with the introduction of heat, but magnetism was not.

Critics of these theories and observation were noted, and Laura found their arguments of merit. Wouldn't it be wonderful to conduct experiments herself? There were also drawings of Gilbert's invention, the electroscope, an instrument that measured forces of electricus. She frowned. The University of Bologna was the only place to see a true model of an electroscope and she was not allowed in its classrooms. The booklet also contained information on subsequent work by English polymath and wordsmith Thomas Browne, who suggested a new name for the essence Gilbert wrote about that might, one day, be catchable and used in everyday walks of life. Browne's chosen word was "electricity." Laura liked the word. *Electricity*.

The cold winter months of 1729 brought storms and ice. It had been a year since Laura started her serious preparation to stand for her laurea. She had gotten no response from her request to the Academic Council, but she wanted to be ready when they did respond. Her tutors had lent so many books and pamphlets that the Bassi library shelves were soon doubly stacked, and the floor so covered with books, there was only a thin passageway to Signor Bassi's desk.

Laura composed letters to Enlightenment thinkers in Germany, France, and other European lands.

Most admired philosopher Mister George Berkeley,

I live in Bologna in the Papal States of the Italian Peninsula, far from your native Ireland. I have enjoyed reading pamphlets on your ideas. You have written: "Others may indeed talk, and write and fight about liberty, and make an outward pretense to it; but the free-thinker alone is truly free." I would agree that the freedom of the soul and mind are of great importance, but how does one take solace in your words if one is not free because of societal or religious constraints regarding gender? I enclose a short essay I have fashioned contrasting your ideas on subjective idealism—the metaphysical doctrine you examine that states that only the mental state exists—for materialism and concrete restrictions of our day are there to affect the mental state. I would venture that this is true; for as a woman, I feel it is especially apt. If you have the inclination and the time, I would look forward to your opinions on my thoughts.

L. M. C. Bassi, Bologna

The days when responses to her letters arrived filled her with excitement. She was elated that these great thinkers were willing to share their work with her.

The salons at the Bassi villa continued, now on a monthly schedule. Professors, students, and interested nobles attended, and Laura's reputation as a well-read young woman who posed interesting questions and insights grew in the city. But as her academic stature blossomed, the number of her social invitations diminished; she was not included in many of the dances, teas, and convivial excursions held at the palazzos of the Cruces or Belanontes or other elite members of the Bolognese. Laura barely noticed, but Signora Bassi remained concerned.

Spring arrived and Laura was up at dawn. She had studied deep into the evening, for Newton's book *Mathematical Principles of Natural Philosophy* had recently been translated into French and she wanted to devour its contents. She tasked Manfredi to grill her on all elements of Newtonian study. She compared Newton's work to that of Robert Hooke on microscopy, chemistry, and physics. She was also fascinated by the ideas on learning, the theories written a hundred years previously from Baruch Spinoza, and the recent works of a young Denis Diderot.

She also wrote to Stephen Gray in England and Abbé Nollet in France, for they were doing new work in electrical conduction.

To the highly respected Abbé Nollet,

I work with my private tutors on many subjects in Bologna. Your writings on theology and science have interested me. The bulletins now announce you have joined the French Société des Arts and are concentrated on applying natural philosophy to practical arts, with interest in electricity. I add my congratulations and include a small essay I have written on this topic. As you can see, it is full of questions. I have written to Stephen Gray but have not received a response as of yet. If you would enjoy a correspondence, I would be most willing to impart your thoughts and questions to those of excellent minds in our fair city.

With utmost respect,
L. M. C. Bassi, Bologna

Laura also sought out academic essays written by women. There were few, but she pursued pen-friendships with them. She wrote to the poet Giuseppa Eleonora Barbapiccola, born in Naples and educated by her uncle; she was a supporter of Cartesian thought and Laura celebrated their agreement on advocating for education of females. She also wrote to the Englishwoman Catharine Cockburn on the need for social change.

Most Esteemed Mistress Catharine Trotter Cockburn,

I have read your argument on moral principles and agree with your perception that they are not innate, but learned individually. Thank you for your support of Mister John Locke's Essay Concerning Humane Understanding. I, along with you, believe that with more open thinking in a patriarchal society, women could enjoy acceptance in academia. Should you care to correspond on this topic and others, I am most humbly one who would return countless thoughts and questions to you.

In respect,
Laura Maria Caterina Bassi, Bologna

For almost a year, Laura waited for a messenger from the University of Bologna to arrive.

"Perhaps Dottore Salti did not receive the letter," she said to Manfredi during a break in a difficult English language lesson.

Manfredi shook his head. "I saw it myself on his desk. And I reminded him I was one of your tutors."

"Did he give any clue to his opinion of my request?"

"No. Dottore Salti chose to ignore my entreaty and paid no attention to the matter."

Laura's jaw tightened. "Then I shall send in another request."

A week later, Laura and her cousin Carlo sat in the Bassi family carriage on their way to the university. Laura's second letter to the Academic Council was in his hand.

"Don't worry, cousin. I'll deliver this to Dottore Salti's office—either directly into his hands or into that of his second, Dottore Balbi. Balbi is a fair man, but it's known that he defers to Salti in all things."

Laura nodded. "If only a council member would attend the salons at our villa."

"Salti now holds his own, with chosen students, at the university. He requires his council to be there. It is a competition."

Laura had heard of these salons. She was grateful that Vincenzo Cruce's sardonic group chose to attend them; she was still unsettled by his dislike of her. She put it out of her mind.

"Carlo, I want the council to understand my great seriousness."

Carlo laughed. "No one doubts that. Have you had any fun lately?"

"I find my work is all I desire." She shrugged off solemnity and teased, "You are dedicated to enough fun for the both of us."

"Signor Veratti has returned to Bologna."

"Who?"

"Your promenade partner. I believe he has attended a Bassi salon. He's my fellow at the university. His father had taken ill many months ago, and he had to put his university studies on hold and travel to the country to be with him."

Laura remembered the tall, kind student who shared his

knowledge of Bach's "Music of the Spheres." "His father's health now?"

"Unfortunately, he passed to heaven. Veratti took care of family matters. And now he is back." They had reached the university. "Here we are." Carlo stepped out of the carriage.

"I wish I could deliver the letter myself. I wish I could move through the university's hallways and classrooms," Laura said.

"But it is not allowed." Carlo waved and strode through the massive gates.

Laura hoped this request would gain a response. How could they ignore her a second time? She knew that her mother worried, for Laura had become reclusive, concentrating only on her studies; she hardly left the house.

The exception had been to attend Eugenia's wedding. Laura, dressed in a new gown and hat adorned with silk flowers, had arrived with her parents. She'd marveled at the sound of two dozen harps echoing in the colossal sacred space of the Basilica di San Petronio. All of Bologna's finest were in attendance, including Count Marsili and Cardinal Lambertini. Eugenia's mother, Signora Mucchi, on her husband's arm, had preened as she walked down the center aisle, elegant in a deep blue beaded silk gown, her hairpieces studded with crystals and pearls. Signora Mucchi curtsied to the groom, the corpulent Count Cabell, who waited at the altar's steps, and then took her place in a large gilded chair that had been placed a few feet from the altar. Eugenia's father had moved to the near vestibule.

Moments later, he emerged with Eugenia. Laura had gasped; she thought her friend looked like an angel—splendid in a cream silk and lace gown, a train that flowed behind her in great ruffles of fabric. Eugenia joined Count Cabell and they took their places on the kneeling bench in front of the bishop. Laura had prayed for her friend's happiness—and knew in her own heart that she was glad to not be married, to not promise to obey a husband in all things.

After the reception, Laura had paid her respects to Cardinal Lambertini. He asked her about her studies; she told him she was hoping to gain permission to stand for a laurea. The cardinal cocked his head, surprised. And, before moving on to the next person waiting for his blessing and attention, he had kindly asked her to keep him apprised of her application status.

And now, Laura thought, as she waited for Carlo to return to the carriage, it was a year later. Eugenia had given birth to her first child—a boy. Laura had made a fine gift of toys from Divertimenti, and assured Eugenia that her child would grow into them.

"Mission served, cousin," Carlo called out. He climbed into the carriage. "Your second request is now on Dottore Salti's desk."

Chapter Ten

"Queen to king's castle five," said Laura.

Dottore Manfredi studied the chessboard and groaned. "It's a good move, signorina." It was the end of a tutoring session on classical mechanics and Laura and Dottore Manfredi were continuing a game of scacchi they had begun the week before. "Strategy is most important in chess. And clearly you are mastering it."

Signor Bassi strode into the parlor and interrupted them. "Laura, there is a letter."

Laura recognized the official paper and seal of the University of Bologna. Her pulse quickened. "Did you read it, Papà?"

"I thought you should be the first." Signor Bassi exchanged a look with Dottore Manfredi.

They waited as Laura unfolded the letter. She read it silently, and then looked up.

"The Academic Council, with Dottore Salti signing his name, makes it clear that queries from women will not be considered. And, it is added, they hope no new requests be made for they are very busy with academic matters."

Signor Bassi took his daughter's hands. "I'm sorry, *mia cara*. There seems to be no way around the edict."

Manfredi stood, his mouth turned downward, his round cheeks flushed with anger. "Did Galileo stop trying to achieve his goals? Did Copernicus? Did Newton?" He looked at the chess set, then at Laura. "Answer me this, signorina. Which piece in scacchi is aggressive but also one of the most limited?"

Laura looked confused. Manfredi insisted on an answer. She took a moment, then touched the piece on the board carved to look like a horse's head.

"The knight?"

Manfredi straightened the wig on his bald head. "It can move three squares—in a two-and-one leap. Take out obstacles in a unique fashion. I believe, just moments ago, we agreed that strategy is very important in chess. Perhaps we can say it's also important in life."

Laura quickly saw his point. "And if the direct approach does not bring satisfaction, other paths must be considered."

"I think so," Manfredi nodded. "I believe Cardinal Lambertini is scheduled to be in Bologna in the early spring. Perhaps he would appreciate a special invitation to a salon held at the Bassi home."

That night, Laura sat at the small table in her bedroom and wrote:

Most esteemed Cardinal Lambertini,

You kindly asked that I keep you informed of my hopes to earn my laurea. To date, my entreaties to the Academic Council have not been welcomed. However, I will not give up for I believe I am capable. As you may know, our home has been a monthly gathering place for academic salons. We would like to extend a special invitation to the salon held during the time of your next scheduled visit to Bologna. It would give the Bassi family, and the academic community that attends the salon, great honor if you would grace us with your presence and, for me, an opportunity for you to judge, for yourself, my capabilities.

Laura signed her name and arranged for the letter to leave with the next postrider to Rome. She knew it might take a week to reach its destination. She hoped that it would reach the hands of the cardinal and that he'd understand how his influence might change Dottore Salti's mind.

Weeks later, on the eve of Laura's nineteenth birthday, Laura walked with her mother to the dressmaker on Via Clavature, a small, narrow street off the Piazza Maggiore. The day was cold and they wore scarves over their woolen hats. Deirdre, now well-fed and sure of her position, strutted behind, proud to be carrying a small bag filled with fabric samples. She enjoyed the admiring gazes of shop assistants for she knew that being a young woman gainfully employed at a fine household made her attractive and she could have her pick of suitors. They passed the convent of San Barbaziano; the nuns, dressed in long brown wool tunics, veils, and white aprons, were just heading out to the poor neighborhoods with their baskets of food. Laura's mother stopped in front of the chapel, made the sign of the cross, and placed a silver scudo in its charity box.

Laura's attention was pulled to the far corner of the street.

There, a thin teenage girl in a moth-eaten wool dress and tattered cape, was trying to get the attention of passersby.

"I solve a mathematics problem, without quill and paper, in less than ten seconds." She rubbed her red nose and chilled cheeks and called out in a proud voice, "See the magic of mathematics in my head. Only half a copper scudo. Signors, *prego*, take time to be astounded."

Signora Bassi and Deirdre moved into the dressmaker's shop. Laura stalled and watched the teenage hawker as a well-heeled banker, in a fine waistcoat and tricorn hat, stopped and called out numbers. Laura watched the girl squint, quickly calculate in her head, and call back: "The answer's two hundred and ninety-five!" The banker flipped a coin into the air; it landed on the street. The girl scrambled to pick it up, calling out for the next customer. A nobleman, exiting the tobacco shop, stopped and posed a problem. It took only a moment for the answer to be sung out loudly: "One thousand and twelve!" The nobleman hurried off, not parting with a scudo. "*Scusami*, signore! A half copper scudo is owed to me!" The girl's shoulders slumped as she realized she was going to be ignored.

Laura reached into her small drawstring purse and moved to the thin girl. "Here is a silver scudo, in advance, for your talent."

The girl's blue eyes grew wide, her chapped fingers quickly putting the money into the pouch attached to her belt. "What's your question of numbers?"

"What would be the total of twenty multiplied by six, multiplied by three?"

A squint of the eyes, then the answer came quickly. "Three hundred and sixty."

Laura was impressed. "You know multiplication." She was

about to ask for another calculation but was interrupted by Deirdre, who had hurried out of the shop to join Laura.

"Your mother awaits you." Deirdre came closer, then whispered in Laura's ear, "You do not want to talk to *zitelle*."

Laura knew of the zitelle—young women with no family, money, or education, who had to fend for themselves; they often lived in Bologna's abandoned buildings. Men preyed on them, offering lodging and food in exchange for favors of the flesh. Many zitelle did not have the fortitude to refuse the predatory men, for the girls had no place to turn.

Laura's voice was respectful as she talked to the girl. "What's your name?"

"Bianca." The girl's eyes swept the street, looking for new customers.

"Where do you study your mathematics?" Laura asked.

"To study takes money. So—nowhere."

Laura was surprised. "But where did you learn?"

Bianca blanched. A mean-eyed member of the Bolognese police force, in his red cap and dark blue *polizia* jacket, was approaching. He grabbed her arm and growled.

"Told you not to be here, *ragazza*."

Deirdre, not wanting to be caught in a struggle, tugged at Laura's shawl. She hissed, "We must go."

Laura ignored Deirdre and stood her ground. "*Carabiniere*, it was me who asked her a question. There's no need to handle this girl."

"Zitelle aren't allowed to disturb passersby." He glared at Laura and slapped his large wood baton into the palm of his hand. "Who are you to tell me my job?"

A voice interrupted. "Signorina Bassi, is there a problem?"

Laura turned to see the tall student—her promenade partner—standing behind her. His deep brown eyes looked solicitous—and protective.

"I'm telling the carabiniere that it was I who have detained this girl. He's under the impression she lingers for no good reason and has suggested I take no interest in his actions."

Veratti was taller than the policeman, but not as thick or muscular. Yet he faced the policeman and spoke firmly.

"This woman's father, Signor Giuseppe Bassi, is a respected lawyer and chancellor in Bologna. He is often at court in the Palazzo d'Accursio, which is close to the civic offices of the polizia. Perhaps you know of him?"

The carabiniere's eyes glanced at Laura, assessing the fine cloth of her coat and her warm boots.

She smiled politely, but her eyes were cool. "If not, perhaps I could introduce you to my father."

The carabiniere took a moment and then let go of Bianca's arm. "Don't let me catch you again, girl." He glowered at Veratti and strode off.

Laura nodded to the medical student. "*Grazie*, signore." She turned her attention back to Bianca. "Are you harmed?"

Bianca shivered, suspicious of kindness. "Have to find another spot to pose my talent. Have to pay for my lodging."

Laura put her hand on Bianca's arm. "Where do you live?"

Bianca pointed to a decrepit house in a nearby narrow alleyway. "That be my fancy palace," she said belligerently, then bolted around a corner and out of sight.

Laura frowned. "I wanted to ask her more about how she learned mathematics."

Veratti gazed at Laura, her intelligent blue eyes, her strong chin, and smooth cheeks. She always seemed concentrated on other things; he wondered how he could gain her full attention.

"I'm pleased to cross your path, for I have a question—"

Deirdre approached, huffing impatiently. "Signorina, your mother waits."

Laura turned to her. "One moment."

Deirdre persisted. "She sent me for you. And it's already been a long time, you talking to the zitelle." She looked over at the dress shop. "See, your mother is there, worried. She is looking out the window."

Laura saw her mother peering into the street and sighed. "Very well, Deirdre." She turned to the medical student. "*Mille grazie*, signore. But I am expected elsewhere." She followed Deirdre to the dressmaker's shop.

"Who was that young man, Laura?" Signora Bassi asked as they entered the shop.

"I don't know his name."

"It's not impolite to ask," Signora Bassi said, trying not to sound critical. "Laura, *prego*, you must think of something else besides your studies."

"Mamma, you must accept what I already know. I don't fit the mold of a young Bolognese woman who attracts suitors and it's silly to even think about it." Laura kissed her mother's cheek. "Don't look sad, for I am not."

But a great sadness did overwhelm Signora Bassi; she had not fully realized how Laura saw herself. Did her daughter think herself unattractive? As one that a man could not love?

Outside, on the street, Veratti lingered in the cold. He could see Laura through the shop's window. He realized, again, he hadn't provided his name. And he hadn't asked the question to which he wanted an answer. He plunged his icy hands into his gloves and thought that perhaps it did not matter. Laura Bassi's family was connected to the highest echelons of Bologna's society and he was only a poor student.

At the supper table that evening, Laura pled her case.

"Mamma. Papà. It's very clear the lack of access to education divides our society. Why should status of birth be such a factor? If those in positions, like the zitelle, were given the chance to learn, their lives could change. And in changing, Bologna could benefit."

"It's fine to care, but trying to fix things is not our place." Signora Bassi sipped her watered wine. "The church will care for their souls if they pray."

"You're committed to charity, Mamma, and give monies to the church. Imagine if your charity was focused on education for those who cannot afford it. What good it could do."

Signora Bassi put her wine glass down and readied her fork to spear a roasted carrot. "The church uses our offerings as they see fit."

Laura spoke softly. "But don't you see, it's only because you and Papà are willing to pay tutors that I'm given the blessed opportunity of learning. It was the luck of my birth. I can't help but think of the actions of Saint Caterina—she taught all who came to her."

"But you're not a teacher, Laura." Her father cut into his roasted lamb and dipped it into the sauce. "I must agree with your mother. It's unseemly for you to approach zitelle. Let me present your ideas to the city advisors."

Laura picked at her meal. She knew that the city advisors, when asked to address any change, made very slow progress.

She recalled Dottore Manfredi's advice: strategy. Perhaps, in this instance, there were other paths to explore.

After the church service on Sunday, Laura sought out Father Stegani to discuss her desire to help educate the zitelle.

"Education, cousin, must reflect the new Enlightenment thinking—on tolerance, opportunity for all, individual liberties."

He was taken aback by her intensity, but Laura continued.

"John Locke in England and Jean-Jacques Rousseau in France write about the mind, how it thirsts for sustenance. I would like to help provide that. I would become their teacher."

"But how and where would you teach the zitelle?" asked Father Stegani.

"Is there not a room or hall here, at the church? This girl, Bianca, has natural gifts. There must be others like her who could benefit. Mister Locke wrote that, depending on their education, nine out of ten people will be good or evil, useful or not. He examines how poverty contributes to actions that society finds unlawful and evil. Isn't it logical that poverty is exacerbated by lack of education? God cannot want that."

Father Stegani knew how frustrated Laura was about not being accepted in the official intellectual community—the professors and students of the University of Bologna. He wanted more for her, too.

"I'll speak to the bishop, Laura. Maybe something can be done."

True to his word, he talked to his bishop. The next week, at the Bassi home, Father Stegani told Laura and her parents he was able to procure funds for teaching supplies, but not the permission to use the church premises for a meeting place.

"But why not?" Laura asked. "In Germany, more than a

century ago, Martin Luther saw the good of all being taught to read. He held classes at his own monastery."

Father Stegani leaned back, not fond of this argument. "Martin Luther committed heresy when he broke with the Church and became a Protestant. He had the Bible translated from Latin into German, another blasphemy."

"He did that to make God's teachings more accessible. How can that be a bad thing?"

Father Stegani was stern. "Be careful, Laura, in the sharing of your thoughts on this. We're living in the Papal States."

Signora Bassi also worried about Laura's argument. She nodded to Nucca to pour more wine. "Shall we change the subject?"

Laura persisted. "Luther believed in education for both boys and girls, rich and poor. I support that."

Father Stegani was adamant. "Laura, I cannot use the ideas of a Protestant to convince the Catholic bishop."

Signor Bassi had stopped eating. "Is there more to the bishop's denial of using a room in the basilica? Is he fearful of his congregation's reaction?"

"There is that, of course," Father Stegani admitted. "There are noble families who would not be supportive of having zitelle in their place of worship."

"That raises a question," said Signor Bassi. "Is it theirs—or is it God's?"

Laura held her tongue. Father Stegani had gone to the trouble of broaching her plan to the bishop, and even though she did not get the response she wanted, she was grateful.

"*Grazie*, cousin. The funding you've procured is appreciated. How to use it well—that will be the problem that will need to be solved."

After Father Stegani had left for the evening, Laura sat in the candlelit library with her parents. She had a book open on her lap, but did not read. She was frustrated.

"This week I'll visit the convents and the monasteries," she said. "Perhaps there will be a place for a classroom."

Signor Bassi sipped his wine and pointed to the books piled all around them. "Our living space has been taken over."

Signora Bassi's eyes were on her needlepoint. "That is true, my husband."

"I have an idea." Signor Bassi turned to his wife. "Rosa Maria, what would you think about converting part of the carriage house into an additional library and workspace for Laura and her tutors? The carriage house is large. And we have need for only one carriage."

"Would that mean we could move the microscope and other instruments from the parlor?" Signora Bassi asked. "And the insect collection that has to be put away when ladies come to tea?"

"Perhaps the renovation could be called 'Laura's classroom.' A place for learning." Signor Bassi's eyes smiled at Laura.

Laura felt hope surge within her. If this was to be her classroom—could it be for her learning, and the teaching of others? Was her father willing to take a risk?

Signor Bassi stood. "I'll draw up plans. Let's see what can happen." He offered his hand to his wife. "Rosa Maria, it's late and you need your rest."

Laura's mother took her husband's arm and they headed up the staircase.

Signor Bassi stopped to look back at Laura. "*Buono notte, mia cara.*"

She beamed at him; she was a lucky daughter to have a father who believed in her so.

~

Over the next few weeks, workmen built new stables in the back area of the villa's property. They converted half of the carriage house into a study and small laboratory. Bookshelves lined the walls. Laura's microscope and scientific measuring devices were set on a long table near a new window. Insect specimens, preserved plants and flowers, and other collections were displayed in glass cases. Her telescope was put in the former hayloft; it was accessible by a new stairway.

Laura, with Carlo as a chaperone, visited the decrepit house where Bianca and other zitelle slept on rough mattresses stuffed with hay.

"I've convinced my mother to agree to offer Bianca a few hours of work in our kitchen, and then a few hours of instruction in my new classroom," Laura told Carlo.

They located Bianca, who was accepting hardened bread at the back door of a *panettiere*.

Bianca was suspicious. "Is there a trick here?"

Carlo shrugged. "Only that my very smart and educated cousin, for some reason, thinks you're special. And she's willing to give you her time and share a love of mathematics."

The day of the first instruction arrived. Bianca appeared at the Bassi villa's kitchen door. Her hair and clothes were washed. Her eyes widened as she looked into the large, warm place and smelled the roasting meats.

"This is fine," she said looking around. "Never been close to such as this."

"Would you like to eat or learn first?" Laura asked.

"Learning." Bianca's voice lowered, as if she were ashamed. "But I wonder if I wouldn't learn faster if my stomach was full."

"Then you shall have soup first." Laura smiled.

The cook set a bowl of lamb and root vegetable soup in front of Bianca. The girl began to devour it just as Deirdre entered the kitchen. She glared at Bianca.

"What're you lookin' at?" asked Bianca, wiping her mouth with the back of her hand.

Deirdre kept her eyes on Cook. "The best houses of Bologna do not allow this. Everyone knows that."

Laura said gently, "If you would like to join any lesson, Deirdre, you are welcome."

Nearly snarling, Deirdre lifted her nose into the air. "I'm not like her." She marched out of the kitchen.

Moments later, the soup eaten, Laura led Bianca outside to the carriage-house classroom. "You must tell me what you most want to learn," she said, remembering the joy she felt when Dottore Manfredi had said those words to her.

Bianca took in the shelves of books, the pieces of scientific equipment, the long wooden board with mathematical problems written in chalk. She clasped her hands over her heart.

"*Bellisima*, beautiful."

Laura had prepared a lesson plan and found Bianca to be quick and receptive. Bianca had never written numbers before; she learned to shape them and put them into the written formulas that aligned with her unusual capacity for calculation. She practiced writing her own name on the board. She stood back, glowing with pride as she looked at her signature.

"So, that's me. That's Bianca."

After her first lesson, Bianca curtsied to Laura in respectful gratitude. "Do you think one day I could be a housekeeper in a fine house? Be of use with my numbers? I've also heard there're now things called 'factories' being built, where there's use for those who know numbers. Maybe that's where I'll find my worth."

"Bianca, it's my opinion that you're of much worth now, as you are."

The girl ducked her head, unused to kindness or praise. "I'll come next time—do my chores with your cook and then apply myself to the classroom." She took her leave.

Laura looked to the small statue of Saint Catarina on the bookshelf. She sent a silent message to her namesake, thanking her for inspiration.

"It's a great satisfaction—to teach," she muttered aloud.

The next week, Bianca arrived with another zitelle, Abriana, who was barely thirteen. They entered the renovated carriage-house classroom. Bianca stood in the doorway, her voice was assertive, as if she wanted to ward off a refusal.

"Signorina, Abriana lives in the same building as me. She wants to work, one day, in a hat shop. Can you teach her so she can get a job?"

Laura looked at the young girl in tattered clothes. Her hands were chapped, her hair uncombed. But her large eyes were hopeful.

"Numbers, reading, and proper handwriting would be the requirements to work in a hat shop. Will you listen and be respectful of knowledge?" Laura asked.

Abriana, her chin quivering, nodded.

"Excellent. Then we will light the fire of learning today."

The next weeks brought more students, all girls with desires for futures in the workforce. Laura convinced her father to let her buy flash cards at Divertimenti. She made a game out of learning the shapes of the numbers and letters. She instructed them all in reading and recitation and the use of quill and ink, teaching each how to write their names without filling the vellum with spots and splotches of ink.

Early one day, as Laura passed out books to the zitelle, she saw movement out of the corner of her eye. Deirdre, wearing her cloth coat and carrying a bag, was at the kitchen door talking to Nucca. Deirdre glared toward the carriage house and then flounced across the courtyard and through the villa's gates.

Laura moved out of the carriage house and called to Nucca. "Is everything alright?"

"We've just lost a housemaid," Nucca said. "Apparently we're not one of the best houses in Bologna."

Chapter Eleven

The night of the April salon at the Bassi home arrived. Laura, with Nucca's help, finished dressing in her room, donning a soft green linen dress with a sky blue belt and sash.

"Hold still, signorina," Nucca said.

"No word today from Cardinal Lambertini?"

"No, signorina."

Laura put her disappointment aside. "I must go over the pamphlets again, Nucca, have everything in my head. I don't want to make a mistake." Laura had spent hours preparing. "Domenico Galeazzi has recently triumphed in his defenses and earned his laurea, and tonight he'll present on the medical field of anatomy. I've questions I want to pose."

Galeazzi had become a regular at the Bassi salons and had begun to seek out Laura's thoughts on various topics. She dared to think they were almost friends.

Laura looked out the window and saw carriages arriving. She could hear her father welcoming the nobles, professors, and students to the parlor, offering them fortified wine and the bites of the cheeses, olives, and sweets that Nucca had set out. And then she heard Count Luigi Marsili's booming voice.

"I have a guest with me, Signor Bassi. Let me introduce you to Marchioness Elisabetta Ratta—she has donated funds to the institute in the name of her recently passed husband. She asked to accompany me this evening and I could not deny her."

Laura headed to the top of the staircase and peered down into the foyer. Who was this woman interested in science? The marchioness was in her early thirties and dressed in the height of fashion. Her cloak was of fine velvet and dotted with felt appliques in the shapes of roses. The hood of her cloak was lined with silk, and when she slipped it off, Laura saw that her golden hairpieces added three inches to her willowy height. The marchioness handed Signor Bassi a package wrapped in brocade fabric.

"Now that I am a widow and free to make my own choices, I've become a publisher of Bologna's finest poets. Please, accept this volume for your library."

Signor Bassi thanked her, and as Nucca took the marchioness's cloak, Laura could see her beautiful chestnut silk dress. The marchioness's eyes landed on Laura.

"You must be the one I've heard so much about."

Laura moved down the staircase and curtsied.

Marchioness Ratta had a wide, toothy smile. "I've been told you debate with the best minds in Bologna." She gave a sidelong look at Count Marsili. "I enjoy seeing a man who listens and appreciates a woman's mind, don't I, Luigi."

Laura thought she saw a blush rise in the count's face.

He chided, "Marchioness, you have become quite outspoken."

Her laughter filled the foyer. "I had to wait until I was a rich widow to say what I think."

Count Marsili's attention was drawn to the courtyard, where a team of horses clomped heavily on the stones. "Is that a Lambertini carriage?"

Laura felt her breath catch in her throat. Had he really come? She peered out the door and saw the cardinal, followed by the twisted and stooped Dottore Salti and his second at the academy, the hefty, long-faced, beaked-nose Dottore Balbi, step out of the large gilded carriage.

Marchioness Ratta leaned into Laura. "The elite of the elite are here. Most exciting."

The charismatic Cardinal Lambertini entered the foyer. His dark red cassock and cloak were perfectly pressed, his large-brimmed burgundy hat brushed to a sheen. Laura curtsied as Marchioness Ratta extended her hand.

"I see it's true, cardinal," the marchioness said. "You're an academic at heart."

Lambertini smiled. "Ah. I go where God leads, and I am grateful He has chosen the scientific revolution to be along my path." He nodded toward Laura. "This young woman is perhaps the truest academic at heart."

The marchioness's high spirits bubbled as she tucked her arm into Laura's. "In truth, I have come to witness her." She turned her bright eyes to Laura. "Shall we be friends?" She glanced at the men, her lips forming a teasing challenge. "Shall we be two women aligned in a world controlled by men?"

Laura was taken aback by the marchioness's playful confrontation, intrigued that she was able to state a criticism in such a charming manner.

Lambertini turned to Laura. "I am glad you have admiring

friends." He looked to Dottore Salti, who looked like he'd just tasted vinegar. "Shall we take our seats?"

Marchioness Ratta reached for the arm of Count Marsili and swept into the salon. Laura slipped into her chair in the back of the room.

Domenico Galeazzi stood at the front of the attendees. "I'm most honored to lead the topic of the evening." His hand pointed to a group of medical students standing at the side of the room. "These are my fellows in studies. I teach them now, but in reality, they are just behind me in their bids for laureas. Tonight, they will aid me and help answer questions."

Laura noticed the broad-shouldered student who had intervened with the carabiniere on her behalf. She observed a steadiness about him, a quiet attention. Laura was aware of a feeling—a warmth igniting in her chest. She quickly looked down at her notebook; she knew she needed to keep her concentration on the evening's purpose: inspiring Cardinal Lambertini to solicit the Academic Council to consider her request to stand for a laurea.

Dottore Manfredi and Dottore Tacconi arrived. Manfredi took a seat near Laura.

"I see the cardinal has graced us." He leaned into Laura. "Do not hold back, signorina."

Galeazzi started his lecture. "To set the scene: Hippocrates, the first established medical scientist known to us, lived about four hundred years before the birth of Christ. It is from him that we have the Hippocratic oath: *First, do no harm.* We also credit Hippocrates with medical etiquette, with advising for a well-kempt and calm demeanor, for recommending short fingernails and a clean environment, for keeping meticulous records and diagnosing ailments through sight, feel, smell, and intuition. Hippocrates was responsible for taking superstition out of disease, for he argued that sickness was not punishment from the gods, but the result of natural or environmental effects on the body. He taught us that many diseases are treatable. He studied organ structure and functions. However, Hippocrates could only go so far, for there was a taboo in Greece against cutting up the human body to peer into its inner secrets."

One of Galeazzi's students stood. "This taboo became a law, supported by the Church, and was in place until the sixteenth century."

Galeazzi nodded and kept his eyes on his study group. "Is there someone who would like to tell us of the first medical doctor who delved into human anatomy?"

Laura quickly stood. "I would venture that it was Claudius Galen, two hundred years after Hippocrates. Turkish, but he made his home in Rome. He dissected apes and monkeys because he saw their similar physiology to the human form. He studied their organs and offered a primary stab at circulatory systems. But Galen did not dare go against the religious edicts against human dissection."

Galeazzi nodded to Laura. "*Grazie*, signorina. And what of Andreas Vesalius?"

Laura was ready with a response. "He worked after Galen, just two centuries ago. Vesalius was Belgium-born. Came to the Italian Peninsula to study at the University of Padua in 1543. In that century, the progressive Pope Clement VII decided to allow dissection of deceased criminals—and thus gave the opportunity for anatomy to thrive. Vesalius was among the first to dissect a body himself, instead of leaving the cutting to a barber or butcher." She enumerated many of Vesalius's advancements, such as investigating and notating intricacies of the nervous system and understanding that the heart was an involuntary muscle, and how Vesalius put together the first human skeleton; she also noted that this skeleton was still on display in Basel, Switzerland.

Laura snuck a look at Cardinal Lambertini. He had not turned to listen to her. But the marchioness had—and she gave Laura an encouraging wink. She caught Manfredi's eye; he nodded his approval and mouthed, "Stay on course."

One of youngest of Galeazzi's group, hoping to make an impression, made a point. "Vesalius's book *De humani corporis fabrica* will be forever on the shelf of the serious medical doctor."

"Perhaps until new discoveries change what we know," said Galeazzi with a frown.

"*Sì*, true, Dottore," the young student gulped. "As we learn, beliefs can change."

Galeazzi took control of the lecture. "And as my interest is in the abdominal organs, I will concentrate today on chapters six and seven—which focus on the internal organs, such as the kidney and its filtering processes, and the lungs—the organs of respiration."

The discussion in the salon continued. Galeazzi distributed drawings of cross sections of the kidneys and lungs, as seen under a microscope. He explained cell structures and systems. There were questions on the physical components and then a series of contentious arguments as the discussion came back to the history of religious opposition to science—and the restrictions still in place.

Laura continued to stand and sit as she contributed, noting many of the Enlightenment scholars' opinions on the separation of church, state, and science. She championed Newton as one of the greatest scientists, reminding all that Newton was also a man of God. "He believed that God's greatest gift to man was free will." She brought up the scientist's words: "'The law of Nature was established by God, as well as man himself. And though man were but a miserable reptile, God gave him thought and conscience, and thus can tell what is fittest to be done.'"

"As opposed to being restrained by the Church," another student added.

There were a few comments of "*Ben detto*" and "Well said" through the room. Others argued the point, taking umbrage at Newton's calling man a "miserable reptile." Manfredi laughed loudly, and called out that Newton was speaking as a poet! Finally, after another hour of opposing opinions and heated disagreements that nearly ended in a shouting match, Laura stood. Her voice rang out.

"We scientists know that with each new discovery, invention, or experiment, we might see the world in a new light. But we are human, and change—for most—is often painful. Resistance can fester and take hold, but must be replaced by patience and even deeper thought. May I point to the Englishman Alexander Pope's recent observation in his pamphlet 'Essay on Criticism': 'Good nature and good sense must ever join; to err is human; to forgive, divine.'"

Marchioness Ratta, energized by the intense debate, burst into applause.

Count Marsili stood and bowed toward Laura. "Excellent end to the evening, Signorina Bassi."

The salon attendees took their leave. Marchioness Ratta and Count Marsili walked to their carriage; Cardinal Lambertini and Dottore Salti followed. Lambertini had not spoken to her. It seemed to Laura as if her latest strategy had failed.

She heard a light cough behind her. "Signorina Bassi."

Laura turned to see the broad-shouldered student. She struggled to put her disappointment aside and aimed to be polite. "I hope you've received no ill will from the carabiniere, signore."

"Gratefully, I've not passed the polizia of late." He smiled, then cleared his throat. "I wanted to ask if you received my gift. I left it here for you over a year ago."

Laura frowned. What was he talking about? "I don't think so."

"A booklet. On electricus."

Laura's face brightened—now he had her full attention. "*Sì.* It's one of my favorites. Unfortunately, the booklet was a victim of an overturned wine glass, and the message and signature became inscrutable. I'm most sorry not to know it was from you."

"It's a small gift," he said humbly. "I would like you to know me by name—Giovanni Veratti. My family is from the countryside; we have a small parcel of land south of Venice. Since my father's death, my brothers work the land, for my future is in medicine."

"*Sì. Sì.* My cousin mentioned your sad circumstance. Please accept my sympathies."

"Of course."

There was another awkward pause.

"I stand for my own laurea—give my lectures and defenses— in just a few months," said Veratti. "I must concentrate on my studies now, but . . . ."

Just then, Galeazzi, standing on the veranda with the rest of his students, waved to him. "Veratti, are you coming?"

Laura dipped into a short curtsy. "Your group waits for you. There is no need to keep them waiting." She moved to the library and looked over her shoulder at him. "*Grazie* for the booklet."

Veratti bowed, frustrated. He strode off to join his study group.

Laura, from the library window, watched the students move off the veranda and through the courtyard and turn toward the city center. She imagined the discussion of science would continue over glasses of ale. She sighed. Was she always going to be on the outside?

The next day, Laura received a small pink envelope that smelled of rosewater. The seal was thick, a silver-colored wax marked with the initials M and R. She unfolded the letter and read the message.

Dear new friend, Signorina Laura Bassi,

Accept my gratitude for an edifying salon. In conversation with Cardinal Lambertini, it has been suggested that you share your knowledge by giving a lecture on botany and poetry at the next meeting of my women's group. I hope you will consent to join us, and edify us with your knowledge. And that, your kindly mother, Signora Bassi will also be my guest.

With highest esteem,
M. Ratta

Wide-eyed, Laura looked to her father and Manfredi. "I've been asked to give a lecture!" Her voice grew higher, jubilant and astounded. "It says here I'll be the guest of honor."

Chapter Twelve

A light rain was falling and the May breeze was warm. Laura and her mother arrived in the Bassi carriage at the Palazzo Ratta on via Castiglione. The ornate gilded gates were open and Laura could see the courtyard, its three fountains rising high in front of the golden-red three-sided palazzo. Liveried groomsmen were on hand to greet each carriage; they held oilskin umbrellas to keep the rain off the ladies as they stepped out of their carriages and made their way to the sheltering colonnade.

"Are you nervous, *mia cara?*" Signora Bassi asked.

"I feel an excitement, Mamma. I've so many facts and ideas in my head that the opportunity to share them feels like a gift." Laura handed a satchel to a groomsman and told him quietly, "*Prego*, take this to where the lecture will be held." She put her slim portfolio, filled with botanical drawings, under her arm and walked with her mother to the main entrance.

Servants took their cloaks and invited them to move up the interior marble stairs. Tapestries and oil paintings adorned the deep pink walls. Laura and her mother reached the top of the staircase and entered a glass-covered atrium filled with exotic flowers blooming around a waterfall. Daughter and mother looked at each other—this was the height of style, fine taste, and wealth.

"What a wonderful day, Mamma," Laura laughed.

Marchioness Ratta, wearing a peacock-feathered hat, a flowing Asian-inspired gown, and long golden earrings, glided across the marble floor to greet them.

"The Bassi women. Welcome. This will be exceptional. Follow me. Your lecture, Laura, will be in the gallery."

Laura and her mother followed the marchioness through the massive receiving room, the sitting room, the library, the morning room, and finally into the gallery. It was studded with gleaming white marble statuary of Venus and Aphrodite and centuries-old portraits of the Ratta family.

"Laura!" Eugenia was dressed in brocade and satin, one hand holding a fur muff. She trilled, "You're the prized speaker today. I'm so proud of you and proud we've been friends since we were children."

Eugenia led Laura to a table piled high with cakes. "You must come and see how my children have grown. You were right. They love the toys from Divertimenti."

The ladies finally settled in chairs and chaises. Laura, in her golden sateen dress and a green short jacket, addressed them.

"I chose my clothes today because I wanted to appear as if I could blend into a garden."

The ladies chuckled and she began her lecture.

"Most exceptional ladies of Bologna, it gives me great pleasure to impart my findings in botany. I know many of you are familiar with the plants and flowers native to the Papal States, so I thought today we could focus on the islands of Greece. We will discuss soil, sun, water and temperatures, and the microscopic examination of seeds."

"Microscopic?" an older countess croaked. "What's that?"

"Scientists, starting with the Dutchman Hans Lippershey in the late sixteenth century, have crafted lenses from glass that are capable of enlarging our view of objects. Eventually, Lippershey—or perhaps it was a spectacle maker in Lippershey's village named Janssen—had the idea of putting these lenses into an instrument that we can put our eyes to, and look through a series of these lenses. It is called a scope. If you put a seed on a slate of glass and look into the peephole of this kind of scope, the seed is enlarged—magnified—so that we see details beyond the capability of normal sight. Would you like to see a microscope?"

"*Sì*," growled the old countess. "Better to see than hear."

Laura motioned for the servants to carry out the three microscopes she had brought with her. They moved around the room so the ladies could see and touch each of the instruments.

The old countess grunted. "No one has told me of these things. Where does a woman learn this? How old are you?"

"Nineteen."

Laura had the servants pass botanical drawings around the room. She quoted from the work of sixteenth-century botanists and explorers such as Linnaeus, Prospero Alpini, and Onorio Belli, and gave a spirited and detailed overview of color, fragrance, and strength of native Greek plants.

"I noticed on my way through the atrium that Marchioness Ratta has fine examples of the deep-red anemone; its seeds are carried in the wind and thus it is also called the windflower. It was written that it was once sacred to the goddess Aphrodite," Laura explained.

Questions regarding the Greek gods surfaced and Laura was able to answer them; she told herself to remember to thank Dottori Greci and Rios's tutelage in the subject. She then talked of the flowers that were used medicinally and those that were toxic and used for poison. Laura segued into Newton's work in botany and plant function, mentioning that the accepted notion of gravity, inspired by the apocryphal tale of Sir Isaac Newton witnessing an apple falling from a tree, was not an actual happenstance but Newton's simple way to explain the concept of the earth's pull.

The gathered ladies, who had never been treated to such a lecture, found their interests piqued.

The old countess loudly muttered. "This young woman is odd—she seems to know very much."

Laura ended the lecture. "It's good to remember that we're living in the Age of Enlightenment, a time meant to give light to dark corners. Preparing for those changes, in my opinion, should be exciting. Not just for men, but for you—and for your daughters."

Eugenia's mother, Signora Mucchi, cleared her throat. "The zitelle are not our daughters. There's talk that you're teaching these wretched souls. To what good?"

"Zitelle?" the old countess moaned. "Those unfortunate girls?"

"Exactly, Contessa," said Laura. "They are unfortunate. I teach them because they want to be able to fend for themselves rather than be at the mercy of those in our society who would use them for deplorable purposes. Plato observed, centuries ago, that the person interested in happiness must depend on self, not on others. That is what the zitelle want—a chance to do that. Education can help them achieve their goals. I want to help if I can."

There was a silence. Signora Mucchi looked around, wanting support for her point of view.

From the back of the room, a male voice sounded. "*Brava! Brava!*"

Laura noticed a young, stylish man in the back of the gallery. He was not tall, but he was striking. Everything made him stand out—from his silver-haired wig to his royal blue velvet waistcoat, lavender linen shirt, dark breeches, and shoes so shiny they caught the descending sunlight visible through the window.

Marchioness Ratta took advantage of the interruption and announced the end of the lecture.

She hurried to Laura and ushered her to the young man. "This is Signor Francesco Algarotti. He is from Venice, but Bologna has captured his heart."

"I call it the 'City of the Fat,'" Algarotti smiled.

The marchioness explained, "Because he loves the farms and foods of our home."

"And the City of *La Dotta*, the learned," Laura said, "because our university is the best in Europe."

Algarotti bowed to Laura. "I would like to write a poem to you."

"That would surely be a waste of your talent, signore," Laura laughed.

Marchioness Ratta patted Algarotti's arm. "I'm about to publish a book of his poems. One dedicated to you would make a good addition."

The next day, Signor Bassi rushed home from the Palazzo

d'Accursio; he carried a dozen bulletins. "There is poem, written to our Laura! It's titled 'Bologna's Lady Philosopher' and calls her a 'mine of inexhaustible knowledge.'"

Laura read the poem, her heart sank. "Oh no. It's filled with hyperbole."

Nucca clucked. "The city must be talking about this."

"Surely the heads of the university are talking about it," said Signor Bassi. "We shall see how it's received."

That night, Laura sat on the window seat in her bedroom. She wondered if Marchioness Ratta encouraged Algarotti to write his poem. She wondered if the marchioness and Cardinal Lambertini could have foreseen the reaction to her lecture at the ladies' salon. Had they embarked on a strategy to sway the most powerful men of the university to reconsider her request? Were they dedicated to helping her?

In the next weeks, Laura was invited to give lectures at various ladies' clubs, at public gatherings, and at Bologna's special occasions. Her popularity grew. The populace began to buzz with opinions about the university's denial of her application to stand for a laurea. People stopped her on the streets and told her of their support. Algarotti continued to write poems, calling her "Bologna's Hypatia" and "The Champion of Great Science and Great Newton."

Late summer arrived and Laura received a note from Marchioness Ratta.

Friend,

My dear Algarotti and I will be attending, as Count Marsili's guests, the defense of a laurea candidate. I feel you, too, would find it of interest. My carriage will stop for you at the start of midday, tomorrow.

With highest esteem,
M. Ratta

The marchioness's carriage arrived at the Bassi villa. Laura, in a blush-rose-colored dress with silk cuffs, white leather shoes, cream stockings, and straw hat, stepped inside the vehicle to join her friends. She carried a small purse; inside was her notebook and graphite *penicillus*—she hoped she'd be able to take notes at the lecture and study them later.

Marchioness Ratta had an elegant picnic basket on her lap and was excited to share news. "Laura, the pope has named Cardinal Lambertini the new archbishop of Bologna."

Algarotti nearly crowed. "Finally, a learned man in a seat of power who sees the good of new thinking." He straightened his lace cravat. "May he live long and may Bologna prosper."

"I'm glad of his recognition," said Laura.

"And the new archbishop is quite impressed with you." The marchioness smiled at Laura, as if she were holding onto a secret. "It can only help, don't you think? He is a forward-thinking man."

The carriage arrived at the institute.

"Ah, there's Count Marsili, waiting for us." Marchioness Ratta gathered her skirts. "Do you know this medical student who is presenting today? Giovanni Giuseppe Veratti?"

Laura was startled. "Veratti?"

"Do you know him?"

"No, no. Not at all," Laura denied. But she did feel a strange added excitement.

Count Marsili opened the carriage door and quickly took the picnic basket from the marchioness. "I've reserved seats for us. It's about to begin."

Veratti, in student robes over a simple wool waistcoat, stood on the dais. A short, curled wig covered his dark hair. He espoused, in Latin, on mathematics, in particular the arithmetic treatises of Luca Pacioli on geometry, Pacioli's mathematical puzzles, and his book *Divine Proportions*. Then Veratti moved on to the post-Renaissance additions made by the Flemish mathematician Simon Stevin and his introduction of decimal points. He spoke on the latest studies, including calculus and the advancements made by the Swiss Bernoulli brothers, their "calculus of variations," and their book *Art of Conjecture*, covering mathematical probability, permutations, and combinations. The Academic Council grilled him.

Laura, jotting questions in her notebook, was impressed by Veratti's steady and quiet demeanor as the council raised complex questions on the subjects.

After two hours, Dottore Salti raised his gnarled hand into the air.

An assistant rang a heavy iron bell and called out, "This is the end of Signor Veratti's defense on mathematics. We will reconvene in one hour for lecture and defense in chemistry!"

The Academic Council moved out of the hall and headed to their private quarters.

Those in the gallery opened their picnic baskets. Marchioness Ratta handed Count Marsili a specially wrapped treat.

"Luigi, it's a new thing called a sandwich. It gets its name from an English earl who was too focused on his card game to eat his bread and meat separately."

Laura noticed their closeness, their enjoyment of each other, how the count smiled every time the marchioness spoke. Laura accepted a few slices of a peach and small wedge of hard cheese. She had little appetite; she was too excited. Veratti's presentation had invigorated her and a now-familiar envy filled her. She wanted to be the person behind the lectern on the dais.

At the end of the day, after Veratti's thorough defense in chemistry, the Academic Council filed out to their chambers. Those in the gallery seats moved into the loggia. Laura stood alone as the marchioness, on Count Marsili's arm, and Algarotti moved through the crowd, sharing gossip and opinions with the gathered academics.

Laura looked at Tibaldi's frescoes—Odysseus's adventures, each one depicting the Greek triumphing over his opponents. She remembered her father telling her that Odysseus's journeys were about curiosity and strength. She felt she understood the Greek's desire to test himself. How she wanted to do the same thing.

"Signorina Bassi. I noticed you in the gallery." Veratti had joined her. He looked tired, but confident.

"It was impressive, Signor Veratti," she murmured. "If it were me on the council, I would assure you of that immediately."

He laughed. "Then we shall have to find a way to get you a seat with the honored professors, for they prefer to let a student suffer."

"How many more topics, in total, will you defend?" Laura asked.

"Twelve. Languages, history, and literature will be in three months' time. Then there will be astronomy, geology, and geography. Finally, areas of medicine. I hope to complete them all in the next two years."

Laura's eyes grew wide. "But aren't you impatient to

complete your laurea and gain special access to everything in the university? And practice your medicine?"

"I don't want to misstep."

"If it were me, I would not be so patient," Laura admitted. "I've heard only those with laureas can have the first choice of laboratories."

Veratti inclined his head. He'd never met a young woman so forthright. "I'm following the recommendations of Dottore Salti and the council."

Marchioness Ratta joined them and congratulated Veratti. "Well done, signore. I can see you'll be a fine doctor one day." She turned to Laura. "The carriage waits." She swept off.

Laura nodded to Veratti, signaling her departure. "*Buongiorno*, signore."

"I've heard you are teaching," Veratti said quickly. "That you have a classroom at your family villa that has also become a small laboratory. I would be most interested to see it."

Laura was surprised. "I teach those who are referred to as zitelle. Some do not approve."

"I do."

Laura took a long look at Veratti and saw his deep brown eyes were kind. "My classroom is simple, but you are welcome to see it." She moved off; she didn't want to keep Marchioness Ratta waiting.

Veratti was pleased with himself. He knew he had defended his work well today—and now, he had permission to call on the very interesting Signorina Bassi.

That visit was delayed, for the city of Bologna was plunged into deep mourning. One of its most generous, Count Luigi

Marsili, had died. He'd been born in Bologna, served in the Holy Roman Emperor Leopold's armies, became a decorated soldier in Habsburg regiments, fought against the Turks, been a prisoner of war, and served as a strong emissary for the Papal States. Finally, he had dedicated his life to science.

Count Marsili's funeral was held at the Basilica di San Petronio. The testimonials and prayers lasted from morning to night, and Archbishop Lambertini gave the final eulogy.

Laura lingered after all had filed out. She prayed for Marsili's soul, remembering the man who, at first, had ignored her and then became her champion. She heard soft footfalls approaching.

Marchioness Ratta, her face covered with a black lace veil, sat beside Laura and reached for her hand. "How I'll miss his generous spirit."

Laura nodded. "It's a surety God welcomed Count Marsili into heaven at the moment of his last breath."

"Is it weakness that makes me angry at God's decision to take him from me?"

"God gives us room for discontent and questioning," Laura murmured. "He also provides the companionship of friends to make sadness easier."

The marchioness squeezed Laura's hand. They sat together honoring the memory of Count Marsili.

It was weeks later and Laura was at her desk, organizing the day's lessons. Bianca nearly flew into the carriage-house classroom.

"I've gained employment, signorina. I'll be a ladies' maid in the Galeazzi household. I've been hired because I can read and write and exchange money in the proper way in the market-place. And Signor and Signora Galeazzi say to thank you for my education." Bianca's once thin and wan face was glowing; her shoulders were now held back and looked strong.

"They're lucky to have your talents."

"I ask permission to continue to work here with you on my one day off a week. I want to keep learning."

Laura felt relief. Bianca's announcement had filled her with happiness, but also a feeling of loss. She'd come to rely on Bianca's tough and energetic spirit and incorrigible curiosity; she was an excellent assistant in the classes and laboratory.

"That is good news, Bianca. We have so much to do."

Nucca entered, carrying a tray with a teapot and small cakes. She interrupted, "You have a caller, Signorina Laura."

"Who is it? I'm not expecting anyone."

Nucca put down the tray. "He's talking to your mother. He says his name is Giovanni Veratti."

Laura was surprised. "Well. Signore Veratti did tell me he wanted to see my small laboratory. You may show him here, Nucca. *Grazie.*"

Moments later, Nucca ushered Veratti into the carriage-house classroom.

"I do not mean to disturb," Veratti said.

Laura introduced him to Bianca and waved her hand to the laboratory. "I told you it was simple."

"But large enough." He took an object from his satchel. It was wrapped in canvas. "I stopped at Divertimenti and found this. It's a toy, but I thought you might find it interesting. May I?"

"Of course," Laura said.

She and Bianca cleared the long table and Veratti untied the canvas surrounding the toy. He revealed a small bag, made of silk and lined with paper, thin silken cords, a miniature straw basket, and four short tallow candles.

"Have you heard of Bartolomeu de Gusmão?"

"I have not," said Laura.

Veratti took a pamphlet from his pocket. "Gusmão was born in a Portuguese colony in Brazil and became a Jesuit when he was very young. He moved to Lisbon to continue his studies in theology. But his interests were more in mathematics and invention." He showed them a drawing in the pamphlet. "He built a floating balloon to convince the king of Portugal that there was possibility of a manned flight—that a person could travel in the air, using a balloon to do so."

Bianca clapped her hands together. "Up in the air? With the birds?"

Veratti checked Laura's interest. "Shall we try?"

Laura nodded. "Absolutely."

Veratti situated the toy's small square basket on the work table and set the short, thick tallow candles in holders in each corner. He muttered under his breath, becoming totally engaged in the experiment.

"Perhaps Gusmão was inspired by the Chinese; they used sky lanterns centuries ago during battles—to give signals to soldiers."

"How and why will this toy rise into the air?" asked Bianca.

"Perhaps it's not fully known, because air is a mystery," Laura said. "We don't know its composition. Is it one element? Or more? We don't know."

Veratti tied the thin silk cords to the basket and then to the silk and paper bag. "What Gusmão understood was that air expanded as it heated—it became lighter."

"And that makes the balloon go up?" Bianca asked.

Laura pondered aloud. "We think of air as weightless, but I believe it's true that we, at times, can feel its heaviness. Sir

Newton experimented with sound traveling through air. He found it to be changeable, depending on circumstances such as the weather. I've always wondered about the sound of thunder—why it sometimes follows lightning quickly and sometimes at a slower pace. There's much to learn about air."

Veratti lit the candles. The three waited, and then, after just moments, they watched as the silk and paper bag, attached by thin cords, began to fill with the air warmed by the candles. The silk began to billow.

"Gusmão presented his ideas to the king of Portugal—and his balloon, fancier and larger than this. It floated through the air for nearly five meters—right past the king's nose."

Their eyes were on their toy. The attached bag was nearly full; the thin cords were stretched from the basket.

Veratti's voice was like a whisper. "Some accused Gusmão of being a wizard, and the Inquisition took notice. But the king was entranced and wanted to hear Gusmão's plans for what he called an airship—large enough to carry a man. Gusmão told him it would contain bellows that the rider could manipulate in case the source of air unexpectedly died and interesting mechanicals would help with directing the airship to certain locations."

"But Gusmão never made this airship?" Bianca asked.

"He died before he could do it."

The toy airship began to rise off the table and into the air. Bianca gasped and Laura and Veratti laughed.

"It's good that Gusmão was not condemned as a wizard," said Laura, her voice filled with awe. "And that science was recognized."

A loud voice pierced their amazement. "What's going on?"

It was Dottore Manfredi. He joined the three in watching the balloon as they caught him up on the details of the experiment.

"Excellent," he said. "Another thing for you to discuss in your salon lecture."

"What salon?" Laura asked. "I am not scheduled for a—"

"You've caught the imagination of the city." Manfredi helped himself to tea and cakes. "Hasn't she, Veratti?"

"It's true," said the young medical student.

The candles had blown out and the toy began to descend; they watched it land back on the table.

Manfredi popped another cake into his mouth. "Now professors and nobles of Bologna are curious about you, Laura. And there are some on the Academic Council who have also shown interest. I suggest, with great vehemence, that it is time for you to lead a Bassi salon."

Bianca gasped. "*Sì. Sì.* That would be wonderful."

Laura was stunned. "I would be the main lecturer? In front of the academics?"

Manfredi nodded. "You father, your other tutors, and I recommend this next strategic action. It is time."

Chapter Thirteen

The night of Laura's lecture arrived. The night before, during a cold October rainstorm, the family had celebrated her twentieth birthday. But Laura's mind was not on her favorite cake, the *torta della nonna*, or the fine sherry that her father had uncorked. She couldn't stop thinking of her lecture and excused herself to her bedroom early, so that she could pour over her notes.

The storm had abated and the skies cleared. A crisp autumn breeze blew through the streets. The academics and nobles who regularly attended the Bassi salons arrived at the villa. Marchioness Ratta arrived with Algarotti; they deposited their cloaks with Nucca and moved into the parlor. Dottore Balbi of the Academic Council arrived, his footfalls heavy on the veranda. He wiped his beaklike nose with his handkerchief and coughed; he was clearly not in the best of health.

Laura waited in her room upstairs. She heard the carriages and horses arriving, was clued into the sound of boots on the courtyard. She pressed her hands together and felt their dampness, she licked her lips for her mouth felt dry. Would she be able to keep the attention of these learned men?

Her father moved into the doorway. "*Mia cara*, it's time."

Laura moved down the stairway. Nucca and Bianca were standing side by side at in the hallway. They knew they wouldn't be able to enter the parlor, but they planned to listen. Laura saw the support in their eyes.

She entered the salon and saw Veratti out of the corner of her eye, standing near the window. Taking a deep breath, she moved to the lecturer's spot. She stood behind a table that supported a carafe of well-watered wine and a crystal goblet, and set her notes on the wooden surface.

Dottore Balbi coughed, the sound raw and loud. He blew his nose into his handkerchief. "*Scusami*, signorina," he muttered.

Laura began by dedicating her lecture to Count Marsili. Then she moved onto Newton, detailing his contributions to science. She worked chronologically, noting Newton's interests and experiments that built on one another, and then listing those that seemed to stem from flights of imagination. Questions came from those gathered, and Laura debated and defended her points of view and allowed for differing ideas. Her experience in teaching in her carriage-house classroom had taught her to strive for clarity and conciseness. Manfredi sat in the back, arms folded, nodding his round head, and he and Signor Bassi exchanged glances. They knew Laura was nervous, but she was still impressive.

Laura continued, "Newton has inspired us to think about gravity, about mathematical forms, about mechanics and hydraulics, about how we see, even about God and the Bible. In the middle of the 1600s, the Frenchman Antoine Arnaud and others became interested in how we think. How we implement logic and how we reason. Newton took Arnaud's ideas—along with those of mathematician Isaac Barrow, and related them to how we approach geometry. Sir Newton made connections. He let us see that we could look at our world as a machine— moving parts that work together. From botany to physics. From nature to man-made instruments. In *Naturphilosophie*, Newton relayed his observations and conclusions and reminded us that our universe is not a stable, unchanging entity. It is always in flux."

The next day, during a tutoring session with Manfredi, a messenger arrived.

Signor Bassi brought the letter into the carriage-house classroom. "Daughter, it is from the university."

Laura's hand trembled as she broke the seal and read the message aloud.

This is to inform you that your application to stand for a laurea at the University of Bologna has been accepted and will be scheduled for May 1732.

"That's six months from now. Unacceptable!" Manfredi yelled. "Not enough time for proper preparation. The council is setting you up for failure."

Laura stood. "I accept the challenge. I've been waiting for a very long time and I don't want to put it off."

Signor Bassi moved to his daughter. "First, let us enjoy the moment. I worried this day would never come. You have earned it, my daughter."

"*Grazie*, Papà." Laura stood and her father embraced her. She could feel his emotion, his pride.

Signor Bassi moved to the door and ran up the stairs. "I must tell your mother," he called out. "I shall bring her down to join us!"

There was barely a moment of silence before Manfredi started making plans.

"You'll begin with no more than three topics," he said to Laura. "We'll demand another date, three months later for another series of defenses. And three months after that . . ."

Laura moved to the window, considering her strategy. "I want to leave no room for a change of mind, Dottore Manfredi. I'll petition to present all subjects in one week's time. It's an opportunity I don't want to disappear."

"Are you sure?"

"*Sì*. And I will be ready."

Bologna's imagination was captured. Their "Hypatia," their chaste and brilliant maiden goddess, was now to face a great test. Would she be able to accomplish this feat? Would she have the mental and physical strength? What if she fainted in front of the Academic Council? What if her voice gave out? What if the pressure was too much?

Part Three

1732–1744

Chapter Fourteen

It was nearly dawn on the day of the defense. It was early May and there was a chill in the morning air. Laura had kept the fire going in the parlor's fireplace all night and candles glowed on the mantelpiece. She sat in a hard-backed chair at the long table that had been added to the room, deep into reading her notes. Piles of books and open pamphlets filled most of the wood surface.

There was a knock on the open door. Laura looked up.

"Mamma."

She noticed how small her mother's shoulders looked beneath her morning robe, how thin her neck was, as if it were getting too weak to hold the weight of her head. Signora Bassi had taken ill again during the winter months, a chill had taken hold in her bones, and she had lost a taste for food. Dottore Galeazzi, who had focused his medical work on internal organs, had spoken to Signor Bassi and Laura about a tumor that was growing inside her.

"Mamma, you should be in bed." Laura stood. "Dottore Galeazzi says rest is most important. I'll take you back upstairs."

"Let's sit, *mia cara*," Signora Bassi said. She lowered herself to the chaise and leaned back against its pillows.

Laura took a shawl from the back of a chair and wrapped it around her mother's shoulders. She could smell the lavender scent of her mother's bath oil and a rose-infused cologne. She knew her mother struggled to retain her dignity during her illness.

Laura reached for her small hand. "Mamma, I hope I do not disappoint."

Signora Bassi eyes filled with tenderness. "I've always worried that you would not ultimately be happy if you didn't choose to follow a woman's well-worn path. Marriage. Taking care of a husband and children." She smiled. "But disappoint? That's the farthest from the truth. My failing was not believing my child could have a unique path. And be so strong."

Laura moved a footstool to the side of the chaise and sat close. "I want to do well today, so your years of worry will not be in vain."

"I am proud." Signora Bassi closed her eyes. "Very proud of my daughter." She drifted into sleep.

Laura yawned. Sleep for her, in the last months, had come in short spurts. She had concentrated on digging deeper into her studies of languages, sciences, natural history, logic, and philosophy. She closed her eyes.

There was a whisper from the open doorway.

"Signorina Laura." Bianca, still in her hat and cloak, was out of breath. "I've run here to help you get ready. Signora Galeazzi has given me the day off. She sends her best wishes and wants you to know she'll be sitting with Marchioness Ratta today in the gallery."

Laura opened her eyes and smiled, "*Tempus est mihi. Tempus ultra aperire fores.*"

"What does that mean?" Bianca asked.

"It's Latin. It means 'It is time for me. Time to open the door.' To more." She looked around the room. "This house has been my refuge. But today, I could step through a gate to a wider field. Full of even more learning."

Hours later, Laura had bathed and her hair had been swept up off her neck and off her forehead. During her defense, she would be wearing a white academia wig and she wanted to appear tidy and not let her curls tumble around her face. Nucca was fussing in the room. She could hear her father quietly moving through the hallway. She knew he was pacing, worried about her.

Bianca entered with newly pressed linen drawers and Laura stepped into them.

Nucca tied the ribbon through the waistline into a double bow. "We don't want to worry about your undergarments coming loose, signorina."

Bianca held out a gauzy chemise, and Laura ducked her head so it could be pulled down over her breasts and rib cage. She sat on the velvet-covered stool and placed her toes into thickly woven white stockings. She unrolled them up her leg to her thigh. Bianca handed her ribbons to tie below her knees so they would not fall or sag to her ankles.

"Nothing must fall today," Bianca muttered, totally invested in making sure Laura would have no distractions during her presentations.

The next undergarment was the soft petticoat.

"No noisy crinoline today," Laura said, stepping into it. She remembered when, at age five, Father Stegani had lifted her onto the hard chair to recite her multiplication tables for her parents. She had worn a stiff crinoline that crunched and swayed and distracted. Today would be different.

"Your corset, Signorina Laura," Nucca said.

Bianca presented the stiff, boned corset, made of inflexible coutil material. The bones of the corset were made of thin strips of whalebone slipped into twelve fabric channels situated in the seams. Laura wrapped the corset around her midsection. Bianca used a bodkin needle to pull the laces through metal eyelets.

Nucca tightened the laces. "Tell me when, Signorina Laura."

"Do not over-tighten. I must be able to use all my breath."

Laura dressed in a blue silk gown, donned her low-heeled shoes. "Not the height of fashion," she mused. "But today I will stand for hours."

Before going downstairs, Laura slipped into her mother's room. Nucca had helped Signora Bassi back to her bedroom and she was now asleep, her breathing soft and shallow. Laura smoothed her mother's quilt and kissed her forehead.

The Bassi family's carriage moved through the streets. Signor Bassi had a set smile on his face; he didn't want to betray his anxiety. Laura sat up straight, holding tightly to her leather-bound notebook. She thought of the day, six months ago, when she was summoned to the institute, to the office of the Academic Council to face Dottori Salti and Balbi.

Salti's gray wig had hung low on his forehead and he rubbed his thin, sour face. "Signorina Laura Maria Caterina Bassi. I've a defense schedule in front of me that must be a mistake. It calls for your lectures to be on five consecutive days."

Laura had told him that the schedule was correct, that she would defend three topics a day for five days.

He had snarled. "It is unheard of."

Laura, keeping her voice calm, had responded, "I know the honored Council has provided this irregular opportunity. I do not want to take advantage of your time and good will." She did not say that she was afraid the chance might disappear if her presentations were stretched over a longer period of time.

The carriage turned toward the main piazza. Laura saw hundreds of people crowding the streets, all streaming toward the Palazzo Pubblica.

"Papà. Look." Her voice was strained. "Where are they all going? Has something happened?"

Dottore Manfredi, his round face damp with sweat, raced up to the window of the Bassi carriage. "I had to push through hundreds to get to you! All these people are here for your day, Signorina Laura." He climbed up next to the driver. "The front entrance will be problematic. Go to the west alleyway of the palazzo. I've someone waiting at a side door."

The carriage driver avoided the main piazza and took narrow side streets. Veratti was waiting at the side entrance to the Palazzo Pubblica.

"I'm certain it will go splendidly," Veratti said as he helped Laura from the carriage.

Laura looked into his dark, encouraging eyes—and quickly moved through the door to the back hallways of the palazzo.

The front rows of the Sala degli Anziani were peopled with professors in tightly curled horsehair wigs and long robes. Behind them were noblemen in frock coats and heavy periwigs.

Marchioness Ratta and Algarotti had procured front-row galley seats on one side, with an unobstructed view of the dais. Signora Paola Galeazzi, the beautiful wife of Dottore Galeazzi, arrived with Eugenia and they sat next to the marchioness. They were three women in magnificent dresses and bright hats in a sea of men. The back benches were filled with university students and clergy, and the balconies were packed with curious Bolognese—shopkeepers, merchants, weavers, butchers, and jewelers. In the highest corner of the balcony, there was a small group of young women—zitelle. They sat with Abriana, who now wore the clothes of an assistant shopkeeper and a hat with a feather. The well-scrubbed zitelle looked excited, but also nervous; they were in an important palazzo with many well-heeled people. Would they be asked to leave?

Bianca slipped in beside Abriana, squeezed her arm, and said, "Signorina Bassi will show them all."

The bell rang. The crowd quieted. Laura, in robe and wig, entered the lecture hall. She climbed to the dais and stood behind a high square lectern. The Academic Council filed in to sit behind a long walnut table just below the dais. Salti took his spot in the middle, in the chair with the highest back. He raised his crooked arm, and the assistant rang the bell again.

Laura's throat was dry. The air felt thick, her ears felt plugged; she could feel the sweat form under her wig. "Dottore Salti and esteemed Academic Council, I am honored to be here before you today."

"Louder!" A deep, irritated voice came from the front row.

"We can't hear you! *Forte! Forte!* Talk louder!"

Laura swallowed hard. She saw Vincenzo Cruce sitting behind Salti, glaring at her. She looked to where her father and her tutors sat. Galeazzi and Veratti were behind them.

Determination strengthened her. She would not disappoint; she would prove that the gates to academia need not be closed to her.

Her voice rang out. "Today, I will be defending three subjects. Tomorrow, I'll do the same and continue each day until the end of the week."

Tacconi, sitting behind the Academic Council with Manfredi, muttered, "I fear she's too ambitious."

Laura widened her stance. Her voice steadied. She spoke in Latin, and took her time to show her fluency in the accepted language of learning, and then moved on to show her knowledge of French, Greek, English, and German.

In the front seats of the gallery, Marchioness Ratta leaned into Eugenia. "I don't understand a word."

Eugenia nodded; she was only able to ascertain the meaning of a few French words. "But she seems to be doing well." She looked to the gathered professors and students. Many were sitting forward, their faces filled with surprise. Eugenia felt a swelling of pride—they must see that her friend was extraordinary.

An hour later, Dottore Salti raised his hand, signaling the assistant to ring the bell. Laura, who had prepared more, was startled. Was she to be rejected so soon?

The council stood, formed a tight group, and conferred. Finally, Salti, with an angry flick of his hand, sat back in his chair and waved to the solidly built, hooked-nose Dottore Balbi to address Laura.

Balbi's voice rang out. "It has been determined that proficiency in languages has been met."

Laura's knees stopped wobbling. She nodded to an assistant sitting on a straight chair in the corner of the dais; he poured her a glass of well-watered wine. As she sipped, she could feel the liquid soothing her throat. She faced the council again.

"*Grazie*. This day is most important to me because I was introduced to the idea of the Enlightenment at a young age and felt a great desire to follow its principles—its call to question, to use critical thinking to examine the known and unearth the unknown. It was Copernicus who, nearly two hundred years ago, wrote: 'To know that we do not know—that is true knowledge.' The words of this Polish scientist resonate today in the Age of Enlightenment."

She continued, moving into the expected Latin. "Descartes, in his *Principles of Philosophy*, states that only God is perfectly wise, and that man is more or less wise depending on his commitment to understanding and gaining knowledge. Descartes wrote about the five degrees—or sources—of knowledge. The first: We learn, from simple existence and experience, things that do not require study. The second: We learn from our senses; the third, from communication with each other; the fourth, from concentration on the ideas of those who dedicate themselves to study and experiment. The fifth is what Descartes points to as forming the base of all progress: questioning. Everything." She paused. "Everything."

Laura took a deep breath and continued. "Saint Caterina, beloved nun and teacher in our Bologna, had a similar realization one hundred years before Descartes. In her seven spiritual rules, she wrote that one must always question and continuously explore in order to come to a deep understanding of the world. I applaud Descartes and I honor Saint Caterina, for I, too, believe that questioning all ideas—in science, philosophy, and society—is commendable and the only way to move humankind forward."

She took a sip of the watered wine, then forged ahead. "There are many fine leaders and contributors in the Enlightenment movement. And because my main interests are in science—specifically physics—my first subject will concentrate in this area." Laura proclaimed that she'd begin with the most recent theories and work backward through time, venturing into the earliest documented ideas of the Greeks and Romans. "I will always embrace the provenance of our sciences and the long history of extraordinary thinkers."

Her two-hour lecture was spirited, passionate, full of anecdotes and specific instruction. The gathered listened attentively; a few students even slipped out vellum from their satchels and took notes.

The bell rang, signaling the end of her presentation. Laura closed her notebook. The council members looked to Salti. He folded his hands on the table and nodded to Balbi to lead the next segment.

Balbi stood. "We'll now move to the questions and answers—Signorina Bassi's defense of her lecture. This will commence in our native tongue."

He acknowledged the council; each was to challenge the depth of Laura's understanding. Pointed questions soon bombarded her, clearly meant to shake her composure, argue with her reasoning, and inquire about her conclusions.

Laura felt the harsh scrutiny. She soon realized the goal was to show her to be unfit.

The marchioness bristled. "They're cruel. They're trying to break her."

Eugenia frowned and leaned into Paola. "I want to kick them on their ankles and hear them howl."

Algarotti, using his *penicillus*, was writing in his notebook, intent on building a new poem. "But our friend is doing marvelously."

Another hour passed. Laura was able to answer all the questions and defend every dissent. Salti raised his arm. The bell rang.

Moments later, in a private room behind the lecture hall, Laura collapsed into a chair.

Signor Bassi entered. "You were impressive, my daughter."

"Perhaps to you, Papà. But what about to the Academic Council?"

"It's very hard to read their faces."

Bianca entered, carrying a picnic basket. "Nucca and Cook packed smoked fish and cheese for you."

Laura nodded. "I will need sustenance."

The crowd did not dissipate during the hour break—in fact, more bodies pressed into the large lecture hall for the second session.

"For my first subject this afternoon," Laura informed the council and those gathered after the break, "I will focus on classical mechanics, one of the first branches of physics that relies on Aristotle's logic and integration for its calculation of quantifiable forces of action and reaction."

She detailed recent theories and equations and noted that the results of these findings could be seen in everyday life, as well as in hydraulics and the machines now important in the fast-growing Industrial Revolution. She noted that Sir Isaac Newton was considered the "father" of classical mechanics, and because of his writings and experiments concerning gravity, motion, resistance, direction, and trajectory, there were also applications of classical mechanics in astronomy, chemistry, and geology. Then she traced Newton's influences back to the groundbreaking work of Copernicus, Galileo, Kepler, and Descartes.

"Over the centuries of excellent questioning, the picture of the world that was presented to us by Aristotle has changed."

She smiled, leaning forward toward those gathered, her eyes twinkling. "The astronomer Copernicus showed us that we are heliocentric, that as much as we would like to think otherwise, the earth—and us on it—revolves around the sun. We know now that humankind is not the center of all things, that we may be privileged, but it does not revolve around us. Therefore, we must participate in understanding our role in the scheme of life."

Manfredi called from the gallery, "*Ben detto!*"

Laura's cousin, Father Stegani, remembered the young Laura asking him to help her study mathematics—and how his knowledge had been so rudimentary. He leaned into Carlo and whispered, "Is she really our relative?"

Carlo snorted. "She surely fell from another tree."

Laura moved from classical mechanics to specifics in hydraulics and then withstood another hour of questions. Finally, the light that streamed through the lecture hall windows darkened as the sun began to set.

The sound of the bell marked the end of the day's presentation. The Academic Council took their leave. Laura, her feet tired from standing for hours, her throat raw, moved off the dais. Veratti, Manfredi, and Tacconi joined her father in the back hallway and shepherded Laura to the waiting carriage. She collapsed inside its confines and closed her eyes.

She had only twelve hours to rest before she would start again the next day.

The next morning, the piazzas and streets near the Palazzo Pubblica were packed. The whole city talked of Laura Bassi. Some saw her as brave. Some thought her foolhardy. No one ventured to predict the outcome of her daunting task. Would a female ever be accepted into the sciences of the University of Bologna? Assistants to Bologna's printers handed out bulletins with news of Laura's initial presentation. Algarotti's printer had worked through the night to set the type of the poet's latest work, which praised Laura's elegance in knowledge and composure. Nobles, fine ladies, and shopkeepers parted with their *scudi* and the first edition quickly sold out.

Laura's lecture started midmorning. "Today, I will examine mathematics, a field naturally aligned with science—for most scientific equations use mathematical forms. I will start with the work of Leonhard Euler of Switzerland and his recent introduction of revolutionary terminology and notation. And then the influence of calculus on Euler's work—a form first explained to us by Newton, Johann Bernoulli, and the German Gottfried Leibniz, and illuminated by Bologna's own Dottore Manfredi—a mathematical methodology designed to deal with constant changes: in dimensions, time, force, mass, length, momentum, and other elements . . . ."

Laura's lecture showed her deep love of numbers, equations, and theorems. When Dottore Balbi stood to lead the defense section, Laura withstood the questions, sometimes pausing to check her notes for she didn't want to flirt with the possibility of making any mistakes. Mathematics needed to be exact. She could hear Salti tapping his finger on the table with exasperation, but she did not allow herself to be intimidated.

Finally, the bell rang to end the morning session.

Laura felt that the afternoon lectures on astronomy and Greek and Roman history were rushed, for Salti called for the bell to be rung before she had completely finished speaking. The question period was also truncated, for her answers were often cut off. Dottore Balbi looked uncomfortable, but he did not try to temper Dottore Salti's rudeness. Laura did not dare point out her frustration to the council—she knew the allotted time was completely at their pleasure. But she worried that she was not being given the opportunity to truly defend her knowledge.

The next two days continued in the same vein. Laura's presentations included lectures on chemistry, biology, geology, anatomy, water, and air. Dottore Salti rarely raised his head and wrote furiously in his notebook and grunted loudly.

At sunset on the fourth day, as the Bassi carriage left the Palazzo Pubblica, people jogged next to the carriage, waving in the air another new poem by Algarotti and shouting their support. Laura, her mind and body spent, thanked them as her father urged the driver to quicken the pace. He knew Laura needed rest. He saw the paleness in her cheeks, her chapped lips, the dark circles under her eyes.

At home, soup and bread were ready and Laura sat with her parents near the fireplace. Nucca fussed over her. No one spoke, but all worried this was too much pressure on her. Would it be worth it? Would the council reward her?

The fifth and final day arrived. Laura carried her notebooks from the carriage to the back room behind the Sala degli Anziani. She stopped. There was Archbishop Lambertini walking toward her—his presence, as always, seemed larger than life.

"Y-your Grace," she stammered, and curtsied. She hoped he would not hear the exhaustion in her voice.

"I've come to witness your final lecture, signorina." His voice was gentle and kind. "The marchioness tells me you've been most extraordinary."

"The council has not given me any indication of their approval," Laura said.

The archbishop lowered his voice. "Ah, *sì*. That would take the sense of power from them." He put his hand on her shoulder. "You must trust in yourself and God."

A short while later, Laura was in place on the dais to start her presentation. Every seat was taken. Bianca, Abriana, and the *zitelle* students were settled in the same balcony bench seats. Veratti, Carlo, and Father Stegani sat with the marchioness, with Eugenia and Paola hoping to provide group support. Manfredi, Tacconi, and the other tutors sat behind the council, trying to gauge their responses. Laura's father leaned against the wall to the side of the dais, much too nervous to sit.

On this last day, Laura concentrated on the work of Newton; she knew it was daring to choose him as her final subject, for Newton's work covered many disciplines and there were those in science with contrary theories on similar subjects.

"Sir Newton appreciated the history of science—he believed all scientists 'stood on the shoulders of the giants'; those who came before them," she said.

Laura acknowledged Newton's eccentric ways but championed his bravery in experimentation and his place as one of the most important thinkers of the scientific revolution. She detailed his major scientific achievements, then moved into Newton's interest in sight and color and covered the salient points in his 1704 book titled *Opticks: or, A Treatise of the Reflexions, Refractions, Inflexions, and Colours of Light*.

This took the entire morning and afternoon—to her surprise, her lecture was not cut off. There was a great quiet in the hall; all seemed to hang on every word.

At the end of the question-and-answer period, the final bell was rung.

The assistant's voice rang out: "This marks the completion of the application, lecture, and defense for a laurea by Signorina Laura Maria Caterina Bassi."

Marchioness Ratta rose to her feet and applauded. "*Brava! Brava!*"

Veratti stood and joined her, as did Eugenia, Galeazzi, and his wife, Paola. The zitelle in the balcony leaped to their feet and joined in the acclaim. It was only a moment later that the nobles and townspeople stood and added approval. "*Brava!*"

Archbishop Lambertini's eyes moved over the gathered, witnessing the wave of support for Laura. And then he looked to the Academic Council. They sat, motionless, waiting for a sign from Dottore Salti.

The head of the council did not react to the crowd, to Laura, or to his fellow council members. He rose to his feet. Vincenzo Cruce moved to his side, ready with the man's cane. The bent, humpbacked Salti, using Cruce's arm for support, hobbled out of the hall. His council silently followed.

Chapter Fifteen

Laura slept. On the third day, as Nucca was bringing in freshly boiled water for the washbasin, she opened her eyes.

Nucca moved to the side of the bed. "Laurina. We were beginning to worry."

"*Buongiorno*, Nucca. Is there word from the Academic Council?"

"No, signorina."

"How long have I been asleep?"

"Three days."

Laura groaned. "Is it not cruel for them to delay a decision?"

"Signor Veratti agrees with you."

"What?" Laura sat up, confused. "Signor Veratti? How do you know?"

"I heard him tell one of the students in the laboratory. He has arrived daily to cover the classes."

Laura dressed and let Nucca arrange her hair loosely and tie it back with a ribbon. She headed to her classroom in the carriage house. Veratti was putting notebooks and materials on the shelves behind Laura's desk.

"Signor Veratti?"

Veratti's eyes lit up when they landed on Laura. "You're rested?"

"*Sì. Grazie.* I'm told you've been meeting with my students."

"I had visited to see how you were, and the students were waiting. And you were sleeping. I thought I could help. Do you mind?"

She realized she didn't mind at all. "I'm most grateful."

"Daughter, you have rejoined the world."

Laura turned to see her father pushing the new rolling chair in which Signora Bassi sat into the carriage house.

"Laura, there are many notes of support and gifts," said her mother. "We've put them in the parlor."

"But no word from the council," Laura reminded them all.

Veratti kept a positive tone to his voice. "They could not deny you."

Signora Bassi pulled on her husband's arm, her eyes signaling him to speak. "*Sì, sì,* Rosa Maria." He turned to Laura. "Daughter, your mother would like to extend to Signor Veratti an offer to sup at our table. As he lives alone, she thinks this will give him a chance at a proper meal."

Laura looked to Veratti. "Where do you usually sup, signore?"

"The lady of my boarding house provides a soup," Veratti explained. "That meets my needs."

"Soup. Is that all?" Laura asked.

"Sometimes there's meat of some kind in it." He smiled. "Its provenance remains a mystery for it is cooked to a gray, indistinguishable state."

Laura laughed. "Our cook will do better."

Signora Bassi's eyes brightened. Perhaps Laura's acceptance of Veratti was a good sign, perhaps her daughter would think of things other than science and hearing from the Academic Council.

Signora Bassi motioned to her husband that she wanted to head back to the main house. "Let's alert Cook."

The dinner conversation, to Signora Bassi's chagrin, focused on electricity and the recent conductivity experiments of Stephen Gray, a British scientist. Laura and Veratti discussed how Gray had draped oily hemp packthread through a house and then draped a length of metal wire on the same path. Gray connected both to pieces of ivory as well as to glass tubes, and then sent charges through each to identify which would be the most viable conductors.

Laura observed, "His work is brilliant and it's a shame he's not accepted into the Royal Academy in London."

"Contentious personality, they say," Veratti observed.

Signor Bassi had also read about Gray. "A lone and irregular person. Apparently, he has no home of his own, and if friends take him in, he's forever setting up experiments all over their homes."

Signora Bassi interjected, "That might not make him a popular guest."

Laura laughed. "And isn't it true that even when he's living in a poorhouse, he continues to set up experiments? We must be grateful for his obsession." She turned to Veratti. "I read that Gray noticed that a static charge within a glass tube could be conveyed outward through the wooden stoppers—those simple corks meant to keep out dust. That gave him the idea that electricity could be conducted from one place to another. Is it true he's made it move over one thousand feet?"

"I've heard that," Veratti said. "And also that he believes the twisted hemp, with additives, conducts a charge in an efficacious way."

Laura mused aloud. "There must be room in the carriage house to set up such an experiment."

Signora Bassi's eyes grew wide. "Would that be safe?"

Signor Bassi calmed his wife. "Rosa Maria, Laura is not about to . . ."

Laura wasn't listening. She turned to Veratti. "We could try to replicate his findings."

Laura and Veratti continued to discuss Gray's theories on how various conductors offered greater and lesser resistance to the flow of electrical energy and his ideas on how to insulate certain materials. They discussed Gray's ideas of polarity, that there could be two different directions to examine in an electrical field. Laura fetched a notebook and began to make a list of what she must gather to set up the experiment.

Signora Bassi tried to change the topic. Had Signor Veratti heard of the new gardens in Bologna? She knew that many young people were taking time to stroll in them. And did he enjoy opera? The family should take advantage of the seats that they bought every year, and since she was not feeling well enough to attend, didn't he think that Laura and a guest should use them?

Signor Bassi smiled, enjoying how his wife wanted to turn the conversation to the social events of Bologna's season, to encourage thoughts of activities beyond erudition. He glanced at Laura and Veratti and realized they had returned to talking of science. No matter the future, he was glad for Laura to have a friend whose interests so aligned with hers.

When it was time for Veratti to leave, Signora Bassi suggested that Laura show him out. The two stood on the veranda.

It was a warm night and fireflies flitted through the trees. The tiny creatures created a magical glow.

"Signor Veratti, I wonder why these small creatures glitter and others do not." She shrugged. "One day, someone will know the source."

Veratti turned to her. "I would like to ask you a great favor."

"What is it?"

"I would like for you to call me Giovanni. *Prego.*"

Laura hesitated and then nodded. "*Bene.* It seems we are friends and it would be appropriate."

Veratti wanted to take her hand, tell her he hoped for more than friendship. But he held back, thinking of the years of study he had left before gaining his laurea and setting up a medical practice. Frustrated, he felt that being content with friendship would have to suffice.

"*Grazie,*" he said.

"And you may call me Laura." Her voice was soft, her eyes still focused on the fireflies.

He wanted to push the blond curl from her cheek, tuck it behind her ear. But he merely joined her in following the glow created by the insects.

"*Bene.* Laura."

She smiled up at him. "Giovanni."

The following day, early in the afternoon, Nucca rushed into Laura's room.

"Signorina! A messenger. From the university. He is here."

Laura, in her robe and warm slippers, bounded down the stairs. Her father was in his dressing gown, holding the unopened letter. Laura broke the seal and read the short request.

"Papà." She looked at him. "I'm to stand before the Academic Council tomorrow."

~

It was midmorning and Laura stood in the Academic Council's conference room. The council was seated at a long table, with Salti positioned at the head. Vincenzo Cruce, wearing the robes of an administrative assistant, stood behind Salti, holding his cane.

"Signorina Bassi," Dottore Salti's voice was rough and cool. "This council has voted. It was not unanimous, but it is what it is." His rheumy eyes looked at each wigged member, as if in doing so, he could change the results. No one met his gaze.

He grunted and looked up at Laura. "It is determined that you have met the necessary criteria . . ."

Laura's heart thumped and she swallowed hard. Had she really accomplished her goal?

". . . and we have decided to award you an honorary laurea."

Laura felt a stab of dismay. What had he said? "Honorary"?

Confused, she blurted out, "What does that mean?"

"It means you have earned an honorary membership in the Institute of Arts and Sciences. It also means, as a woman, your presence at the university will not be necessary."

"Necessary? But it's what I want. I want to teach. And I want to work in the laboratories, to be able to set up experiments, spend hours in the university library, to consult with peers."

"Peers? Do not imagine, in any way, that you are a peer."

"But you've noted that I've met the criteria—"

"The tradition of our university will not be sullied. I believe it is in Corinthians that the Apostle Paul instructs: 'Let women keep silence in the churches, for it is not permitted them to speak. And if they will learn anything, let them ask their husbands at home, for it is a shame for women to speak in the church.' It's in the Bible, signorina. And you must see that the university could be called academia's 'church.'"

His words hung in the air. Laura wanted to pound her fists angrily on the table, to challenge harshly.

But she took a moment and then said, evenly, "And it is quoted in Genesis that Jesus said, 'So God created mankind in his own image, in the image of God he created them; male and female.' There it is, Dottore Salti. Jesus embraced both men and women."

Salti's face was dark. "Interpretation. Do remind yourself that I've studied quite a few years longer than you. And I know what is best for the Institute of Science."

"With great respect, Dottore, the Enlightenment has been of great benefit to the institute. Its precepts encourage the interrogation of old ideas and all previously held 'interpretations.' My goal is to lecture at the university. I have experience teaching already."

Salti snorted. "Teaching zitelle is not teaching at the level of a university."

"That is true, of course, but I've prepared myself to teach at the higher levels. I agree with Aristotle: 'Those that know, do. Those that understand, teach.' I've proven, in my defense, that I do understand. I desire to use my perception, recognition, judgment, and experience to share knowledge with students at all levels."

Salti's voice grew colder. "I will not debate. Is your recalcitrance a signal of your rejection of the laurea?"

Laura raised her chin. "I will not accept 'honorary.' I will only accept what I've earned: a full laurea, with all its privileges. Including lecturing in the university classrooms."

"Learn to be content, signorina."

"I cannot be content with this decision, Dottore Salti. I press for new consideration."

"No!" Salti's loud outburst echoed in the room, and the council members stiffened. "No."

Salti nodded toward Cruce, who handed him his wooden cane, and he hobbled out.

There was a public outcry. As soon as the decision of the Academic Council reached the streets of Bologna, Algarotti wrote a poem denouncing the council's position. Placards of support were set in shop windows. Pamphlets followed; most were supportive, but there were a few that suggested Laura Maria Caterina Bassi had overreached, that females should know their place.

Laura paced in the Bassi parlor as her father poured fortified wine for her tutors.

Tacconi helped himself to fresh figs and tried to soothe the tension. "The council has recognized you, signorina. Made it clear that your tutors have done well by you. An honorary laurea is an accomplishment. Perhaps Dottore Salti's advice—to be content—should be taken."

Laura took a step toward Tacconi. "You cannot feel as I do. A man is rarely told 'no.' He's free to make the best—or worst—of himself. A woman, if she agrees to be an ornament, is patted and appreciated for a moment, like a sweet confection in the mouth that disappears. She is told to be content to be decorative. I suggest, with great respect, that men look deeper into women's souls. There is a hunger."

Tacconi opened his mouth to speak, but Laura did not give him a chance.

"There's a rising discontent. I see it in my students—

the zitelle. I see it in my friend, Eugenia—it may appear she has everything—social standing, a husband, children. She has fulfilled society's expectations. But I know her. When we were children, we both had visions of different lives; she wanted to see the world, understand different peoples and customs. She still longs for that, but she's learned to keep her desires secret. Men who give up dreams are often considered weak. Women who let go are considered amenable." She looked to her father. "Papà, I'm sorry. I don't want to be amenable."

Manfredi took Laura's side. "'Amenable' is not a stimulating state of being. I find the council to be shortsighted and mean. I quote Newton: 'I can calculate the motion of the heavenly bodies, but not the madness of people.'"

Signor Bassi hated to see the injustice done to his daughter. "You've presented fifteen subjects. That's more than any man has done in pursuit of a laurea at the University of Bologna."

Laura looked into the fiery glow in the fireplace. "The only way I can see to change their minds is to do more. I did not present on electricity because it is a new field and there is so much unknown. But I will present on it—and also on the ideas of atoms; their mystery, their possible structure and power. I could also go deeper into mathematical physics."

She made a list, writing her thoughts down on a piece of vellum. "I'll compare the Frenchman Jean-Jacques Rousseau's arguments against science, coupled with William Blake's pointed advice to scientists to desist from trying to understand the complexities of the world and leave God's work to God—compare those thoughts to the most recent Enlightenment thinking. I'll go into Voltaire's philosophies—the ones that had him banished from France, and how he champions Newtonian thought. And changes in the structure of education." She placed an "x" next to this idea. "*Sì*. I would like to speak of educational reform, the work of Locke, Luther, and Rousseau."

Tacconi shook his head. "How would you get the Academic Council to even consider another series of lectures?" He looked to Manfredi. "She must see reason. She must stop trying to change things."

Manfredi took a bag of dates from his pocket and offered one to Laura. "In my opinion, there is always a path. If we find it and walk it, it could lead to a place where our soul—and happiness—can rest."

Laura accepted the succulent fruit. "*Sì*. Strategy, Dottore Manfredi. As the knight on the chessboard finds its way toward the opposing king, I, too, will find my path."

A surprise visitor arrived at the Bassi villa the next day with Marchioness Ratta.

"Laura, let me introduce you to Princess Faustina Pignatelli Carafa of Colubrano," said the marchioness. "She's most interested in your classroom."

The petite and beautiful princess grabbed Laura's hand. "I must tell you, I'm doing all I can, with my father's influence, to help secure you another series of lectures. I, too, love science and wish to study at the university here. You're lighting the way for me and other women. *Grazie mille*."

"The light is dim at the moment."

"I believe you can help make it happen." The princess examined the laboratory's instruments and tools and books on the bookshelf. "I was instructed in Naples, where my family resides, by a wonderful tutor, Nicola De Martino, who taught me and my brother. He thought Sir Isaac Newton walked on water." Her light laughter filled the room. "And he instilled that belief in me, too. I hear we agree."

"I hold Sir Newton in great esteem," Laura said.

"Laura, take strength in this." The marchioness took a serious tone. "We are bending the ear of every man who can influence Dottore Salti. Consider us your allies."

In the weeks that followed, missives from academics and Laura's pen-friends from all over Europe flooded the Academic Council's offices. Many had read Algarotti's poems about the erudite female scientist who had famously earned a laurea, but was being kept from taking part in the university. Bulletins petitioning the Academic Council to attend Laura's next lectures and reconsider their position were nailed to trees and posts.

Dottore Tacconi predicted the entreaties would fall on deaf ears and let Laura know he would not be her advocate. "I've been offered a post to head a medical college at the University of Pisa. I wouldn't want to jeopardize their decision by being too vocal on your behalf. I'm sure you understand."

Laura congratulated him, accepted his decision, and hid her disappointment. Her father reminded her that Tacconi was always one to act in his own best interests. Laura wondered if the tutor was happy in his vacillations; she knew she could never be.

May turned to June and the birds of summer nestled in the trees. Manfredi arrived at the Bassi villa with a basket full of early blackberries from his garden. He found Laura in the carriage-house classroom.

"I've heard rumors that the Academic Council is looking to set aside time on the calendar for you," he said.

Laura looked up at him, her face serious. "*Sì*. My father and I received a letter. They have given me two weeks to prepare."

Chapter Sixteen

Laura's next series of lectures were announced and excitement bubbled through the city. Because of the great interest, the venue was moved to the Archiginnasio, the largest building of the University of Bologna.

The sun rose on the day in late June. A festival atmosphere filled Bologna. Market stalls lined the Piazza del Francia near the university. Performers juggled and danced. Children played tag while their parents gossiped and wagered on the outcome of Laura's bid for a full laurea. People carried picnic baskets for they were not about to relinquish a seat. And, for the first time, women filled nearly a quarter of the lecture hall.

Laura began her first lecture. She referred to the work of Giuseppa Barbapiccola of Naples, a poetess who wrote under the pen name Myristic.

"She refers to Descartes' five degrees of learning and points out that contrary to arguments by Homer, Herodotus, and even some thinkers today, the intellectual capacity of the female is equal to a man's."

Laura paused. An unease spread through the gathered. This was a topic that was not discussed.

She continued, "Myristic writes that females are not intellectually inferior out of nature, but because of their lack of education."

The women leaned forward. Laura was championing their minds, their abilities.

Cruce, sitting behind Salti, called out, "For a woman to say this means nothing!"

Laura continued, "Myristic herself had no opportunity to study at a university; she had to struggle to find tutors and learn through her own resources. Yet she took on the task of translating Descartes' *Principles of Philosophy*. These are Rene Descartes' words: 'If one looks carefully and clearly, women should not be excluded from the study of the sciences; they are not inferior to men in terms of the greatest virtues.' It is with Descartes' inspiration and with Myristic as inspiration, as well as the learned Bathsua Makin and her treatise 'Education of Gentlewomen,' and writings by Mary Astell—a woman who opened charity schools in England to teach women aching to learn—and, importantly to me, with the inspiration of Saint Caterina of Bologna that I move on to my lectures today."

The zitelle, flanked by Bianca and Abriana, stood together at the back of the huge hall, hanging on every word.

Dottore Salti and the Academic Council sat in silence, their faces set. They gave no support or encouragement. They waited to judge.

Laura covered her chosen topics, concentrating first on the hard sciences and moving into the philosophical questions of the place of science in everyday life and its relation to theology and the Vatican.

The bell was rung, and this time, Salti pushed himself to his feet and growled the first question. "You seem to favor the English, German, and Swiss and their scientific views of the world. What about those of the Italian Peninsula?"

Laura could see the trap Salti was setting. She was prepared. "It's well known that the contributions of mathematicians like Bonaventura Cavalieri and Saccheri, physicist and astronomer Galileo Galilei, physiologist Giovanni Borelli, and astronomer Zucchi have had great influence in Europe. We have many erudite naturalists who have given us a deeper knowledge of how plants and creatures exist, such as Andrea Cesalpino, who, over a hundred years ago, advanced botany, observing minute details even without the aid of a microscope. The Italian Peninsula celebrates numerous physicians who have advanced knowledge in organs and muscles and circulation of blood—including Dottore Galeazzi, whom I'm honored to see in the gallery today. Galeazzi often points to his good fortune to have the work of Signors Giovanni Morgagni and Jacopo da Carpi before him. The University of Bologna and the Institute of Science are leaders in academia. The greats of the Italian Peninsula have contributed to what all scientists know today, and for that we are grateful."

Salti stared at Laura, then sat down. He did not participate in the rest of the questions posed to her.

In the days that followed, Laura defended more theses. Town bulletins announced on the last day of her presentation that in recent months, she had completed lectures on sixty-one subjects and that no other student or academic at the university had accomplished this before. The news bulletins praised her, reporting that the luminescent Laura Maria Caterina Bassi, her voice nearly worn out, her mind and body exhausted, did not miss answering one question.

Laura—along with the people of Bologna—waited for four months for the council's decision. Finally, on one of the last days of October, Dottore Salti's carriage arrived at the Bassi villa. Nucca showed him and Dottore Balbi into Signor Bassi's library. Laura's father offered them wine; Salti gruffly declined.

"We are here to alert you, Signor Bassi, that the decision on your daughter's award has been reconsidered. The council will now—"

Signor Bassi held up his hand. "*Perdono, dottores,*" he said. "I believe you need to be speaking to my daughter."

"Are you not head of this household, Signor Bassi?"

"Laura is a learned person who stands in her own right," said Signor Bassi. He nodded toward Nucca, who hurried off.

Nucca knew Laura was in the carriage-house classroom; Bianca was assisting her in a lesson. Laura received the news of the villa's guests and paled.

Bianca whispered, "Don't allow any meanness, Signorina Laura. If there is, give them no attention."

As Laura followed Nucca, a feeling of serenity came over her. She realized she was tired of striving for Salti's approval. She would not judge herself by his evaluation; she felt confident in her own value.

Laura entered the library. Dottore Balbi gave a slight bow, acknowledging her. Salti, leaning on his cane, did not meet her eyes.

She gave a short curtsy. "*Buongiorno, Dottori.*"

Salti's thin face drooped into a scowl. "I shall tell you of the decision and take my leave."

"*Bene*, I'm ready," said Laura.

Salti spoke. "On this day, June 27, 1732, the council has reconsidered and has agreed to award Signorina Laura Maria Caterina Bassi with a full laurea and membership in the Institute of Science."

He gave a sharp nod and marched out of the library. Nucca hurried to open the door for him.

Dottore Balbi bowed again to Laura and smiled. "*Congratulazioni*. Well deserved."

A week later, the city's leaders organized a lavish ceremony at Bologna's Main Hall. Laura became the first female to become a member of the Institute of Science at the University of Bologna. She walked through the center aisle, passing her parents, her tutors, and Veratti, and moved onto a stage. She was presented with an ermine cape, signifying a full laurea, and a university ring. Notes of congratulations from Cardinal Lambertini and others were read. The French ambassador to Rome presented her with a silver crown of laurels. At the end of the ceremony, as the gathered dispersed into the piazza, copies of Algarotti's poems were handed out freely. A special bronze medal had been made; one side featured Laura as the Goddess Minerva, the Roman virgin goddess of wisdom and strategic warfare, and on the other side was the Italian phrase "Only you can see Minerva." The medals were quickly sold as the city celebrated.

Marchioness Ratta, Princess Carafa, Eugenia, and groups of young women congratulated Laura.

Princess Carafa leaned in. "You've opened a door, my friend. *Mille grazie.*"

"Let us hope so," Laura said.

Eugenia kissed her on both cheeks and held up the coin. "Minerva? Who thought to call you that?"

Laura laughed. "I don't know. It's a bit much."

"You're twenty-one years old," Eugenia teased as she looked toward the nearby Veratti. "Perhaps it's too early to be called a 'virgin' goddess."

Laura shook her head. "Signor Veratti is a fellow scientist. That's all. Do not fret—your oldest friend will remain a happy maiden *professoressa* and take delight in your children."

Eugenia's mother, Signor Mucchi, joined them. "I told your mother years ago that your interest in science and education would make you odd." She softened and held out her hand. "And it is still so, but I applaud you."

"*Grazie*, Signora Mucchi." Laura was elated. She thought of the times as a child when she had felt like an outsider, when Signora Mucchi's criticism had stung.

"I will congratulate your mother that this is now over and you can concentrate on finding a husband who will accept . . . all this." Signora Mucchi moved to Signora Bassi, who sat in her rolling chair, a fine silk shawl over her shoulders, a proud smile on her face.

Eugenia stomped her foot. "My mother can be intolerable. I'm sorry, Laura. Today you have given all the women here something to think about, the possibilities that could be. Only think of that."

Laura did concentrate on what a laurea would mean for her future. She'd now be able to be part of the university. She'd soon walk into a classroom, wearing her academic wig and robes.

She'd face a group of students and teach her beloved science. Standing behind the lectern, she'd speak to the university's exceptional students, share her comprehension of Newtonian precepts. Questions would be asked. A discussion would follow and maybe—just maybe—a significant new idea would be born.

That night, Veratti joined Laura, her parents, and tutors in an outdoor community supper in the Piazza Maggiore. Vendors and local shopkeepers sent Laura baskets filled with sausages, breads, and cheeses.

"They're too generous," Laura said.

"They're happy for you," said Veratti. "As am I." He toasted Laura with his wine, and a moment later, asked to be excused for a minute.

"Where is he going?" asked Signora Bassi.

"I don't know," said Laura. Her attention was pulled in all directions; young girls wanted to touch her and university students stopped by to ask questions on science.

Veratti returned with a covered pewter bowl and four spoons.

"What is it?" asked Laura.

"It's new—it's called cream ice. A combination of egg yolks, sugar, and cow's cream. It's boiled together and then set on ice and salt and put into an icehouse. An endothermic reaction occurs, and finally, when the mixture is cold, it is churned." He lifted the top of the bowl. "And we have cream ice. We must eat it right away, before it melts." He handed out spoons.

Laura took a bite and sighed with pleasure. "Delicious." She turned to her father. "Papà, what if we build a small icehouse near my classroom? If we do the digging now while the ground is soft, then build the structure and cover it with dirt and sod—then, in the winter when the ground freezes, we'll add straw and salt and ice. If done properly, we should have a year-round cold storage place." She took another bite of cream ice and laughed, her eyes full of fun. "We can consider it a grand experiment to make cream ice all year long."

Signor Bassi toasted Veratti. "My palate thanks you."

Laura smiled at Veratti.

His heart leapt, he was glad to make her happy.

A letter arrived the next week. Laura sat in the Bassi library to digest its contents.

"Dottore Salti has still managed to set restrictions," she said to her father.

The letter stated that although Laura was now a fully paid member of the institute's faculty, she would only be assigned times to lecture three times a year, and these lectures were to be held at public ceremonies. She would not be assigned to teach university classes or allotted time in the laboratory for a female would certainly distract the males' attention.

Laura felt her chest get tight, her ears hot. How could she be denied when she had done exactly—in fact, more than—what was required?

"Laura," her father ventured, "perhaps you can get others to write to the council. It has helped before."

"I will find another way." She was gritting her teeth. The injustice rankled her.

Laura glanced at the scacchi board; she and her father had a game in progress. She thought of strategy and walked to the desk to write a response.

Esteemed Dottore Salti,

I look forward to the time when your restrictions will be lifted. In the meantime, as a full member of the university who is not allowed to use all the laboratory materials, I would hope to be provided funds to better my own home laboratory, I will wait for your approval of this expenditure.

L. M. C. Bassi

Postscript: My first public lecture will be on water, a natural element of all bodies: De aqua corpore naturali elemento aliorum corporum parte universi. *I will announce that it is upcoming; therefore, please inform me of the earliest date this public lecture can be held.*

Salti approved the funds.

Laura mulled things over. "I know Dottore Salti is not generous—it's his way of keeping me from the university. But now, on a small scale, I can truly dip into experimental physics," she told her parents and Veratti, who had become a weekly guest at the Bassi supper table. "Setting up my own proofs will expand my understanding in a significant way."

Veratti knew Laura was making the best of the unfair situation. "Even in a small laboratory, a difference can be made," he said. "And I hope you'll allow me to help, in any way."

Signora Bassi stole a look at her husband: Veratti and Laura seemed well-matched. "Very kind, Signor Veratti," she said. "Know there will always be a place here at our table for you—especially on the days that work in Laura's laboratory keeps you from your boarding house suppers."

When not assisting physicians with their patients or

preparing for his next defense, Veratti worked with Laura in the carriage-house laboratory. With a stronger telescope, they studied the heavens. They were able to replicate some of the mechanics of a new weaving machine called the flying shuttle. With a more advanced microscope, they followed Robert Hooke's experience in the viewing of cells. They made plans to build a vacuum pump. They set up experiments in dynamics, magnetism, and electricity, and pored over the century-old writings of the Roman-born Evangelisto Toricelli on water-based and mercury barometers and then mimicked his earliest experiments.

Signora Bassi often sat in the parlor in the early evening, when the sun was setting, watching as the candles burned in the carriage house. "Husband, do you think they ever talk about anything other than science?" She looked to him; he was busy reading a recent pamphlet on the components of the new pocket-size sundials.

He raised his head. "I think they find their conversations satisfying, Rosa Maria."

"Laura's turned twenty-three years old."

"She's happy. What else can we want?"

"Grandchildren," Signor Bassi said softly. "Giuseppe, I would like to live to see her know the happiness of a husband and children."

Signor Bassi moved to his ailing wife's side. He took her hand. "You'll be well again, *mia cara*. I know God will not take you from me."

In late 1735, Veratti presented his knowledge on astronomy and languages. Three months later, he gained approval of his defenses in medicine and science. He became the assistant to Dottore

Balbi at the institute and prepared for his final defense. His free time was spent with Laura in the carriage-house laboratory.

One day, a group of university students arrived—they'd heard of Laura's work in experimental physics and wanted to participate. It was not long before the group grew larger; Princess Carafa joined, Bianca attended on her day off from the Galeazzi household, and a few of the zitelle, after their weekly lesson, lent their interest.

A short time later, Laura received a letter from Dottore Salti, stating his displeasure that university students were choosing to work outside the official institute's walls.

Laura replied:

Esteemed Dottore Salti,

In response to your letter, I remind you that I am most willing to conduct my experiments in the university laboratories. I am also happy to report that, to date, there has been no issue of inattention due to women and men working together.

L. M. C. Bassi

Laura did not receive a reply to her message. However, there was a steady growth in the number of students arriving to take part in her work. It wasn't the same as being on the university campus, walking the long hallways to the doors of a lecture hall, entering into a dedicated classroom of learning, having an entire classroom stand and accept her as one of advanced knowledge. However, the discussions, arguments, and proofs of science were energizing and Laura looked forward to the progress made in her own laboratory.

The new year arrived and an elegant carriage, sky blue and featuring painted flowers, trees, and flying birds on it, pulled into the Bassi courtyard. Signorina Anna Morandi, in a deep rose embroidered cape, stepped out. Her skin was pale and translucent, her eyes green, her hair a soft strawberry red. She asked Nucca, in a quiet and shy voice, to see Laura. Nucca showed her—and her large driver, who had retrieved an oversized trunk that had been attached to the back of the carriage—to the laboratory where Laura was deep into reading Voltaire's latest pamphlet.

"D-Dottoressa Bassi," Anna said in a breathy, stuttering voice. "I attended your most recent lectures and was g-gratified when you were awarded membership at the University of B-Bologna." Her gloved hands fluttered in the air nervously and then she tapped the leather top of the trunk. "May I show you something?"

Laura nodded, curious. The servant undid the trunk's buckles and lifted the lid. He took out a life-size anatomical figure: a headless torso of a man carved out of a thick, solid wax. The servant placed it on the worktable. Laura gasped. It was extraordinary—it highlighted the fine detail of the musculature, the delineation of tendons and sinew.

Anna's hand shook as she pointed to the figure. "Th-this is m-my work."

"You carved this?" asked Laura.

Anna nodded to the servant. He reached inside the trunk, brought out a detailed foot, then a hand, then a skull, and then a fully detailed arm.

Anna's voice was barely above a whisper. "I study b-books and pamphlets on anatomy. If I could see the actual body up close, I know I would d-discover there are d-details still to be added. As you know, only students at the university have access to the Hospital of Death, where corpses can be c-cut and studied. I'm eighteen years old, and I want to be able to be part of the science c-community."

Laura recognized the passion behind Anna's desire. She asked for permission to hold the skull and Anna nodded. Laura saw the detail, the delineated occipital bone, the four major sutures, the finely carved mandible.

She met Anna's eyes. "I shall see how I can help you."

Anna's voice got higher, lighter, as if these words fulfilled her greatest hope and caused a light-headedness. "I'm not a polymath, l-like you. My focus—my interests are solely in anatomy."

Laura invited Anna to sit so they faced each other. "To my mind, Signorina Morandi, science has advanced so greatly and is now so multifaceted that targeted study is what is needed." She patted Anna's gloved hand. "I count Dottore Galeazzi as a friend. I know he would like to see your work. Would you allow me to share it with him?"

Domenico Galeazzi and his wife, Paola, arrived at the carriage-house classroom the next day. Laura and Anna, with Dottore Manfredi, greeted them. Galeazzi silently studied Anna's wax figures and gazed at her detailed drawings. Finally, he turned to the pale Anna.

"Signorina, I'm impressed. I would like to commission more of these wax figures."

Anna's shy face began to glow; a burst of color filled her cheeks. She stood straighter.

Laura pressed, "Perhaps Signorina Morandi could visit the Hospital of Death."

"I could attend at her side," Dottore Manfredi said, "if that would be necessary."

Galeazzi shook his head. "It is not possible for a female to visit. It is not done."

"Surely, Dottore," Laura interjected, "there's room for exception. Her talent is so fine."

Galezzi turned to Anna. "However, I will find funds for you, and if you'll allow, I'll consult so that your work can be even more specific. And, with your permission, I'd like to use your figures in my lectures."

Anna, torn between disappointment and elation, nodded.

"You would want Signorina Morandi there to explain her work," Laura said.

Galeazzi sighed. "I don't make the rules, Dottoressa Bassi. She would not be allowed. But I will give her credit."

"This is science, Dottore Galeazzi." Laura was peeved. "There should be no barriers."

Galeazzi turned to Laura, ready to bring an end to the discussion. "I'm most grateful, Dottoressa Bassi, for the introduction."

When the Galeazzis took their leave, the reserved and timid Anna grasped Laura's arm. "It is something, Dottoressa."

Laura's eyes sparked with frustration. "But not enough. Dottore Manfredi and I shall work on finding ways to petition for your acceptance to the university. And I'll introduce you to Princess Carafa—she and Marchioness Ratta are gathering support for her application. We will forge a pathway for women." Laura smiled. "I won't forget my promise. I know how important it is."

Chapter Seventeen

In 1737, Veratti, in a deep blue wool waistcoat and breeches, stood in front of the council and presented his final lecture in physics. The lecture was comprehensive, the defense stellar. The following day, Veratti received word that he had earned his laurea and been assigned to teach classes in natural philosophy and medicine. Laura was the first to call him "Dottore"—and the Bassi family celebrated his accomplishment.

February snow was falling. It was thick and sticking to the cold stone streets of Bologna. The winter sun had set an hour ago and oversize candles, set onto posts in Piazza Maggiore, were lit for a special occasion. It was Candlemas, a holiday that celebrated the Virgin Mary's purification and the first entry of the child, Jesus, into a temple where he was presented to God. The working class of Bologna, holding glowing tallow candles, stood in the piazza as clerics led them in prayer.

Laura, Veratti, and Signor Bassi stepped from the Bassi carriage in front of Basilica di San Petronio. They moved into the vestibule. Each was given a candle made of precious beeswax. The golden glow of the flame warmed Laura's face; the smell was special, more sweet and flowery. They entered the nave of the tremendously vast basilica. Nobles and city officials, the favored churchgoers, walked in a slow circle around the perimeter of the massive space, candlelight moving with them. The three joined the procession.

Father Stegani said Mass and the monastery choir sang hymns. Laura bowed her head and thanked God for her good fortune and prayed for her mother's health. As the celebration came to a close, the gathered shared good wishes for health and a blessed year. Signor Bassi walked out with other city officials and Laura and Veratti made their way past the side chapels. The paintings and statues of saints were lit with candlelight.

They approached the altar dedicated to Saint Caterina, and Veratti put his hand on Laura's arm. "A moment, *prego*."

Laura, pulling her fur-lined cape closer for warmth, gazed at the visage of Saint Caterina. She thought of the classes that she still held in the carriage-house classroom for the zitelle, how many had gone on to find employment in shops and the homes of noble families. She said a silent prayer, asking for the saint's intervention with those still denied access to the university. She prayed for help for the growing number of women who asked her for letters of recommendation and influence.

Veratti took out a long, thin box covered in dark green velvet. Laura was suddenly aware of his silence and the tension in his body.

"Your father and mother have given me permission to ask you this—it concerns the future."

She felt a tingle of apprehension. "Please make yourself clear, Dottore Veratti."

His voice was low and gruff. "I would be honored if you would consider this question."

"Which is?"

"To accept me as your husband."

Laura's mind was a jumble of thoughts and memories; all at once she could envision all the postulated theories and experiments she and Veratti had sent up in her laboratory, the ones that remained unprovable. How the expected—or hoped for—outcomes remained elusive, the constant tease of answers that seemed determined to stay hidden. How the proofs hung in the air, just out of reach.

"Laura. *Prego*. Be my wife."

Then she realized that the answer to this surprising question was abundantly clear. And she reveled in the clarity. She smiled.

"*Sì*, Giovanni. I accept you, knowing you understand me. And I, you."

Veratti, overcome with relief, wrapped his strong arms around Laura. He brought her close to him; they could feel each other's breaths.

"Laurina. I've wanted to kiss you for so many years."

"Then do not wait longer."

Laura lifted her lips to his and felt her first kiss. She closed her eyes and longed for it to last for a very long time. What was this feeling that started in her toes and climbed through her spine and caused a headiness in her brain? Her heart was beating faster; she felt the flush in her cheeks. She didn't know a kiss—this feeling of closeness—could bring such changes to her body.

And then she pulled back. Her laughter echoed in the large empty space.

Veratti looked at her, confused. "What's so funny?"

Laura leaned into him, set her head on his shoulder. "I was just thinking how happy my mother will be to plan a wedding."

Bologna was in an uproar. Speakers stood on the corners of the piazzas, stating that their virgin goddess, their "Minerva" should not—could not—marry. The populace argued that her duty was to the city of Bologna; she was their symbol of cultivation and learning and feminine grace. A marriage would sully that and distract her from her sciences—from representing the city when dignitaries visited, from sharing her presence at events in the churches and cathedrals and basilicas of Bologna. Marriage would keep her from being solely theirs: Laura Maria Caterina Bassi, an iconic symbol of Bologna.

Eugenia's carriage arrived at the Bassi villa. She raced to the carriage-house classroom to find her friend.

"Laura, the news is extraordinary!"

Laura looked up from her study of a prototypical electrostatic generator and grimaced. "Bologna is not happy."

"It won't keep you from marriage. Will it?"

Laura shook her head. "No." She smiled. "Imagine, Eugenia. Me. Married."

"*Sì*. I can. I do!" Eugenia laughed.

Laura wiped her hands on a cloth, her voice now filled with worry. "Some people are saying hurtful things. That Dottore Veratti has no personal fortune, that he's marrying above his status. But my family does not descend from nobles."

"*Prego*, you cannot listen to them. And besides, you're Laura Bassi," Eugenia told her proudly. "You've made your intellect a new class of nobility."

"I simply take great pleasure in my work," Laura smiled.

"It's surprising to hear a woman say 'work.' Only men seem to claim that. Despite all a woman does at home, or even in the marketplace with her family's goods, we are accustomed to using the word 'duty.'"

"As a wife, I'll have 'duty' and my work. I won't stop, Eugenia."

"I know. But let's concentrate on the marriage first. I want to give you a party. I want to help your mother plan."

"You've been married ten years already. You must know everything."

Eugenia hugged her friend. "Come to tea at the end of the week. Now I must get home—my daughter has a dancing lesson. Remember when we took dancing lessons?" She hurried off.

Laura called after her, laughing. "I only took one!"

The people of Bologna continued to voice their displeasure. Father Stegani, at a family dinner, suggested that Laura make a statement, with hopes to appease their concern.

Laura resisted. "It's my life."

"Bologna loves you," said Father Stegani. "They feel, because of their support of your struggle, they share in your life."

Laura announced a lecture in the city hall. People crushed into the space, eager to be in her presence. First, she spoke on her latest readings and experiments, and then read a poem—on love and freedom of the heart—written by Algarotti for the occasion. She let the beautiful words resonate.

And then, she announced, "Bologna, *vi amo tutti*, I love you all. I want to tell you why I will marry. Because I know I've chosen the most suitable person, for Dottore Veratti walks the same path as I—one of learning and passion for scholarship and insight. He celebrates my work." Laura's eyes found Eugenia's in the crowd. "I'm certain he will never—never—dissuade me from my path of work. He does not desire me to be anyone but myself."

On February 7, 1738, there was a break in the cold winds that gusted through the stone streets and alleyways of Bologna. The sky was a bright blue at midday and the sun lent a golden glow to the red buildings. The Bassi carriage arrived at a side entrance of the Basilica di San Petronio. Carlo and his father, Laura's uncle, stood at the entry; they were there to make sure Signora Bassi was gently settled in her rolling chair. Signor Bassi stepped out of the carriage and offered his hand to Laura; she emerged from the vehicle in a cream-colored silk gown and a white velvet, fur-lined cape. Nucca and Bianca had piled her hair on top of her head and placed pearls and crystals to glint in her curls. The date of her wedding had been kept a secret; she would announce the event to Bologna later, for she wanted this day to be private and personal, for herself and Veratti, for family and closest friends.

Father Stegani waited with Eugenia and Count Cabell, Marchioness Ratta, the Galeazzis, and Laura's tutors at the side chapel dedicated to Saint Caterina.

Veratti, in a deep green velvet waistcoat, dark brown breeches, and shined leather boots stood apart. He remembered the first time he'd talked to Laura; their promenade to Bach's "Music of the Spheres." Over the years, he'd only dreamed of this day. He heard footsteps on the marble floors and turned to see the Bassis approach. He gave a sharp intake of breath. He had never seen Laura so beautiful.

Veratti and Laura knelt in the front pew and Father Stegani celebrated a short Mass. Then Laura and Veratti moved to the altar. Signor Bassi stood next to his wife; both had tears of joy in their eyes.

Laura had chosen a passage for the marriage ceremony, written by Saint Augustine. Father Stegani's warm voice rose as he read the words. "What does love look like? It has the hands to help others. It has the feet to hasten to the poor and needy. It has eyes to see misery and want. It has the ears to hear the sighs and sorrows of men."

Laura turned to Veratti and added her own words. "And love has the heart to feel all for another."

Veratti looked deep into Laura's eyes. His voice was husky with emotion. "That is, indeed, what love is."

Chapter Eighteen

Veratti moved into the Bassi home. Another housemaid was added to the workforce, and Nucca, her hair now completely gray, became the head of the villa's staff. Although her steps were slower, she carried herself with a new pride, and kept a watchful eye on Signora Bassi.

One morning, as Nucca was about to take Signora Bassi's morning tray downstairs, Laura entered her mother's room, her face heavy with seriousness. "Mamma. Nucca. I want to ask you an important question."

Signora Bassi and Nucca were silent. Why was Laura's demeanor so solemn?

"*Sì*? What is it?" asked Nucca. "Is there a problem?"

Laura took her time, speaking slowly, keeping a smile from tugging at her face. "The question is this: Is Signora Bassi ready to be a grandmother?"

It took a moment, but then Nucca shrieked and grabbed Signora Bassi's hand. "*Nonna!* You will be *nonna!*"

Signora Bassi's body quivered and tears spilled down her face. She reached out for her daughter. "*Mia cara. Mia cara.* Laura, you will be a mother! It is *magnifico!*"

Laura kissed her mother's wet cheeks. "I hope to be like you, Mamma. You must stay well so you can hold your first grandchild in your arms."

But Laura's wish did not come to pass. A month later, as the late summer sun descended in the sky, Laura read Dante's *Paradiso* to her mother. Signor Bassi was setting up a chess game for the nightly contest.

Signora Bassi reached for her husband's hand. "Giuseppe."

Signor Bassi sat beside her. "*Sì*, Rosa Maria. I am here."

"I've had a good life. So much love. God is calling me now." She closed her eyes, her lips parted, her mouth lost its form, and her face lost its color.

Nucca, who had taken to sitting in the hallway outside Signora Bassi's room, hurried to find Veratti. He entered the silent room and felt for Signora Bassi's pulse. But all knew that one of their most beloved was now gone from them.

Five months later, Laura, exhausted from a hard childbirth, reached for her newborn son. Veratti handed the baby to her and she marveled at his skin, his eyes, his tiny hands. She looked to her husband and said, "Surely no one can doubt that God is a master scientist."

A year later, Bologna's attention was focused on its political—and spiritual—future. Pope Clement XII had died in February 1740, and the Vatican's cardinals had been sequestered for nearly six months, debating and jockeying to elect a new pope. But the process had stalled for there was no majority agreement. It was now late summer and no new pope had been elected. The University of Bologna and other academic institutions on the Italian Peninsula were waiting for news, for Clement XII had been frugal, a reaction to the corrupt financial machinations of his predecessor's advisor. Monies requested for education and especially the needs of scientists at the university had been ignored.

And then, just before dawn broke on August 17, 1740, the sound of pounding horses' hooves pulsed in the quiet. A rider, pushing his horse to the limit of the animal's physical capability, rode into Bologna. The rider pulled the animal to a stop in front of Basilica di San Petronio and slipped off his horse, barely able to stand. He nearly crawled up the steps that led into the church. His leather jerkin was darkened with sweat and dust from his three-day ride. He reached for the long iron handle of the thick door, but his muscles could not put forth enough effort. His eyes closed and he slid down the door, close to collapse.

"Do you need help, my son?" Father Stegani had just arrived to ready the altar for early Mass and hurried to the man.

The rider whispered. "The pope. The pope has been elected."

Father Stegani's eyes grew wide. "Who is our new pope? Tell me." He leaned his ear close to the messenger's mouth.

At the Bassi villa, Laura, seven months pregnant, was sound asleep. Suddenly, the deep, powerful sound of the bells of San Petronio rang through the city.

Veratti, sleeping next to her, sat up quickly. "What could be so important?" He bounded out of bed, worried there had been a disaster or that someone in Bologna needed help.

Bianca knocked on the door. "Dottores! There is a rumor. A pope has been elected!"

Veratti flung open the door. "Who is it, Bianca?"

Bianca's voice was hushed. "They say it is Bologna's own Lambertini." Her fingers made the sign of the cross.

Laura was stunned. Could it be? Prospero Lorenzo Lambertini, Bologna's most favored son, a man who loved learning, who embraced science? A man who had encouraged her, recognized her, and approved of her passion for science? This could be a great day for the Enlightenment! Energized, Laura threw off her bedcovers and willed her heavy body to stand.

Nucca had joined Bianca in the doorway. She clucked in caution. "Dottoressa, you cannot go out—not in your condition."

"I must, Nucca. My blue dress has been adjusted. I'll add the white kerchief. And my new straw hat! I'll wear a cape over my shape, even though it is the height of summer." Laura turned to Bianca. "Will you take care of the children?"

Signor Bassi burst into the room, his cravat at an odd angle. "I'll get the carriage for us."

"To the church first, Papà. And then to the Institute of Science." Laura moved behind her dressing screen. "Nucca. *Prego*. We must be quick."

A short time later, Laura sat between her father and Veratti in the carriage. The streets were filled, the people of Bologna cried with excitement, and the carriage moved at a slow pace. Bulletins and flowers were tossed through its open windows. Laura placed her hands on her bulging abdomen. "I fear this could be a dream."

"It's not, my daughter." Signor Bassi studied one of the bulletins. "This tells us that after the last six months of deliberation and voting, Cardinal Lambertini's reputation for deep learning, his gentleness and wisdom, and talent for conciliation finally won out over the more conservative—and ambitious—candidates."

Veratti nodded. "The cream ascended to the top. Lambertini is a man of God and of principles."

Signor Bassi looked at another bulletin that had been offered to him by a passerby. "He has chosen his pontifical name. Benedict XIV. It is done."

Laura squeezed Veratti's arm. "If only Leonardo da Vinci's plans for human flight had come to fruition—we could fly to the church."

Finally, the carriage reached Basilica di San Petronio and they joined the throngs in prayer. Then they made their way to the university, where the courtyards were filled with scientists, writers, mathematicians, historians, philosophers, doctors, and lawyers all talking of the new hopes and possibilities for academia. Surely Pope Benedict XIV would change the Vatican's policies; all congratulated each other on their good fortune.

It was late afternoon when Laura, exhausted, finally sat at her writing desk and penned a congratulatory letter to the new pope.

Your Holiness,

May I add my note of felicitations and great excitement to all of Bologna's. I also add my prayers for your health and, as always, celebrate the wisdom that flows justly through you.

Laura Maria Caterina Bassi

Laura's family grew—two more children were born in the next three years. Her first two sons, Giovanni Francesco and Ciro, were strong and playful; Flaminio was thoughtful and always had a smile on his face. Nucca and Laura decided that a *bambinaia*, a child's nurse, must be added to the villa's staff. When Caterina was born, Laura and Veratti were concerned about her quiet nature, her lack of appetite, and overall weakness. Laura, who had been actively teaching and conducting experiments in the carriage-house laboratory, canceled her participation in the classes and sat in the nursery with her sweet daughter in her arms. She rocked her, sang to her. But Caterina's heart was not strong enough and the family was soon placing her small coffin in the cemetery next to Laura's mother.

In the following months, Laura grew thin. She prayed for understanding, spending hours with Father Stegani at the Basilica di San Petronio and sitting alone in the chapel dedicated to Saint Caterina. She knew in her heart that her beloved baby was with God, but she prayed the rosary all through the day, trying to find solace in God's decision.

Bologna mourned with Laura. Algarotti wrote a poem. Eugenia sat with Laura for hours in the Bassi parlor, reading from travel journals, wanting to take Laura's mind off her lost child. Letters of condolence arrived from across Europe, for Laura's correspondence with some of the finest thinkers of the era had continued and friendships had flourished. She had replicated many of the inventors' experiments in her laboratory and written up her proofs, for which they were grateful and now they wrote of their sorrow for her sad event. Over the years, numerous articles in European magazines had extolled Laura's accomplishments and she'd become a role model for women who hoped to become recognized scholars and scientists. These women, too, sent their thoughts and prayers. The university students who arrived daily to work in the carriage-house laboratory joined Dottore Manfredi and Veratti in teaching the growing number of zitelle and overseeing the laboratory. All waited for Laura to grieve—and to come back to lead one of the most vibrant places of study in Bologna.

Spring turned to summer. Laura sat at the parlor table watching Flaminio nap and Giovanni Francesco and Ciro at the chessboard. There was a knock on the door, and she turned to see Bianca.

"Buongiorno, Dottore," Bianca said. "I have something to ask you."

"*Sì?*"

"I'm happy working at the Galeazzi home, but I find that one day a week in the laboratory is not enough. Is there a possibility I could make your laboratory—and your home—my endeavor? Be your assistant?"

"I'm not working on anything right now, Bianca."

"But today is a new day." Bianca's voice was hopeful. "When I stood on street corners, offering the answers to math problems, I could not see the next day without worry and disappointment. You changed that for me. You showed me that we must reach out and help each other. That is where opportunities are born. I want to tell you that I will always be at your side—in the laboratory—and in your home—if you agree. In gratitude and respect."

"*Grazie*, Bianca. But . . ."

Bianca handed her two letters—one larger with a dark green seal, the other of a creamy heavy vellum with a silver seal. "Nucca asked me to give these to you; they've just arrived, addressed to you. They could be very important. To you. To science."

Giovanni Francesco, unaware of the import of the moment, looked up from the chessboard. "Mamma, that is your favorite thing, science."

Ciro added, "Mamma, you said I could be a scientist one day. I'll start after I take brother's king."

Giovanni Francesco and Ciro bickered about who was winning the game. Laura looked back to Bianca. She saw the entreaty in her eyes.

"*Bene*, let me have the letters." Laura reached for the larger one and opened it. "This is from a Dutch scientist. His work in electricity—"

"I'll alert Dottore Veratti that you'll join him in the laboratory with the news in the letter," Bianca interrupted, speaking fast. "*Prego*, let us go now."

Laura hesitated, and was surprised to see sudden tears in Bianca's eyes, a quivering in her lips.

"The laboratory, Dottore Bassi—it is where you shine," Bianca's voice caught in her throat. "Where you must be. I'll alert Nucca to send the child nurse and I'll wait for you in the laboratory." She rushed off.

The *bambinaia* arrived moments later. "Shall I watch the children, Dottoressa?"

Laura wasn't listening. She was now reading the smaller letter with the silver seal. Then she stood, quickly gathered a notebook, and hurried to the carriage house.

Bianca nearly crowed as Laura entered the laboratory. "I told you she was coming!"

"It's good to have you in your laboratory." Veratti moved to Laura and kissed her cheek.

"*Sì. Grazie*, my husband." Laura moved to her desk and searched for a pamphlet. "Do you remember, last year, when the

German scientist Ewald von Kleist made an accidental discovery? The description is in a 1745 pamphlet." She found it and held it up.

"I've read Kleist's report, *sì*," said Veratti. "On his discovery concerning electricity."

"*Sì*." She turned to Bianca. "Kleist was experimenting when his generator came into contact with a nail that had been inserted into the cork of a medicine bottle. A short time later, he touched the nail and received a shock. He realized that residual energy—electricity—somehow had been stored in the nail and the jar."

"But how?" Bianca asked.

"Kleist did not understand it, but realized the truth of it." She patted Bianca's arm. "It's a reminder that it's possible to know the 'what happened' and sometimes the 'how' of a natural process, even if we do not, as yet, know the 'why.'" Laura waved the first letter in the air. "I've just received word from Holland. Pieter van Musschenbroek. I've corresponded with him in the past. He's conducted work on the same concept."

She shared the letter: Musschenbroek wrote that he'd invented something he called a Leyden jar—a glass container filled with water, wrapped inside and out with wires. He placed an iron rod in the vessel and connected it to an electrostatic machine.

"He found that when a person touched the iron in the jar, he experienced a tingling shock," Laura told them. "And, most extraordinary, the rod, the jar with the fluid and wires stored the charge—and it was viable for several days."

Veratti was amazed. "He was able to store energy? For days? Not moments? I would like to witness this."

"And that will be possible." Laura bubbled with joy. "For in his letter, he tells me of the permission he's granted the

Frenchman Abbé Nollet to set up this experiment in laboratories across Europe. Abbé Nollet has just done so for King Louis the XV at Versailles." Laura held up the second letter, the silver seal now broken. "This one is from France. From Abbé Nollet—he is responding to one of my letters. He wants to come here, to our laboratory!"

Bianca hugged herself with excitement. "I'll arrange every-thing for his comfort. For I'm now your new assistant—isn't that right?"

Laura laughed and grabbed Bianca's hands. "*Absolutamente.* Indeed you are." She looked to her husband. "Shall we prepare for Abbé Nollet?"

Chapter Nineteen

Jean-Antoine Nollet arrived. At forty-four, he was a dozen years older than Laura, and he was boisterous, full of infectious verve. He regaled Laura and Veratti with stories of studying theology at the University of Paris and being consecrated a deacon in the Catholic Church, earning the priestly title of Abbé.

"Has a certain ring to it, don't you think? But, alas, I tossed the clerical robes, *oui*, for science. It's the study of electricity that consumes me, night and day," he said. "If we can learn to grab it, own some of its mystery, it could change how we live in this world. Let me tell you how I lined up one hundred and eighty soldiers in front of King Louis XV and strung wires among them. I had them all hold hands, so flesh connected. I had the first soldier place his hand on the rod in the large Leyden container, and an electric pulse was relayed down the line of soldiers, causing them to jump—almost simultaneously. The king *etait excite*—adored it. Had me do it again in Paris, with two hundred monks. I placed them in a wired circle that was about a mile in circumference. Then I discharged the energy stored in a group of Leyden jars. The speed of the electricity's propagation—*incroyable*—a quiver and a bounce! The king adored it even more."

"It's most exciting." Laura was enchanted with Nollet's puissance and animation. "And now you will help us build Leyden jars here? And experiment?"

"*Oui. Oui.* Gather all the students who would like to participate. We shall have an extraordinary event. Is there a nearby field at our disposal?"

The next week it was time for the Leyden jars to be built. Laura, finishing her morning dressing, looked out her bedroom window. She spied a small youth, waiting at the door of the carriage house. She hurried out.

"Did you need something? May I ask why you're waiting here?"

His high, adolescent voice was serious. "My name is Luigi Galvani. I've signed up to work with Dottoressa Bassi and Abbé Nollet."

"I'm Dottoressa Bassi."

The youth bowed. "You're most respected. I'm honored to work with you."

Laura was confused. "I'm sorry, we're expecting university students today."

"I am one."

"How old are you?"

Galvani worked to lower his voice. "I'll be thirteen in ten months."

Laura smiled. "You're too young to be enrolled at the university."

"I was admitted this year. I took tests and withstood interviews. The Academic Council could find no reason to deny me."

He took his letter of acceptance from his pocket. "In case you think I'm telling tales."

Laura looked at the proof of his status at the institute.

Galvani continued. "I'm most interested in electricity. I've tried to create a Leyden jar on my own, but my materials are limited."

"The other students who want to work with Abbé Nollet will have had more experience."

"But no one will work as hard as I."

Laura unlocked the carriage-house door and led Galvani into the laboratory. "I'll have to see if you're useful. I want to remeasure the length of wires we will use as conductors."

She handed him a thin rope that had been studded with measurement marks and pointed to a pile of wires. Then she placed a *penicillus* and a piece of vellum on the long wooden table.

"I'll want to see your notation. As you know, Sir Isaac Newton often produced a hundred pages of notes a day. He thought it the most powerful way to track thoughts and experiments."

"*Sì*, Dottoressa. Science began anew with Sir Newton's work on gravitation and force. I would be honored to emulate him."

"Good." Laura heard the sounds of the house, the children running down the stairs. "I must check to see if my family and Abbé Nollet are having their breakfast and are in fine spirits." She pointed to the wires. "Let's see what you do."

Laura hurried out, not at all positive that this young Galvani would succeed.

Galvani did not disappoint. His measurements of the wires were exact. And he quickly made himself useful to Abbé Nollet, running errands and taking notes when needed. Leyden jars were being constructed when Dottore Galeazzi and his wife, Paola, and their daughter, Lucia, age seven and dressed in a pink velvet cape and lavender wool hat, arrived.

Galeazzi bowed to Nollet. "I appreciate your work."

"And I yours." Nollet grinned. "Dottore Veratti has told me you share his interest in how electricity might be used in medicine."

"*Sì*, that's true. I hope you find Bologna beautiful."

Abbé Nollet grinned. "Dottoressa Bassi's home is excellent, her cook excels, and the company in this laboratory is very fine. If Dottoressa Bassi is not careful, she may have herself a permanent houseguest."

Laura laughed. "*La mia casa e la tua casa.*"

Lucia padded around the laboratory in her small, soft leather boots, fascinated with the scopes and simple machines. When she reached young Galvani, she untied her cape and placed it on a chair.

"What are you doing?" she asked.

Galvani glanced at the young girl, then moved his stool to one side so she could get closer to the diagrams he was drawing. He told Lucia about the experiment and how it would be set up in a field. Lucia leaned in and asked for details on the making of the Leyden jar. Laura glanced over at the youngsters; she'd grown fond of Luigi Galvani, and she was glad to see how patient he was with the bright and inquisitive Lucia, that he did not find a girl's interest odd or misplaced.

The next week, despite Dottore Salti promising a degradation of academic points, more than a hundred Institute of Science students took part in Nollet's field experiment. There was twice that many onlookers gathered to picnic and observe, including Laura's cousin Carlo, the poet Algarotti, the marchioness, the princess, Signorina Anna Morandi, and other women who no longer felt unwelcome in a community of scientific inquiry.

Laura saw Dottore Balbi arrive with the aging but spry Manfredi. She went to them and curtsied to Balbi. "Dottore, you honor us."

The long-faced Balbi bowed. "Your personal laboratory has become known for its experiments in physics. You're Bologna's pioneer in this. I'm curious to see what you have in store for us." He nodded and moved on.

Dottore Manfredi stood with Laura. "If you cannot enter the university classroom, you bring the classroom to you."

"*Sì*. It seems so." Laura sighed.

"You deserve to be at the university. To use its resources. To stand behind one of its lecterns and teach," Manfredi said. The Academic Council's barring of Laura made him furious, but despite his outspoken support, there had been no change.

Laura was focused on today's experiment. "Dottore, I'm nervous. All these people have come to witness something extraordinary. Will they be disappointed?"

Manfredi took an orange from his pocket and gave it to her. "Science can be temperamental at times. That is why it's good to take solace in a ripe fruit."

Laura laughed. Was food his answer for every tense moment?

"Dottoressa Bassi! We are ready! *L'heure est arrivé!*" Nollet had arranged the human chain of students in a figure eight. They held hands and other student volunteers threaded conducting wires through their arms.

Nollet called out, "*Fait attention!* Release the energy in the Leyden jars at my signal. *Un, deux, trois!*"

He dropped his arm. The nearest student to the apparatus reached for the iron rod—and immediately there was a near-simultaneous, involuntary jerk and jump speeding through the human chain.

The participants' mouths were agape. What had happened? The onlookers gasped—and then shouted with glee. Could they do it again?

Nollet waved his arms. "*Non, non*, we have stored *juste assez*—only enough for one! Wait until science figures out how to keep it longer!"

Laura shouted over the crowd to Veratti. "The proof is only a split second, Giovanni! If a person blinked, he could have missed it!"

"But it worked!" he shouted back. "Success!" He moved closer and leaned down to speak into her ear. "Laurina, Nollet is here because of you. You have brought this to Bologna. *Fantastico*."

The next day, the city's bulletins extolled the experiment and Dottoressa Bassi's participation in hosting Abbé Nollet. Dottore Salti was not pleased and sent a letter to remind Laura that allowing students of the institute access to her laboratory could cause a lack of focus on their more important studies at the university. Laura sent back a respectful note, reminding Dottore Salti that she would be happy to conduct her experiments in the institute's well-stocked laboratories and would await his attention to assigning her time and place.

Dottore Salti did not respond.

Days after the success of the experiment in the field, Nollet sat at the long table in the Bassi-Veratti laboratory, designing a new undertaking. He drew a framework with a horizontal beam supported by two pairs of sloping legs of thick wood.

Nollet looked over at Galvani. "You could be just the right size!"

Laura, intent on writing up the results of the field experiment, looked up. "Right size for what?"

"A replication of Stephen Gray's experiment. The experiment that won Gray some of the attention he deserved, even the Copley Medal from the Royal Society of London. It's called 'The Electric Boy.'"

Galvani stood quickly. "I will be the 'Electric Boy.' I would consider it an honor."

Laura and Veratti oversaw the students' building of the trestle while Nollet and student volunteers studied Otto von Guericke's instructions on building a sulfur globe.

Nollet told the students, "Guericke, after providing us with excellent plans for a vacuum pump, turned his attention to electricity. *Bonne chance a nous!*"

Galvani, working as Nollet's assistant, asked, "Do you want me to ground the crystalline sulfur?"

"*Oui*, into a powder and then we will melt it and pour the liquid into a hollow piece of thick, round glass."

The smell of rotten eggs filled the laboratory. "Is it supposed to be so offensive, Abbé Nollet?" asked Galvani.

Laura called from the other end of the laboratory, "The odor is a sign you're doing your job well!"

"*Oui, oui*," said Nollet. "Scientists can use smell just as well as their eyes, ears, and touch! *Certainement!*"

Once the sulfur cooled, Nollet carefully broke the glass; the sulfur was now in a solid, spherical shape. He spitted the center of the sulfur ball with a metal rod.

"We will use the rod as an axle, so that we can turn the ball as fast as possible. If we do it properly, a glowing heat will come from its center. Then we can put the ball in contact with wool, carpet, wood, or anything we have a mind to, and take notes on the different levels of frictions and what kind of sparks we might make!"

"*Sì.*" Laura remembered when she was young, how fascinated she was by touching the metal door handles on cold, dry days and feeling the sharp tingle. Now she knew of the certain elements that contributed to make up the experience, but she still didn't know the "why." She hoped this experiment would bring her closer to a deeper understanding.

Nollet observed the spherically shaped sulfur. "Guericke was content to keep the ball on a wooden base and bring small objects to it. He showed how the static electricity attracted feathers and paper and other puny things. But Stephen Gray's imagination was more expansive. We shall see what he did with the same concept." Nollet's eyes were bright with enthusiasm. He turned to Laura and Veratti. "Shall we arrange for a show? How many people can fit inside this small laboratory? Shall we say tomorrow?"

"Laura, it's your birthday tomorrow," Veratti said.

"And a man never asks a woman's age, *n'est-ce pas?*" Nollet chuckled.

"I'll be thirty-six," Laura said. She teased, "Aging is part of science, *non?* Should we not document changes as we see them?"

Nollet puffed out his chest and guffawed. "I choose to ignore it. I will not let aging get in the way of experiments."

Laura laughed and agreed. "Oh. Never. And how wonderful to celebrate tomorrow's experiment on my birthday."

That night, as Laura dressed for supper, Giovanni Francesco

and Ciro played tag in their parents' room while Flaminio sat on the bed, cooing his appreciation.

Laura looked to Veratti. "Husband, do you think tag would be more challenging with four children?"

Veratti buttoned his waistcoat. "I don't know. I hadn't thought about it."

"Perhaps it's time to think on that." Laura smiled.

Veratti, finally getting her hint, moved quickly to bring Laura into an embrace. "Laurina, *cara*, are you happy?"

"*Assolutamente.*"

"Perhaps you should rest. Take days off."

Laura kissed her husband. "How could I miss 'The Electric Boy'?"

The next day, Signor Bassi took an early leave of his office to join the students and friends gathered in the small carriage-house laboratory. There were three sulfur globes in the center of the room. They were of varying sizes, all inserted with handled rods so they could be turned. Dottores Manfredi and Tacconi arrived just as Galvani's youthful frame, dressed in breeches, stockings, undershirt, and linen overshirt, was lifted into a simple netting made of silk cords and suspended, six feet off the ground, from the horizontal beam. He rolled onto his stomach.

Nollet, enjoying having an audience, called aloud, "Luigi, are you comfortable? *Bien?*"

"*Sì*, Abbé Nollet," the boy said.

"Do you know what is going to happen, Luigi?"

"We're going to witness electrical activity."

"I assure you—and all here to scrutinize this—there will be no pain," Nollet announced to the gathered as he spun with arms outstretched. "Just science."

He nodded to the volunteer students, who began to crank

the rods. "Use your strength! *Utilise ta force!* We want them to spin quickly—*vite, vite!*" He grabbed a handle on one of the iron rods himself; soon he was breathing hard, his round face had become sweaty, and the linen collar of his shirt was drenched.

"Look, the sulfur balls are glowing!" Princess Carafa called out, pointing to the spinning sulfur globes.

Laura exclaimed, "It is light! It means they are near their utmost!"

Nollet gave a signal to the volunteers to move their carts with the spinning sulfur globes on them toward Galvani. "Get closer, *mes amies.* Closer!"

Nollet positioned his cart to touch Galvani's feet. "What do you feel, Luigi?"

"Pulses of energy," Galvani said.

"The air is charged with electricity!" Nollet held his hand out to Marchioness Ratta. "Would you touch the boy's hand, Madame?"

The marchioness approached Galvani and touched his outstretched hand. "*Dio mio!* I too feel the tingling and small shocks!"

Nollet asked Laura to open a book and hold it in front of Galvani's hand. "Reach for a page, Luigi!"

Galvani stretched his hand toward the book. The open page, attracted to his "electrified" body, floated up toward him before he even touched it. Galvani controlled the turning of the pages of the book without actual contact!

"Don't let up—keep the sulfur spheres spinning!" Nollet instructed the volunteers. Another burst of effort from the volunteers and the sulfur globes shone even brighter. "*Tres bien!*" He turned to Laura. "Dottoressa Bassi, good friend, will you now close the window curtains?"

Laura quickly moved to the window and pulled the thick velvet curtains shut, blocking much of the light.

Nollet's commanding voice rose. "And now, Dottore Galeazzi, would you reach out your hand to touch Luigi's nose?"

Galeazzi approached Galvani. He reached his hand toward the boy's nose. Before his finger could touch flesh, a *crack* was heard, and a bright spark of light flew between Galeazzi and Galvani. "Ah!" Galeazzi shouted. "My body too is energized. His energy has come to me! Extraordinary!"

Nollet's experiments, aided by Dottoressa Laura Bassi, were the talk of Bologna even after the Frenchman had moved on to other areas of Europe. Over the next years, Laura was asked to give lectures on the elements of electricity at ladies' clubs and public gatherings. She wrote to Dottore Salti, asking to schedule a lecture and experiment at the institute, but there was no response.

In the spring, Laura gave birth to another boy, Giacomo. His brothers doted on him. Veratti tried to insist that Laura take time to rest, but she pointed out that the first volume of *Encyclopédie* had been published and she couldn't wait to read it.

"Giovanni, it's genius what the Frenchmen have done— Denis Diderot and Jean le Rond d'Alembert. To document all the latest thought and work in one reference book. In my correspondence with Monsieur Diderot, he states they hope to publish a volume yearly—and he thinks the endeavor might grow to over thirty volumes."

Veratti sat on the edge of the bed and tucked one of his wife's curls behind her ear. "The *Encyclopédie* will be here next week, Laurina. Do not over-exert."

Laura, focused on her reading, continued, "The publication will help all thinkers—across Europe and beyond. It's a wonderful way to share the best of the Enlightenment."

Veratti sighed. "As a doctor, I insist you stay in bed. As a husband, I know my advice will be ignored. But I'll ask Cook to make a broth for you, and I expect to hear that you've eaten well."

Months later, the leaves on the trees had changed to a brilliant orange and gold. Laura spent long hours in the carriage-house laboratory inspired by the *Encyclopédie*; she was intent on researching and replicating many of the referenced experiments. She was also deep into preparing one of her yearly lectures for the institute. Galvani, now seventeen, sat at the next desk, working on his latest project. Twelve-year old Lucia Galeazzi sat with Dottore Manfredi at a corner table, where they discussed Newton's Laws of Motion. Her father and mother had visited Laura's classroom the year before to tell her Lucia was very interested in science.

"I now know what your father felt, Dottoressa," Galeazzi said, "not wanting to deny his daughter." Galeazzi had asked if Lucia could study in the Bassi-Veratti laboratory—for there was no other place that would accept a girl.

Laura had agreed. "Of course," she said, adding, "but shouldn't something be done about this inequity?"

Galeazzi had shrugged. "Changes come slowly."

Laura was tired of hearing that and pointed out, "Changes come very slowly when people who can gain attention, such as yourself, do not speak up or take action."

And now, on this autumn day, a messenger arrived with a letter bearing the seal of the Academic Council. Laura opened it and groaned in frustration. She slammed the letter, and her fist, on her desk. Lucia and Dottore Manfredi were startled.

"Dottoressa Bassi?" Galvani ventured. He'd never seen Laura angry. He always found her to be calm and patient when she faced obstacles in the laboratory.

"Dottore Salti has denied my choice of topic for my lecture," Laura said. "He doesn't think speaking at length on experimental physics is productive."

Manfredi groaned. "Will that man never stop?"

Lucia was confused. "Shouldn't you be able to choose your own lecture topic, Dottoressa Bassi?"

Laura threw up her hands, "That makes sense, doesn't it, Lucia?"

Galvani frowned. "Dottore Salti prefers only theory. I don't agree, of course."

Just then, Veratti entered the laboratory. Laura turned to him.

"Husband, it's clear to us that experimental physics is important. Why does that escape Dottore Salti and others? Theory is a necessary beginning, but we must engage in proofs to learn more."

"It's clear as day!" Manfredi, cranky, bellowed. He turned to Lucia and repeated himself. "It is clear as day. Write that down."

Veratti settled next to his wife. "I'm in agreement, as you know, Laurina. And Dottore Balbi sees room for both theory and experiments."

"He's Salti's second," Laura said. "I must ask him to influence Dottore Salti."

Veratti took her hand. "Wife, things have changed."

Laura's brow furrowed. "Why do you look like you have a secret to tell me?"

"It's not a secret." He nodded toward Galvani, Manfredi, and Lucia. "All can know this. Dottore Balbi has taken a new post. He's been named the head of Collegio Montalto—the college at the university aimed at educating a wider populace and providing free instruction to students of the Marche province."

"He's a good choice," Manfredi called out.

Laura agreed. "*Sì*. He cares about his students."

A smile tugged at Veratti's lips. "Dottore Balbi has asked me to be his second."

Galvani and Manfredi clapped their hands.

"*Buone notizie*. Good news!" said Manfredi

Laura's eyes lit up with joy. "Well done, my husband. A very high appointment at the university." She immediately recognized the possibilities. "You'll be in a perfect place to influence Dottore Balbi—advise him to include experimental physics in the curriculum at Collegio Montalto."

Veratti chuckled. "I have a feeling you and I both will be trying to influence him."

"We'll tell Dottore Balbi that it's imperative to keep up with the latest knowledge—if we do not, our fine University of Bologna will suffer," said Laura. "And that the doors must be open to women."

Part Four

1745–1766

Chapter Twenty

It was late in the next year, when the first snow fell, that it was announced Pope Benedict XIV would have an extended visit in Bologna. Laura was surprised to receive a letter from his secretary, Professore Scarselli, stating that the pope would be gratified if Dottoressa Bassi would agree to a personal meeting with His Holiness. Laura and Veratti talked for hours about the invitation—what could the pope want to talk to Laura about? She had written to him, over the years, about her desire to teach in the halls of the university, how she was continually blocked. Did he find her entreaties bothersome? Was there a problem? An opportunity? She wanted to prepare, but she didn't know what to prepare.

Laura counted the days before the meeting. Finally, the day arrived.

Nucca sat in a chair in Laura's dressing room and clucked as Laura dressed carefully. "You cannot hide your delicate condition, Signora Laura. Perhaps the pope would prefer to wait until you've given birth."

Laura laughed. "I'm not in ill health, Nucca. I'm not contagious. I am only pregnant. A natural state that men should understand, for they are partially responsible." Laura could hear her children in the nursery. She placed her hands on her belly. "I'm hoping for a girl, Nucca. Wouldn't the addition of a girl to the family be *favoloso*?"

An hour later, Laura, feeling a little anxious, arrived at the impressive and elegant Palazzo Lambertini, an edifice that stretched over a quiet block in the center of Bologna. Pope Benedict XIV made use of his familial home when he was in the city; he housed his travel staff and cook and others of the papal entourage in one wing of the massive estate. Professore Scarselli, the pope's officious and very protective secretary, looked surprised when he met Laura. He kept his eyes from her protruding belly and led Laura through wide hallways adorned with centuries-old portraits of the Lambertini nobles.

"Professore Scarselli, you must be very busy in your office," Laura said, trying to make conversation.

"I am in charge of the pope's calendar, his correspondence, arranging his reading—as you know, His Holiness is interested in many things."

"We are all glad science is among them," Laura said as they arrived at the high-ceilinged, wood-paneled library.

Fires roared in the two enormous fireplaces at either end of the room. Pope Benedict was at his desk, reading.

He stood when she entered and glanced at her condition. "Is this a convenient time?"

"I'm capable of conversation and experiments and many

things while carrying a child, Your Holiness. One should never underestimate a woman."

The pope smiled. "Would you include the ability to partake in a game of chess?"

"Of course."

"I believe we've promised each other a game and years have passed without its actuality." He waved his hand to a decorous chess set on a fine walnut table.

Laura settled in a large comfortable chair. The pope motioned for her to begin.

She reached for a pawn. "White, to play."

Pope Benedict made the next move, muttering, "I wish more cardinals played chess." He poured them glasses of fortified wine. "Tell me, how is the institute faring? From your point of view."

As the game progressed, Laura realized the pope wanted her to fill him in on the status of the university's scientific community.

He explained himself. "I've been looking at the records, and I see that the Institute of Science has published only four pamphlets in the past year. Not too long ago, the yearly average was fourteen. What has changed?"

Laura spoke carefully. "Perhaps some of the professors are set in old ways. New ideas and methods are not part of the curricula. Perhaps the intent to teach what is known—and not venture into what could be—is slowing the imagination."

Pope Benedict sat back. "Ah. Dereliction can lead to stagnation."

Laura moved her knight to take out one of his towers.

The pope frowned and focused on the chessboard again. "It's

most important to me that the University of Bologna remain first on the Italian Peninsula. And it's with concern that I see the universities of Rome and Pisa and others gaining in reputation."

"An increase in funding would help, Your Holiness. I've heard complaints from lecturers that new equipment needs to be purchased and the laboratories updated."

"You've heard? Not witnessed?"

"No woman is allowed privileges at the university, Your Holiness, even if she is one who is married and mother of many children."

"And that is why you give leave for university students to participate at your personal classroom and laboratory?"

Laura realized the pope had kept abreast of the controversy. She wondered if Dottore Salti had complained to him and that was the reason why she'd been called for a meeting. She defended her actions.

"Teaching gives me great joy, Your Holiness. And conducting experiments. I give any person interested in learning the opportunity to participate."

"Commendable." He made another move on the chessboard. "Since you were a young girl, you've impressed me as one who finds ways to move forward, despite great obstacles."

"There are other women wanting to join the university ranks, Your Holiness. Could I tell them that you might help get their applications approved?"

Pope Benedict was careful in his response. "You may tell them that I admire all intelligence, be it in a man or woman."

Laura tried to keep the frustration from her voice. "Actions that support your beliefs would benefit these women, Your Holiness. With great respect, words and wishes are not enough."

The pope sipped his wine. "I'd like to know more about their petitions. Would you keep me informed?"

"Your Holiness, can a man understand what it feels like to be at a patriarchal mercy? To be waiting for studied consideration and decisions of a man concerning their future? Women have thoughts of their own and wills of their own. And desires."

Pope Benedict frowned. "Perhaps I can't understand. I've had the good fortune to make my own decisions concerning my path in life."

Laura leaned forward. "Women would cherish that freedom, Your Holiness. Are you familiar with the work of the English poet John Milton? These words of his I hold dear: 'Nothing profits more than self-esteem, grounded in what is just and right.' I believe freedom, respect, and opportunity provide self-esteem. And women deserve it just as much as men. Mary Astell in Great Britain made a good argument: 'If God had not intended that Women should use their Reason, He would not have given them any, for He does nothing in vain.'"

Laura watched as the pope moved a chess piece and remained silent. She flushed. "I speak too freely?"

Pope Benedict pursed his lips. "What kind of shepherd would I be if I did not allow anyone—man or woman—to speak freely?"

Laura saw a muscle pulse in the pope's neck. Was he displeased? Nevertheless, she felt the need to continue. She folded her hands on her belly.

"I've read your writings, Your Holiness. How you wish to bridge the gap between religion and scientific discoveries . . ."

"I see science as a way to glorify God."

"As do I, Your Holiness. But what Bologna needs—the

university and even my humble laboratory—is something even beyond your personal patronage. It is support from the Vatican. Monetarily—but also in recognizing all—women as well as men—as people who have rights to pursue their destinies. Build a bridge. *Prego*, show that God believes in all of us."

Three months later, Caterina, a healthy girl, was born. Laura marveled at her daughter's alabaster skin and blue eyes and her penchant to reach for the Saint Caterina medal that Laura wore around her neck. Veratti kissed Laura and his daughter, and the boys stood around their mother's bed, wide-eyed.

Ciro, now tall and full of mischief, wrinkled his nose in confusion. "What are we going to do with a sister?"

"Love her, let her play with you, and let her be who she wants to be," Laura told him. "Will you promise me to do that? All of you?"

The boys nodded solemnly.

Chapter Twenty-One

"I was born in Como. I've studied with the Jesuits and at the Benzi Seminary, and now I will learn at the University of Bologna. I've come to call at your villa because Abbé Nollet told me you are a great supporter of Newtonian thought and suggested I also study with you, Dottoressa Bassi." Twenty-year-old Alessandro Volta did not look impressed with the simple Bassi-Veratti laboratory. "The university has more equipment."

"Sì, it does," said Laura.

"But Abbé Nollet says there is more excitement here."

Laura was not sure she wanted this judgmental young man working in her space. "What is it that you wish to work on, Signor Volta?"

"A better storage of electricity. The Leyden jar is not capable of enough. I plan to design something extraordinary."

Laura's interest grew. "Admirable. I cheer you on in that endeavor. And anything that has to do with electricity—you're welcome to work on it here." She motioned to Galvani, who was thumbing through pamphlets at the bookshelf. "May I intro-duce Luigi Galvani? He is about to stand for his laurea at the university and also has a great interest in electricity."

Volta bowed to Galvani. "I too plan to earn my laurea. You, apparently, are ahead of me—but I'm fluent in French, English, German, and Latin and many subjects. I shall catch up."

Galvani shot a look at Laura. Who was this extremely con-fident, entitled person?

Volta moved to Galvani's desk and looked at the diagrams. "Signor Galvani, what's your focus?"

"At this moment, conductors," said Galvani. "And 'animal electricity.' I'm exploring how different metals, perhaps like copper and zinc, in various combinations, might increase conduction."

"I have an idea that chemicals can also act as conductors."

"Nonbiological agents?" asked Galvani.

"We must be ready to give up even the most attractive ideas when experiment shows them to be wrong," said Volta.

"Wrong? I don't think I am wrong."

"Have you read the work of Erasmus Darwin? What of the ideas of the French chemist Charles du Fay? Du Fay questions Stephen Gray's theories."

"Gray's work won him the Copley Medal," Galvani shot back. He was not sure he was going to like Alessandro Volta.

"I can share du Fay's paper. It was published in a volume called *Philosophical Transactions*—part of the French Academy of Sciences."

"I have great respect for Stephen Gray," said Galvani stubbornly.

"And I, for du Fay," Volta retorted. "Perhaps we shall have some interesting conversations."

Laura went back to her work, smiling to herself; she was always happy when there were constructive disagreements. Perhaps Galvani and Volta would push each other to move the understanding of electricity forward.

In the winter, Pope Benedict XIV made an announcement: The Vatican was creating, and financing, a special group of twenty-four Bolognese academics in various areas of science. The group would be called the Benedettini and its mission would be to increase scientific productivity. Each of the appointed scholars would earn one hundred liras a year and be expected to present and publish a learned paper annually, focused on advancing scientific inquiry.

Laura and Veratti, sitting in the parlor with their children, were ecstatic upon learning the news.

"The pope has given Bologna a great honor," Veratti said. "And he'll surely nominate you to be part of the Benedettini, Laurina; he holds you in high regard."

"I shared many ideas with him and he seemed to listen." Laura lifted her tired feet onto a footstool and sighed. "And it would be an honor to serve the pope."

Six months later, summer days warmed Bologna. Laura was in the parlor, explaining a mathematical formula to her oldest child, Giovanni Francesco. The other children played with the *bambinaia*, but continually called to Laura for attention. "Watch me, Mamma!" "Look at me spin, Mamma!" "Look how I can kick the ball, Mamma!" Laura applauded each and looked over at her aged father, now nearing his eighth decade, reading a story to baby Caterina. Laura got up to refill his empty wine glass.

"Laurina?" Veratti called from the courtyard, bounding up the steps of the veranda.

Father and daughter straightened as he entered the parlor.

"Tell us, Giovanni," said Signor Bassi.

Laura had been waiting all day for the news. "Husband, was the list of the Benedettini announced?"

"*Sì.*" Veratti's face was unhappy. He told them the first fourteen members of the Benedettini had been announced. "The list is conservative. It includes the president of the institute and the heads of each scientific section. That means Salti as head of the Academic Council, Galeazzi as head of the School of Medicine, Balbi as head of Collegio Montalto, and others in similar positions."

Signor Bassi grunted. "Some forward-thinking. Some not."

"Why only the first fourteen? He announced a council of twenty-four," Laura said.

Veratti continued, "It was announced that the chosen fourteen will be responsible for naming the remaining members. Laurina, you will be among the ten, surely."

Laura was not so sure. There were those among the fourteen men already confirmed who would stand in her way.

The unusual heat of September was excruciating. Laura moved Nucca's favorite things to the parlor, where the growth from the mature trees in the garden shaded the room. The children, one by one, spent time there, quietly reading or dancing or singing songs—whatever Nucca wanted. Cook made broth and cooled it; it was the only thing that Nucca's stomach could digest. In the early evenings, Laura read to her; Nucca favored the epic poetry of Dante, remembering how Laura used to recite it to her mother. Invariably, Nucca fell asleep as Laura read.

One sweltering night, Laura, tired after a long day, also slipped into sleep. Veratti entered and saw that the napping Laura's breath was soft, her chest moving up and down. But Nucca's chest was absolutely still.

Veratti woke Laura, and that night, she sat next to the woman who had been her caregiver, supporter, and friend to the Bassi family for five decades, praying for Nucca's safe passage to heaven.

Days after the Mass and funeral for Nucca, the list of those chosen to fill the last ten spots in the Benedettini was posted. Veratti rushed home from the university and found Laura soothing Paolo, who had a slight fever. She'd been up with him all night, and Verratti noticed that her face was pale too.

Laura saw his solemn look. "Tell me," she said.

"The list of the final members of the Benedettini has been posted. I am on the list."

"Good." Her smile was genuine, but tired. His hesitation foretold the next part of the news. She pressed him. "But I'm not?"

"The committee has made a mistake, Laurina. Dottore Salti oversaw the final choices; that means it's a vote against experimental physics. Wife, I'm sorry."

Laura's anger flared. "Let's face what it really is. It's more than a vote against experimental physics. It's a slap in the face of women." She stood quickly, then grabbed onto a table, for she felt woozy.

"Laurina, be careful. You're doing too much."

"Giovanni. *Prego*. Let me be. I must write a letter."

Most esteemed Holiness,

As the final list of the Benedettini has been posted, I feel there is an oversight. I do not want to be presumptuous, but I feel I have your support and respect for my scientific endeavors. I request that you alone be the judge of whether I deserve a place on your esteemed council. I thank you, most deeply, for considering adding me as the twenty-fifth member of the Benedettini.

Laura Maria Caterina Bassi

Months later, on a cold winter day, Bianca, now head of the Bassi-Veratti household staff, entered the library. She handed a letter to Laura, who was sitting with her father, Dottore Manfredi, and Veratti.

"It's from Professore Scarselli, Pope Benedict XIV's personal secretary."

Laura read the letter and shook her head, staggered at its contents. "I cannot fathom if his Holiness received my letter or if it was intercepted by his secretary."

"What is the response?" Manfredi asked.

"Professore Scarselli suggests I prove my worthiness for such an exception by giving a public lecture and dedicating it to the pope. And that I also publish a scientific treatise and dedicate it to the pope. And follow that with a book dedicated to the pope."

Manfredi reached for the bowl of roasted chestnuts, held one close to his weak eyes, and cracked it open. "What is this absurdity? Those already chosen did not write books and pamphlets and dedicate them to Pope Benedict."

Signor Bassi shook his head. "Of course not. Laura must always do more."

Veratti was angry. "Laura's lectures, her continuing work with students and scientists across Europe, her experiments, her dedication to education of the community—and making Bologna feel part of science—should have already secured her a position."

Laura looked out the window toward the carriage house. "I must keep my focus on my laboratory proofs. I cannot be chained solely to a desk writing papers or a book on what is already known. I want to keep moving forward."

The men in the room agreed. "*Ben detto.*"

Laura looked to Manfredi, who was enjoying chewing the tasty chestnut. "I know what you'll say, Dottore Manfredi. Strategy. But I'm tired of having to do that. I'm tired of always being on the outside."

Signor Bassi looked at his daughter. "It is so. The battle has been long. But, my daughter, it is not in your nature to give up."

For the next year, Laura wrote a series of letters to Pope Benedict XIV, outlining what she saw as worthy contributions she could make to the Benedettini. She signed each one "The twenty-fifth member of the Benedettini."

Word of Laura's not being included spread through Europe. The Vatican received letters from Enlightenment scientists and philosophers, each stating their support of Dottoressa Bassi as the twenty-fifth member of the Benedettini. The young Henry Cavendish, who, through letters, had shared with Laura his early theories on inflammable air, wrote from England of his support; Roger Boscovich, the Jesuit who had long been pen-friends with Laura regarding his work in astronomy, sent the pope letters from Dubrovnik. Voltaire, the philosopher, poet, and a voluminous letter-writer, shared his support of Laura with Pope Benedict XIV. He also sent Laura a copy of his letter, and she shared it with Veratti.

"Monsieur Voltaire is very generous, Giovanni. I'm most grateful."

Veratti read the letter aloud:

I would like to visit Bologna to be with Signora Bassi, to pay philosophical homage and reverence to the glory of her century and sex. As there is no Bassi in London I should more happily enter the Academy of Bologna than the English one, even though it may not have produced a Newton.

On a winter's night, Laura settled into bed. It was late and the children had been rambunctious after supper. She had read to them from "The Fisherman and the Genie," a tale in *One Thousand and One Nights* that had recently been translated to French. The boys and Caterina had gathered containers from the kitchen, opening each and pretending that a magical genie was appearing and granting them three wishes.

Veratti sank into the soft bed next to Laura. "What would you wish for, my wife?"

"I think you know, Giovanni." She closed her eyes as he wrapped his arms around her. She leaned her head on his shoulder. "Health and love for my family would be first."

"And?"

Laura laughed softly, drifting into sleep. "A complete understanding of God's plan for the universe."

"That's a very big wish," Veratti chuckled. He loved the feel of her breath slowing as she allowed herself to relax.

"And, one day, to feel accepted and appreciated—as a

lecturer and equal at the University of Bologna." Laura's eyes closed. She was asleep.

A month later, Bianca entered the Bassi-Veratti home laboratory, her face filled with worry. Laura, who was working at a microscope next to Volta, stood.

"What is it, Bianca?"

"Cook has told me your father is not able to keep the food in his stomach. And that he looks to be fighting a great pain in his chest."

Laura quickly closed her notebook. "Signor Volta, we'll continue at another time."

Volta nodded. "Of course, Dottoressa. Please tell Signor Bassi I wish him good health as quickly as it can be acquired."

Laura, with Bianca following, hurried to the back door of the manor house. They raced through the kitchen and up the servants' stairway. Laura pushed open the door to her father's bedroom.

"Papà?" Laura had to swallow her dismay. Her father's face was a grayish color and there were beads of dampness on his forehead. "Bianca, send for Dottore Veratti."

Signor Bassi rallied. For weeks, Laura spent most of her time in his room. She read while he slept. When he was awake, they played chess and she listened to his recollections—of his moving to Bologna from his small village, meeting her mother, and how he fell in love with her the moment he saw her.

"Rosa Maria was the most beautiful. God is surely happy to have her by his side."

Laura patiently waited as his frail hand moved his chess pieces across the board.

"And how proud she was to have a daughter dedicated to family. Laura, *mia cara*, she knew your talent could take you anywhere, away from her. She relished having you here, with us, always."

"Papà, there's nowhere else I'd ever want to be."

It was summer when Signor Bassi's head fell to his chest and a long creaking exhalation of air passed his lips. Days later, he was buried next to his Rosa Maria. Laura stood next to Veratti; he had to hold her up, for her sorrow consumed her.

"He believed in me always," she whispered. "He did everything he could to open the doors of knowledge and opportunities." She suddenly felt very lonely. "I shall miss my papà."

Chapter Twenty-Two

More than a year later, in late October, Laura celebrated her thirty-ninth birthday. The wind swept the autumn leaves from the trees and the air took on a chill; the Bassi-Veratti children began to dream of building snowmen. Pope Benedict XIV announced another extended visit to Bologna. Again, he asked Laura to meet with him.

Professore Scarselli joined Laura in the long hallway that led to the Lambertini library. "You are quite the letter-writer, Dottoressa Bassi."

Laura glanced at Scarselli. Was he being snide? She could not be sure. "When I have something worthy to ask—or to share—I find it an excellent form of communication."

Scarselli opened the door to the library, bowed coolly to Laura. He departed.

Pope Benedict took Laura's hand. "My sympathies for the passing of your excellent father."

"*Grazie*, Your Holiness."

"He was the one who taught you scacchi. Is that right?"

"Sì. When I was a young girl."

He moved to the chess table. "Another game? In his honor?"

Laura took the seat across from the pope. She reached for a pawn to make her first move. "White to play."

She wondered if Pope Benedict would bring up her request to join the Benedettini. Veratti had told her about dissension among the current members; many of the conservative academics had blocked ideas for advancements at the university. Was the pope aware of the discordance?

If so, he gave no clue. The pope played silently.

Laura decided to bring up another topic. "Your Holiness, please pardon if this request is improper. Dottore Veratti, my husband, has applied to be the physician at the Santa Maria Maddalena monastery for nuns."

"He has a laudable reputation in academics and in medicine." The pope moved a chess piece forward.

"The rules, it seems, are against him," Laura continued. "They state that a man needs to be fifty years old to medically care for the nuns, and, as Dottore Veratti is only forty-four, his application has been put aside. He is most capable, of course, and the extra money he would earn would go to building up our home laboratory, where I work with many deserving students."

"Those rules on age have been in place for a long time; I believe they were set by the Vatican Council in the sixteenth century."

Laura, vexed by antiquated thinking, divulged her opinion. "To be held to the ideas of those nearly two hundred years ago and not question them—it seems to go against all that is the Enlightenment."

"Ah." The pope rubbed his chin.

Laura wasn't sure he was listening to her, but she continued. "Of course, if I had been appointed to the Benedettini, with the salary of one hundred liras, this added employment would not be as necessary for our family and our laboratory."

Pope Benedict dodged the topic of the Benedettini. "I shall see that Dottore Veratti's age not be a concern."

"*Grazie*, Your Holiness." Laura moved her tower further down the chessboard. The match continued; both played at a quick pace.

"How many children do you have now, Dottoressa?"

"Six. All run through the house . . . it can get quite loud. God called two—one girl and a boy—when they were just babies, and there is sorrow still at their passing . . . ." She remembered the months of sadness. The days that had felt so dark. Of each precious life and its loss.

"God's decisions are not always understandable."

Laura rallied. "But we're grateful. God blessed us with six healthy children. Caterina is the only girl. Paolo is the youngest."

Pope Benedict moved another chess piece and glanced quickly at his opponent. He'd always noticed Laura's intelligent eyes, but now he also saw a weariness. This woman took care of a family, her laboratory, her experiments and students, and served the city of Bologna by continuing to speak at engagements. Did she ever have time for herself?

Laura continued, "It seems the family interests are divided. Caterina, at her young age, has already told us she will be a nun. And our oldest, Giovanni Francesco, is focusing on theology. The others—it is all science and mathematics for them."

"A mother and wife—and teacher—has many tasks. Perhaps adding the Benedettini to your list would have been too much."

Laura saw her opening. "Your Holiness. The voice of a

female should be in the fabric of all areas of life. And science is no exception."

"Each of us has only so much energy."

Laura was quick to reply. "I'd like to expend less energy convincing men to allow me access to the science and world of knowledge that I love."

"Ah." Pope Benedict fell into a silence again. He moved another chess piece.

"I apologize if that sounded disrespectful, Your Holiness."

"I'm willing to hear the truth. You've always been forth-right."

"Then may I also say this: I dislike feeling the need to apol-ogize for saying what I believe."

Pope Benedict reached for his goblet of wine and observed, "Men rarely apologize."

"And women do it too frequently. Often for no good reason. It is unjust, isn't it, for a woman be held to another standard?"

The pope sipped his wine and reached for a chess piece.

Laura gave a soft chuckle. "As an example, would I need to apologize for pointing out that I'm about to say 'Checkmate'?"

Pope Benedict, surprised, studied the game board. He saw she was correct, and laughed. "You were successful in moving my mind to other topics. Congratulations." He leaned his elbows on the table and held his hands together. "I know you appreciate the thinking of Monsieur Voltaire."

"I don't always agree with him, but he always provides food for thought."

The pope nodded. "I've been thinking of his words of late: 'Every man is guilty of all he does not do.'"

Laura hesitated; she didn't want to misstep or offend. "What do you feel you've not done, Your Holiness?"

Pope Benedict lifted his broad shoulders and let them descend with a contemplative shrug. "Of course, people have regrets, no matter how much effort they've put in to live an exemplary life." He looked at her as if he'd made a decision. "This seems a good time to let you know I've decided to add a twenty-fifth member to the Benedettini. This person is to have full voting rights, and will be expected to question everything, push the study of science forward, and attempt to fix all stalemates on the council. Most importantly, it will be made clear that this person is entirely of my choosing."

Laura strove to keep her face calm. Was she to be disappointed again?

"It also happens that this person is a very good chess player. Do you happen to know Dottoressa Laura Bassi?"

On the day of her first Benedettini meeting, Laura stepped onto her villa's veranda. Veratti was close behind. There, standing next to the carriage, were Dottore Manfredi, holding onto Lucia's arm, and Galvani and Volta.

Manfredi bowed to Laura. "You've come far, *mia studentessa*."

Galvani and Volta jockeyed to be the first to shake Laura's hand and wish her an excellent meeting.

Galvani held her hand the longest. "I know you'll fight for experimental physics. *Grazie*."

Lucia approached Laura. "So many young women look up to you, Dottoressa Bassi-Veratti. You've made my life richer."

Laura squeezed Lucia's arm and thanked her for her support.

Laura and Veratti arrived at the institute for her first Benedettini meeting. She took her place across from the stooped and sour Dottore Salti and arranged her notebooks.

Salti, who had taken on the role of council moderator, opened the meeting. "I've now entered my eighth decade and have led the institute since its inception—and the Benedettini for nearly three years. We now have someone in our presence who's been a thorn in the institute's side for a good portion of the last decades."

Veratti growled and started to stand.

Laura put her hand on his arm. "*Prego*. Please sit, Dottore Veratti." She looked around and saw the unwelcoming eyes of the conservatives on the council. "If you feel a prick due to my existence, I'm sorry. But I'm here and I will not back down."

There was a heavy silence in the room. Then Dottore Galeazzi stood.

"It's to the Benedettini's benefit to welcome its twenty-fifth member. I know of Dottoressa Bassi's fine work and academic rigor. She is most deserving. May I say welcome."

"*Ben detto. Ben detto*," approved Dottore Balbi.

Salti snorted and glared at his former second. Laura noticed that Balbi did not meet Salti's gaze.

The council knew they could not deny Pope Benedict's personal choice, and soon, they focused on their tasks.

In the next years, Laura worked to revamp university courses, added the study of Newtonian physics, lobbied for greater financial support from the Vatican, and supported new experiments by young physicists, chemists, and mechanical engineers. She championed the publications of all the members and was gratified by the continuing and growing esteem awarded to the University of Bologna.

Laura also advocated for the acceptance of women into the university and complained to Veratti and Manfredi that Salti led a series of successful charges against her proposals. She did not want to be content with small steps, but she celebrated each of them. Princess Faustina Pignatelli Carafa, who had continued to study privately and published *Problemata Mathematica*, was finally granted the opportunity to earn a laurea and, after successful lectures and defenses, was accepted into the university's Institute of Science. She continued to lobby for the anatomical sculptress, Signorina Anna Morandi, and finally, with Dottore Galeazzi adding his support, Anna was allowed to study at the Hospital of Death. Anna did not choose to stand for a laurea for she had no desire to be a polymath; she wanted to concentrate solely on anatomy. Lucia Galeazzi was content to set a personal path of knowledge, spending her time in the Bassi-Veratti carriage-house laboratory, assisting Laura and being tutored by the now nearly blind but clear-thinking Dottore Manfredi. When a Frenchwoman, the Marquise de Chatelet, sent Laura her translation and commentary on Isaac Newton's book *Principia*, Laura promoted its contribution to Newtonian mechanics and the marquise's ideas surrounding kinetic energy. The book was adopted as a university text. The news of these women's accomplishments reached other universities in Europe and, along with Laura's letters of support, paved the way for other persistent women to begin successful lobbying for academic studies.

In early winter, Laura, wearing the academic wig and robes of her station, walked alone in a long hallway of the Institute of Science. Veratti had remembered a pamphlet he wanted from his university office and had hurried off to get it; they'd arranged to meet at the carriage. Suddenly, there was a surge of students leaving a lecture hall; she waited for them to quickly disperse, wishing there were female faces among them.

Vincenzo Cruce, wearing the robes of an administrative assistant, moved out of the lecture hall and turned to walk down the hallway. He saw Laura and stopped. Now, at age forty-eight, Cruce's freckles had faded and his face had settled into a sulky grimace; his dissatisfaction of not earning the high marks needed for a laurea and his subsequent position had marked his dour demeanor. He scowled at Laura.

"A woman is to be escorted on university grounds by a husband or an administrator. Why do you not know your place?"

Laura's resentment rose but she kept her voice steady. "I'm a member of the university, Signor Cruce. This is a place I belong."

"God created man to lead, women to follow and serve. I will never recognize a woman's right to stand as my equal. I concur with John Knox, Calvin, Aquinas—and those today who see merit in the truths these great men spoke. That the presence of women, wanting to assert and claim places next to men outside the home, is unnatural and monstrous. Aquinas repeated for us the words of Saint Paul in the Corinthians: 'man is the head of woman.' It will always be true that a woman's intellect is inferior to man's."

Laura remembered his cruelty to her when she younger, how hard he had worked to exclude her. But now, she noticed how his anger consumed him. She realized she felt pity.

"I'm sorry for your beliefs. You will miss out, I'm sure, on the possibilities of excellent dialogues and companionships—of knowledge beyond short-sighted, antiquated texts. And, most importantly, Signor Cruce, the respect a woman could give you, if you returned it in kind."

Cruce bit his lip and hugged his books to his narrow chest. "You'll be known as the odd one in the history of this city. You will be derided." He walked off quickly, his weak shoulders hunched.

A short time later, Laura sat in the carriage with Veratti. She did not share the details of her exchange with Cruce. She realized she'd grown beyond his ability to hurt her.

Chapter Twenty-Three

The new year dawned. Bologna's streets were icy, and many chose to stay home, out of the cold. Laura sat in her parlor reading. She'd gathered a series of pamphlets documenting the work of an inventor in the British colonies of America; his name was Benjamin Franklin. Giovanni Francesco, now sixteen, sat on the windowsill, reading passages of the New Testament. Giacomo was solving mathematical problems on the abacus. Ciro and Flaminio were at the chessboard, Caterina was working on her embroidery, and Paolo, the youngest, rolled a small ball that he'd gotten for Christmas across the floor. He ran to pick it up, and rolled it again.

"Look, Mamma," Paolo exclaimed. "I can kick the ball in different directions just by changing the way my foot hits it."

Laura mumbled, "Interesting, Paolo." She was deep into reading Franklin's *Experiments and Observations on Electricity Made at Philadelphia in America*. In it, Franklin documented several years of personal experiments in electricity.

Veratti entered the room and Laura waved for his attention.

"Listen to this, Giovanni. Mister Franklin's theory is that lightning is a large-scale releasing of electricity." She rubbed her tired eyes. "I remember sitting on my windowsill when I was a little girl, wondering about the source of lightning. And how, from the moment I first heard about it, I was fascinated with the idea of electricus. It's extraordinary to think they are connected." She read on and relayed the information. "It seems Mister Franklin met the Scottish scientist and lecturer Archibald Spence, who was speaking on Newtonian physics and electricus in Boston, America. Doctor Spence introduced this Mister Franklin to Musschenbroek's Leyden jar and Franklin was inspired. He even took over selling tickets to Spence's lectures and encouraged him to add theatrical elements." She looked up at Veratti. "I wonder if they included the 'Electric Boy'?"

"They're doing these electrical shows in London. Apparently they're very popular events."

Bianca had entered to check the fire in the fireplace. "Have you corresponded with this Mister Franklin?"

Laura shook her head. "Not yet." She continued reading. "It seems when Doctor Spence returned to Scotland, Mister Franklin bought the equipment and began to design his own experiments."

Veratti poured himself a glass of sherry. "I've heard him called 'Doctor' Franklin."

Laura chuckled. "It seems he stopped going to school when he was not yet ten. That he took on the title of 'doctor' simply because he liked the way it sounded." She waved another pamphlet in the air. "He also publishes an almanac on astronomy and weather under the name 'Poor Richard.'"

"There are stranger stories from this place called America.

They're very interested in freedom—perhaps that includes adding whatever title they want to their names." Veratti sat by the fire.

Paolo climbed onto his father's lap and pulled at his neck. "Who is Doctor Mister Franklin, Papà?"

"He's an inventor," Veratti said.

Giacomo called to his brother, "Paolo, that means he has an idea for something that doesn't exist yet. He thinks it and then makes it."

Laura's eyes scanned the pamphlet for more information. "One of Mister Franklin's first inventions was a pair of swimming paddles; he designed thin pieces of wood and tied them to his hands so that he could swim faster. And then he invented a stove, cast from iron. The stove can be used instead of a fireplace to heat a room."

"But I like a fireplace," Paolo pouted, holding his small hands out toward the warm flames.

"Mamma, do you have a favorite invention of Doctor Mister Franklin?" Flaminio left his chess game and perched near Bianca, who was adding a log to the fire.

Laura smiled. "Well, you know I like to explore everything about electricity."

"You always talk about it," observed Caterina, pulling the needle and thick thread through the linen on her embroidery hoop.

"Mister Franklin had an idea and built what he called a 'lightning rod.' It's made of iron and has a thin brass wire attached to the top. He placed the rods in the ground and on tops of buildings. His idea was this: If he could attract the bolt of lightning to the rod, it would keep the lightning from striking a person or from hitting a roof and setting it on fire. He waited for a storm and then witnessed that his idea had merit. The lightning bolts were indeed attracted to the rods—it was as if he were controlling nature. He called it 'grounding.'"

Ciro grinned. "That would be fun to watch." He took the pamphlet. "Mamma and Papà, can we make some lightning rods?"

"We can start tomorrow in the laboratory." Veratti smiled. "Remember when we showed you the Leyden jar?"

Ciro nodded. "Where the energy of electricity can be held."

Giovanni Francesco raised his eyes from his reading and laughed. "Remember when you touched the sulfur ball and your hair stood straight up off your head? You looked very strange, Ciro."

"At least I dared do it!" Ciro defended himself.

"I did it too," Giovanni Francesco bantered. "It's just that you did it a dozen times."

Veratti was studying one of the pamphlets. "Franklin writes about how he used the electricity stored in the Leyden jar to send electrical shocks to the limbs of paralyzed patients. He witnessed some movement when the shock was administered. There was even a slight change in ability to feel . . ." Veratti read on silently, and then his voice dropped in disappointment. "But after a short period of time, most patients relapsed." He reached for his notebook and jotted down a reminder. "I want to discuss this with Galeazzi."

Laura looked at Bianca and her family—those closest to her. She felt great gratitude for this warmth, that her children were curious and constantly learning. "Who would like to hear about Mister Franklin's famous kite experiment?"

The children were all ears. Even Giovanni Francesco and Giacomo pulled their chairs close to the fire.

Laura wove the story. "It was a day in June in Philadelphia,

America. Over a year ago, in 1752. Everyone in the city felt a storm approaching."

Ciro loved exact details. "You mean they saw the clouds get dark and felt rain and wind begin?"

"Exactly, *mio figlio*," assured Laura. "Most people go inside, if they can, during a storm. But Mister Franklin wanted to use the thunder clouds to test out a kite he'd made for an experiment."

"Kite? I like to fly kites," said Paolo.

Caterina, eyes still on her needlework, queried, "Why did he want to do it in a storm, Mamma?"

"He had another idea about lightning—and lightning, as we talked about, often arrives when there is a storm," Laura reminded them. "Franklin's kite was made of a large silk handkerchief. He tied two strings to it, one made of hemp and one of silk. He put a large house key into his pocket and carried a Leyden jar and a coil of wire with him. He walked out to a field just as the storm began to rage."

Flaminio asked, "Did he do the experiment all by himself, Mamma?"

"His son was with him. They attached a length of wire to the top of the kite, to work as a lightning rod—to attract the bolt of energy. Franklin knew that the hemp string, when it got wet in the rain, would be able to conduct a charge. He reached into his pocket and took out the house key and slid it onto the hemp—and then—let the kite rise in the air!"

"Did it go high?" Paolo asked.

"They had to keep the kite close enough to see if something happened. And soon, the frayed edges of hemp began to stand up—just like your hair did in the laboratory, Ciro!"

Ciro laughed. "Experiments are wonderful, Mamma and Papà. I want to be a scientist too!"

Laura continued. "Then Franklin moved his finger near the key and he felt a jolt—a spark!"

"Like when I touched the sulfur ball!" Ciro exclaimed.

"*Sì, esattamente*. He wondered if his idea that lightning was a form of electricity was true," said Laura. "Then Franklin moved his knuckle near the key and the spark happened again! And Mister Franklin was able to collect the energy generated in his Leyden jar. Just like when using the sulfur ball." Laura scanned the pamphlet, quickly translating the English. "Here is what Mister Franklin wrote: '*The rain wet the kite and twine and conducted the electric fire freely, and it streamed plentifully from the key when approached by the knuckle. The key and phial were charged.*' So now we know." Her eyes were bright; she looked to Veratti. "Lightning is electricity. How I would've loved to have been there!"

Caterina put down her needlework and approached her mother. "Would you go far away to America to meet Doctor Mister Franklin?"

Laura smoothed her daughter's hair. Her answer was quick. "I could not leave my beloved Bologna."

Caterina leaned her head against Laura's shoulder. "I'm glad, Mamma. I want you always to be here."

"Does that mean we'll try the experiment ourselves in the next rally of thunder and lightning, Mamma?" Ciro asked.

Later that evening, Laura sat down to write a letter to Mister Franklin. She congratulated him and asked for even greater detail about his experiments. Could it be that the elusive understanding of electricity was now being harnessed? What was it in the sky that served as a master conductor? What other ideas did Mister Franklin have for its use?

In May 1758, Laura felt another great loss. Pope Benedict XIV, suffering from gout, died at the Vatican. Wreaths of mourning were placed on all the doors of Bologna. Laura and Veratti attended several Masses and joined in eulogies held at the Lambertini palazzo. Algarotti recited poems and Father Stegani read from the pope's philosophical writings. Laura sat with the elderly and still elegant Marchioness Ratta; they shared their memories of the strong and kind man and his love of science, the pope who used his position to make changes in education and religious understanding. They hoped that Benedict's innovative policies would not be put aside. Those at the university wondered if the newly elected, meek and conservative Clement XIII would be friend or foe to the Enlightenment. His first actions did not bode well; he defended the religiously conservative Jesuits and he ordered plaster fig leaves to be fashioned and used to cover the private areas of the classic statues in the Vatican.

"The world keeps changing, Giovanni," said Laura to her husband as they walked the short distance from the carriage-house laboratory to the villa. "There is war in this new place called America. England, Russia, Austria, Prussia, Spain, and France all want to claim lands on this new continent. It's so far away, perhaps the people there should govern themselves."

Veratti shrugged. "Mister Franklin has said as much, but he and other Americans are not organized enough to make themselves heard. And Britain seems to be vanquishing the others. They've already claimed sovereignty in India and want to keep expanding. We shall have to see if the Americans and British can get along."

Their children bounded out of the villa, happy it was the end of the workday and they would have their parents' attention.

It was only months later, in December 1758, when the unique comet, predicted by England's Royal Astronomer Edmond Halley in 1705 to return to streak through the skies, made its presence known. Halley had died sixteen years before, but Laura was glad that he was proven to be correct. She and Veratti eagerly read the reports of the comet with the long tail and blazing brightness—and shared the news with the blind Dottore Manfredi.

Laura told him, "It's been decided, as of this year, it will now be referred to as Halley's Comet."

"Excellent." The mathematician and tutor who had always stood by Laura, giving encouragement and strategic advice, was gratified. "I've lived in the most wonderful times," he said. "Newton, Halley, Musschenbroek, Kleist, Gray, Guericke, Giovanni Cassini, Gottfried Leibniz—the list is long."

"You, and your work in calculus, can be considered among these greats, Dottore Manfredi," Laura said. "And I am most grateful you shared your acumen with me."

Dottore Manfredi kissed her hand, his voice barely above a whisper. "And I am blessed that you shared your life with me."

In the autumn of the next year, Gabriele Manfredi's massive memorial was built in Bologna's Monumental Cemetery. It featured carvings of angels carrying tablets of mathematical calculations to the heavens. Laura placed flowers at the site every week and sat on the nearby bench, mentally keeping her beloved tutor abreast of the latest work of those dedicated to the Enlightenment.

The Carnevale of Anatomy was part of the yearly citywide carnival held before the arrival of penitential Lent—the weeks of fasting and praying before the holy Resurrection day of Easter. The popular event was first celebrated in Bologna in 1637. All of Bologna vied for tickets to the Anatomical Theatre at the Archiginnasio, anxious to watch physicians dissect a newly deceased corpse and reveal its organs and muscles and bones—while lecturing and sharing their expert comprehension of the workings of the human body.

This year, more women than ever before bought tickets. And Laura had been asked to give the opening night speech.

Laura and Veratti arrived at the Archiginnasio in Carnevale costumes—bright, glittering robes and gloves, painted masks, and outrageously feathered hats.

"The idea of the masks is an excellent one," Laura told her husband. "They give anonymity and mystery. People feel the permission to do and say things they wouldn't do if they could be easily recognized."

"Do you plan to dance on a table or blurt out your real feelings regarding Dottore Salti?" Veratti teased.

"First of all, you know I rarely dance." Laura laughed. "So 'no' to your first suggestion. As to confronting Dottore Salti, I've heard he's to retire to his home in the countryside. We shall not butt heads any longer."

"So then, at this Carnevale, we'll celebrate even more."

They entered the loggia of the Anatomical Theatre. Laura appreciated the wooden statues of the famous physicians lining the walls—among them Hippocrates, Galenus, Mondino de Liuzzi, and the Renaissance physician Gaspare Tagliacozzi, who was portrayed holding a nose in his hand for he, in the 1500s, was thought to be the first to attempt reconstructive surgery. A statue of Apollo, the god of medicine, was in the center of the theatre's ceiling. Laura and Veratti moved closer to the theatre's entrance and stopped, stunned. There, illuminated by candles shimmering in wall sconces, were Signorina Anna Morandi's wax figures. Some were carved to show musculature, some revealed the intricacies of inner organs, some were over five feet tall and highlighted skeletal structure. The shy medical artist stood in a darkened corner, her silver and crystal mask covering her pale cheeks and chin. Her large green eyes were free to watch the reactions of the theatregoers. Laura and Veratti hurried to her.

"Magnificent," Laura said.

"It's thanks to you, D-Dottoressa, that Galeazzi has t-taken me under his wing."

"It is your talent, Signorina Anna," Laura replied. "Believe that."

Veratti congratulated Anna and moved off to join Dottore Galeazzi and student Galvani, for the three of them were to be part of conducting the opening presentation for the evening. Princess Carafa and the marchioness, in elegant Carnevale costumes, joined Laura and Anna just as Eugenia, wearing a full gold mask and a hat of fur, rushed up and whispered to Laura.

"What is this shocking surprise I've heard about—what will we witness this evening?"

"It will astonish," Laura promised. "But you must wait."

Laura gave her arm to Marchioness Ratta and they headed

to the doors of the theatre. There, Dottore Balbi stood with Volta and Laura's cousin Carlo, who had gotten plump due to his success and love of food.

"Cousin," Carlo grinned at Laura, "you look elegant. Not at all like the gawky child I first tormented."

"I don't want any spiders down the back of my dress tonight," Laura teased.

"Not on such an occasion." Carlo laughed and kissed Laura's cheek. "Very proud, cousin," he whispered.

Volta shared a conspiratorial look with Laura; he knew the plan for the evening.

Dottore Balbi did not. He bowed to Laura. "Dottoressa Bassi, what is this marvel we hear of?"

The marchioness patted Dottore Balbi's arm and smiled. "Learn patience, Dottore. My friend Laura never gives away secrets."

The ladies swept into the candlelit theatre, which was built to seat the audience on three sides. They took seats in one of the front rows. Carlo, Volta, Dottore Balbi, and Father Stegani sat across the stage from them.

Moments later, a loud gong sounded.

Laura moved to the stage. The musicians finished a rendition of a sacred singspiel, written by an Austrian who had recently created a sensation with his precociousness—a ten-year-old named Wolfgang Amadeus Mozart. Laura, now accustomed to using her voice to reach crowds, welcomed the audience and spoke of Pope Benedict XIV. All in the audience bowed their heads in silent prayer.

"We dedicate the beginning of this night, our special marvel, to this pope, who will go down in history as one who believed in the tenants of the Enlightenment," Laura said. "There are now studies in science—specifically in medicine—that are contributing to longer lives, greater health, and increased understanding of the human body." Laura raised her hands and told the audience she knew they were excited to see a dissection. "And you shall. But you will also witness electricity."

The audience buzzed. Most had no idea what to expect.

"Let us set the stage," Laura said.

University students who had regularly studied at the Bassi-Veratti laboratory, in full masks and robes, carried in a stretcher to the center of the arena. On it was a corpse, covered in cloth. The students lifted the lifeless body onto a marble slab. Laura continued, weaving a picture to engage the audience.

"We've all seen bolts of lightning. Powerful bursts of energy that blast from dark clouds toward the ground. We've seen lightning's craggy sparks—and they are magnificent. They are the result of what is called 'electricity.'"

Galvani swept in, wearing a long and curled white wig and a half mask. His academic robes were open; his dark velvet waistcoat caught the light. He pushed aside a velvet curtain to reveal an elaborate set of Leyden jars and sulfur globes of various sizes.

Laura's voice rose to fill the theatre. "What would you think if you could see that electrical spark here, inside this theatre, tonight? And witness its possibilities?"

University students carried in a trestle; a student volunteer was already suspended in a net attached to the upper horizontal beam.

Laura announced, "We will show you the 'Electric Boy'!"

As Galvani orchestrated the replication of the experiment he and Laura had participated in with Abbé Nollet—the turning of the sulfur globes and activation of the Leyden jars—Laura explained the process to the audience. When the hanging student was surrounded by static electricity, and the ends of his hair lifted toward the ceiling and he was able to turn the pages of a book without actually touching it, the audience was astounded. There were initial ripples of fear, and then awe, and then grand hurrahs. Laura had added more elements: the attraction of a long piece of shimmering silk material to the waving arms of the electrified student; feathers tossed into the air were pulled toward and stuck to the glowing sulfur globes. Then there was the final element: the person reaching to touch the electrified student—and the sparks of light appearing in the air. Gasps and cries of wonder filled the space and questions were shouted from every corner.

Laura, mistress of the experiment, held up her hands. The audience quieted.

"But we must remember, we are in the Anatomical Theatre. What can this electricity mean to medicine? Do we have any answers to that question—or is this area of science just at its beginning?"

Galeazzi and Veratti, in long wigs, masks, and robes that added to the mystery and theatricality of the evening, moved onto the stage. Veratti pushed a cart topped with a draped object. Galeazzi pulled off the fabric to reveal the still body of a sheep. The animal was shoved and prodded, clearly showing that it was lifeless. Galeazzi instructed the masked assistants to crank the rods inserted in the sulfur balls again, to activate the energy.

Laura told the audience about how, in ancient Greece, fish that had inner light were used to treat headaches and other ailments. "Has anyone seen these eels or glowing fish?"

A few men in the audience shouted that, indeed, they had. One also called out, "And what made the light?"

Laura enjoyed the audience's interest. "Exactly science's question! We ask, is there some sort of electricity in these fish? And tonight we ask, is there some sort of electric charge in the human nerves or muscles?"

Laura felt the excitement of opening Bologna's minds to new concepts, new understandings. She told them of Mister Franklin of America's work, his relaying electrical shocks to paralyzed limbs. The audience leaned forward. They had no idea what they were about to see. Veratti and Galeazzi touched the sheep with electrically charged rods and the sheep's body jerked on the cart—its limbs reacting spastically whenever touched.

The audience gasped. Was the sheep coming back to life? Would it make a sound? Would it run across the stage?

Finally, the cloth covering the human corpse was plucked off. Laura reminded the audience that the body was recently deceased; its soul was not present.

"God has provided this opportunity because He loves his creations and He has deigned to share possibilities of helping those in pain or paralysis—with the magic of the electricity."

Veratti placed conducting rods into the deceased man's mouth and ear. Galeazzi used the charged sticks to touch the shoulder of the corpse. Its arm jerked into the air! Shrieks from the audience drowned out Laura's explanation. Galeazzi touched the thigh— and the entire leg of the deceased body jerked.

The audience exclaimed in wonder. "*Che diavolo? Dio o diavolo?* God or devil?"

Laura called out, "Science! God's gift of science!"

Marchioness Ratta held tightly to the princess's arm. "So wonderfully disturbing," she whispered. "I may faint . . . if I do, will you catch me?"

Princess Carafa had to shout to the marchioness over the din. "Don't faint! You don't want to miss a thing!"

The electric charge was doubled and tripled.

And then Galeazzi touched the rod to the corpse's abdomen. The body sat up!

"Oh! *Dio mio!*" the audience roared, their amazement bringing them to their feet. Many people made the sign of the cross and raised their arms to the heavens!

Onstage, Laura called out, "Is electricity an integral part of all life? Do the fluids in our body, like our blood, respond to electricity? What causes our hearts to beat? Is electricity inside us? Or outside? Or both? Can we harness it on a long-term basis? Will we discover how electrical shocks might have lasting effects? These are questions of the university, of those who embrace knowledge and hope to understand the world. Let us study forever, and allow Enlightenment!"

Dottore Balbi, surrounded by the academic community of Collegio Montalto, felt the energy of the crowd; he enjoyed Laura's ability to entice an audience to thirst for knowledge.

Onstage, Laura caught Veratti's eye. She nearly hooted with glee. How wonderful to share science!

Weeks later, the light in the laboratory was fading as Laura and Veratti wrapped up their work for the day. Bianca had swept the floors just an hour ago and had gone inside to help get the children ready for bed.

"It's like the winter sun is against us," Laura said to Veratti as they placed the tools onto the hooks on the wall.

"The price of candles is rising and oil is dear." Veratti yawned.

"Spring is just around the corner. I will welcome it. Longer days of light will save us money."

Laura looked around. "If only we could capture lightning in a bottle and make it last for an entire night."

Veratti reached for her shawl and wrapped it around her shoulders.

She leaned against him, placing her hand on his. "Gio, isn't it wonderful news about Lucia and Luigi?"

Veratti kissed the top of her head. "The night Galvani finished his defenses and earned a laurea is the night he proposed to Signorina Galeazzi. Who does that remind you of, *mia cara*?"

Laura turned to look at him. "I hope they enjoy the happiness we do, Giovanni." She teased. "We've gotten older together. I see the wrinkles around our eyes."

Veratti laughed. "But I feel as if we've just begun. And I feel there is much more ahead."

Laura opened the drawer to her desk, took out a piece of vellum, and handed it to him. "I've taken to writing poetry, my husband. I wrote this for you."

Veratti raised an eyebrow. "Really?"

"Algarotti will not feel any envy, I am sure." Laura smiled.

Veratti read the poem aloud.

"If there ever comes a day, when we can't be together,
promise to keep me in your heart.
I want to stay there forever."

Veratti folded the paper and put it into his waistcoat's pocket. "I will cherish it. But, *mia cara*, don't get any ideas about resting on past accomplishments."

Laura heard the strident sound of horses' hooves and wooden

wheels on the stones of the courtyard. She moved to the window. She saw Dottore Balbi getting out of a carriage.

"Were you expecting Dottore Balbi?" Laura asked.

Veratti frowned. "I shall open one of our best sherries. Shall we receive him in the library?" Veratti was quickly out the carriage-house door.

A short while later, Balbi rubbed his hands and held them toward the warm flames of the library's fireplace. Veratti poured sherry for all of them.

"It's most pleasant you've chosen to visit, Dottore Balbi," Laura said, wondering if the reason for his presence would be made clear.

Balbi cleared his throat. "I'm here to relay the decision of the heads of the Collegio Montalto."

"What decision?" Laura asked. She looked at Veratti. "Does this concern you as Dottore Balbi's second?"

"I don't know," Veratti told her. "Perhaps we will find out if we listen."

Dottore Balbi continued. "As you know, Dottoressa Bassi, the Collegio Montalto is now one of the most successful divisions of the University of Bologna."

"It has become so, under your leadership," Laura said. She nodded toward Veratti. "I know the hours that Giovanni keeps there, and he tells me yours are often even longer."

Balbi sipped his sherry, savoring it. Then he put the small crystal glass down, his face very serious. "I have a proposition, Dottoressa. The college is in need of a new lead preceptor of the Department of Physics. The administration met today and would like to offer it to you."

Laura was stunned. "What? *E vero?* Is that true?"

It had been more than thirty years since she earned her

laurea. She had expected to teach then, but had been denied. It had remained a dream—a vision of entering a lecture hall to teach the science she loved. It took her a moment to speak.

She turned to Veratti. "Did you know of this?"

Veratti shook his head. "I knew that your name had been discussed. But it is the decision of Dottore Balbi and the administration." His eyes were wet with happy tears and he growled, the emotion catching in his voice. "It's well deserved, Laurina."

"Your answer?" asked Balbi.

"I don't know. It will depend." Laura paced in front of the fireplace.

Balbi was surprised. "Depend on what?"

Laura set her terms. "I would expect to be able to shape the curriculum. And help to hire faculty that would carry out that curriculum."

"And?" Dottore Balbi frowned, waiting for more.

"I want experimental physics to be accepted as a respected field of study. I want to encourage the study of Newton's work, and include subjects like electricity and atoms and elements that need deeper understanding."

Dottore Balbi hesitated. "Dottoressa, we desire your leadership. I will agree to your terms."

Her voice was calm and strong. "I am not finished yet, Dottore. I must be free to advocate for changes in the university's policy toward the admittance of women."

"*Sì*. Understood."

"And see progress."

Balbi's raised his eyebrows. And then nodded. "*Sì*. More women with abilities and commitment. I will work alongside you on that and diligently work for progress."

Laura held Balbi's eyes. "And I must be paid commensurate

with the men. This is a large responsibility and I expect to be paid equally. My salary must match that of the highest paid lead preceptors."

Laura waited. Veratti dipped his head and clasped his hands; he too waited for Balbi's answer.

Dottore Balbi raised his glass of sherry to Laura. "Agreed. And now, will you state your acceptance?"

The first day of Laura's tenure as chair of the Department of Physics at the Collegio Montalto dawned. It was 1766, and she was fifty-five years old. Veratti helped Laura into her long cranberry-colored robe and she reached for her academic wig.

She saw herself in their bedroom mirror. More than three decades ago, she had received her laurea and assumed that teaching at the University of Bologna would immediately follow. It had been so for her husband, for Galeazzi, Galvani, and the countless men who had successfully defended their knowledge and proven great understanding.

"It is unconscionable that it has taken so long, *mia cara*. That you had to carve your own path, build your own laboratory," Veratti said.

Laura studied the gray hairs that now framed her face. "Giovanni, *sì*, the injustice will always be infuriating. I will never be at peace with it. But this day has come."

Bianca waited in the Bassi-Veratti courtyard, next to the carriage. She handed Laura her notebook and curtsied. "*E quasi ora.* It's about time," she said.

Laura stepped into the carriage; she would take this ride alone.

The horses pulled the carriage through Bologna. Laura took

in the elegant palazzos and villas, the offices and shops, the fountains and wide piazzas. How she had loved to share her city with the fine scientists and thinkers who had visited Bologna to meet her, to work in her laboratory. Her ardor for her city swelled. Truly, it had earned its title, *la dotta*—city of "the learned." She felt a great pride; she knew she'd been part of it.

Uniformed guards stood at the closed gates of the university. Laura's carriage pulled to a stop. The head guard strode to the window of the carriage.

"Name?"

Laura recognized his look, one that took pleasure in using his power to deny entry. She announced, "Dottoressa Laura Maria Caterina Bassi."

The head guard stepped back and raised his staff in the air. "*Aperto! Aperto!* Open!" He bent low to Laura, waving his arm in a sweeping bow. "You are expected, esteemed signora."

The words hung in the air. There was a perfect ring to them. The massive iron gates opened.

Only moments later, Dottore Balbi walked with Laura toward her lecture hall. She was aware of the sound of their footsteps on the marble floors; his heavier, hers lighter. She looked at the large portraits of esteemed faculty of the university—poet and humanist Francesco Petrarch, renowned poet Dante, architect and mathematician Leon Battista Alberti, astronomer Copernicus, the alchemist Paracelsus, botanist Aldrovandi, the engineer Giovanni Cassini—and more gold-framed paintings, done in vibrant, rich oils.

Laura smiled. "I feel inspired, Dottore Balbi."

Balbi was not listening. "Ah. Here we are."

A teaching assistant waited at closed, heavy oak doors. He

nodded to Balbi and the head of the Collegio flicked his hand, signaling the doors to open.

Laura breathed deeply, filled her nostrils, and felt her chest expand. The path to the lectern looked long. She straightened her academic wig and squared her shoulders and took her first steps. Her heels clicked on the floors as she walked through the doorway slowly. She could feel a heaviness; the air was thick. She saw, out of the corner of her eye, that each place on the benches was filled—that the students, in their dark robes, were so tightly packed that their shoulders touched. Every space along the wall was taken. She took in a sea of expectant faces. There was no sound. All eyes were on her.

Laura walked at a steady pace toward the dais. She was aware of the sound of her solo walk, of her low heels—ones she had chosen knowing she would be standing for hours. She reached the dais and placed her notebook on it. And then she looked up and willed her voice to reach the farthest corners of the hall.

"Congratulations, *studenti*, on being learners. Congratulations, *studenti*, on being thinkers. Congratulations on having your own mind, thoughts, and ambitions. I will never harm your individuality, your right to follow your own path. My hope, as your *professoressa*, is to instill in each of you the passion to keep the Enlightenment present by questioning all. Questions can usher in progress. We will celebrate discovering new answers to the questions of our world."

She opened her mouth to continue, but was interrupted. She saw Galvani in the middle row—he was bringing his hands together, clapping. Volta was beside him, doing the same. Many of the students who had worked at the Bassi-Veratti laboratory joined, and it was only a split second later that the entire body of students had risen to its feet and were applauding. They shouted "Dottoressa! Dottoressa Bassi!"

Laura was overwhelmed. No matter how many times she raised her hands for quiet, the tribute continued.

Finally, she walked out from behind the lectern and leaned toward them. She whispered. They had to break their applause to hear her. A hush fell on the room.

"Today, *miei meravigliosi studenti*, I will speak to you on Sir Isaac Newton, a thinker and scientist and a man dedicated to experimentation . . . ."

Epilogue

Laura Maria Caterina Bassi held her chair in physics at the University of Bologna's Collegio Montalto for the rest of her life, and remained, for over a century, the only female to hold such a position. Pope Clement XIII, an active supporter of the conservative Jesuits and their educational policies—ones that excluded women—was the leader of the Papal States until 1769. He was followed by a Franciscan friar who took the name of Pope Clement XIV; he was mostly ineffectual and often ill. In 1774, Clement XIV was succeeded by Pope Pius VI, who focused his energies on combatting continual Vatican corruption, and was not known as an advocate of the universities. Laura continued her uphill battle for open enrollment of women at the University of Bologna and spoke at salons and at ladies' clubs advocating science and women's rights in education. She always kept the doors of her laboratory open to any woman interested in science.

Her death, on February 20, 1778, at age sixty-seven, was

mourned across Europe and especially in her beloved Bologna. The city arranged an elaborate funeral; her body was dressed in the ermine cape and silver crown of laurels that Cardinal de Polignac had presented to her in 1732, the day she became the University of Bologna's first official woman graduate. Her body was carried from her home and across the city to the Institute of Science; it was followed by a solemn procession of colleagues, students, and the Bolognese who admired and loved her. At her burial, many eulogies were given and she was referred to as "an Enlightened Catholic"—as a person who saw no conflict between the pursuit of new knowledge and the traditions of faith.

Luigi Galvani, at age twenty-six, was appointed assistant professor of anatomy at the University of Bologna and led Europe in the study of "animal electricity," or bio-electricity; he proposed, through experimentation, that fluid bioelectric forces exist within living tissue. The galvanic cell and the galvanic scale are named after him. The arguments between Galvani and Alessandro Volta continued and they pushed each other to greater insights in electricity. Volta won his fame as a pioneer in chemical electricity; he invented the "voltaic pile" using electrochemical cells—the voltaic pile is better known as the battery.

Dottoressa Bassi is remembered as the first woman to teach within the walls of one of the highest universities in Europe, as a pioneer of championing experimental physics and Newtonian thought to a wide academic populace. She presented papers on mathematics, pneumatics, fluid dynamics, mechanics, optics, and electricity, and authored twenty-eight papers, the majority of these on physics and hydraulics. Most of these papers have been lost, but the few surviving display Laura's talent for mathematics and her commitment to the Newtonian method. Her children followed in their parents' footsteps and joined academia, dividing interests in theology and science.

Laura's portrait now hangs in the Institute of Science at the University of Bologna.

About the Author

Jule Selbo is an award-winning screenwriter, playwright, and novelist. She has written feature films, and written and produced television series for major studios and networks. Credits include George Lucas's *Young Indiana Jones Chronicles*, HBO's *Women Behind Bars—Prison Stories*, and the feature *Hard Promises*, starring Sissy Spacek; her Disney credits include the animated features *Hunchback of Notre Dame Part Deux*, *Cinderella II*, and *Ariel's Beginning*. Her plays *Boxes* and *Isolate* have won regional theater awards. Her novels include *Find Me In Florence* (2019), *Dreams of Discovery, A Novel Based on the Life of John Cabot* (2019) and *Pilgrim Girl* (2005, co-written with Laura Peters). She is a professor at California State University, Fullerton, and has written books on screenwriting and film history, including *Screenplay: Building Story Through Character* (2015), *Film Genre for the Screenwriter* (2015), and *Women Screenwriters: An International Guide* (2016, edited with Jill Nelmes), contributed to *Journal of Screenwriting* as well as anthologies on film and essays in magazines such as *Décor Maine*. She is a writer on the podcast *MeetCute*. She holds a PhD in film from the University of Exeter in England and holds seminars on writing in the USA and internationally.

NOW AVAILABLE FROM THE MENTORIS PROJECT

America's Forgotten Founding Father
A Novel Based on the Life of Filippo Mazzei
by Rosanne Welch, PhD

A. P. Giannini—The People's Banker
by Francesca Valente

A Boxing Trainer's Journey
A Novel Based on the Life of Angelo Dundee
by Jonathan Brown

Building Heaven's Ceiling
A Novel Based on the Life of Filippo Brunelleschi
by Joe Cline

Building Wealth
From Shoeshine Boy to Real Estate Magnate
by Robert Barbera

Christopher Columbus: His Life and Discoveries
by Mario Di Giovanni

Defying Danger
A Novel Based on the Life of Father Matteo Ricci
by Nicole Gregory

FUTURE TITLES FROM THE MENTORIS PROJECT

A Biography about Rita Levi-Montalcini
and
Novels Based on the Lives of:
Amerigo Vespucci
Andrea Doria
Andrea Palladio
Antonin Scalia
Antonio Meucci
Artemisia Gentileschi
Buzzie Bavasi
Cesare Becaria
Father Eusebio Francisco Kino
Federico Fellini
Frank Capra
Galileo Galilei
Giuseppe Garibaldi
Guido d'Arezzo
Harry Warren
Leonardo Fibonacci
Maria Gaetana Agnesi
Mario Andretti
Peter Rodino
Pietro Belluschi
Saint Augustine of Hippo
Saint Francis of Assisi
Vince Lombardi

For more information on these titles and
the Mentoris Project, please visit
www.mentorisproject.org

CPSIA information can be obtained
at www.ICGtesting.com
Printed in the USA
LVHW032136231220
675033LV00020B/296